Irish Heat

Michelle Maree

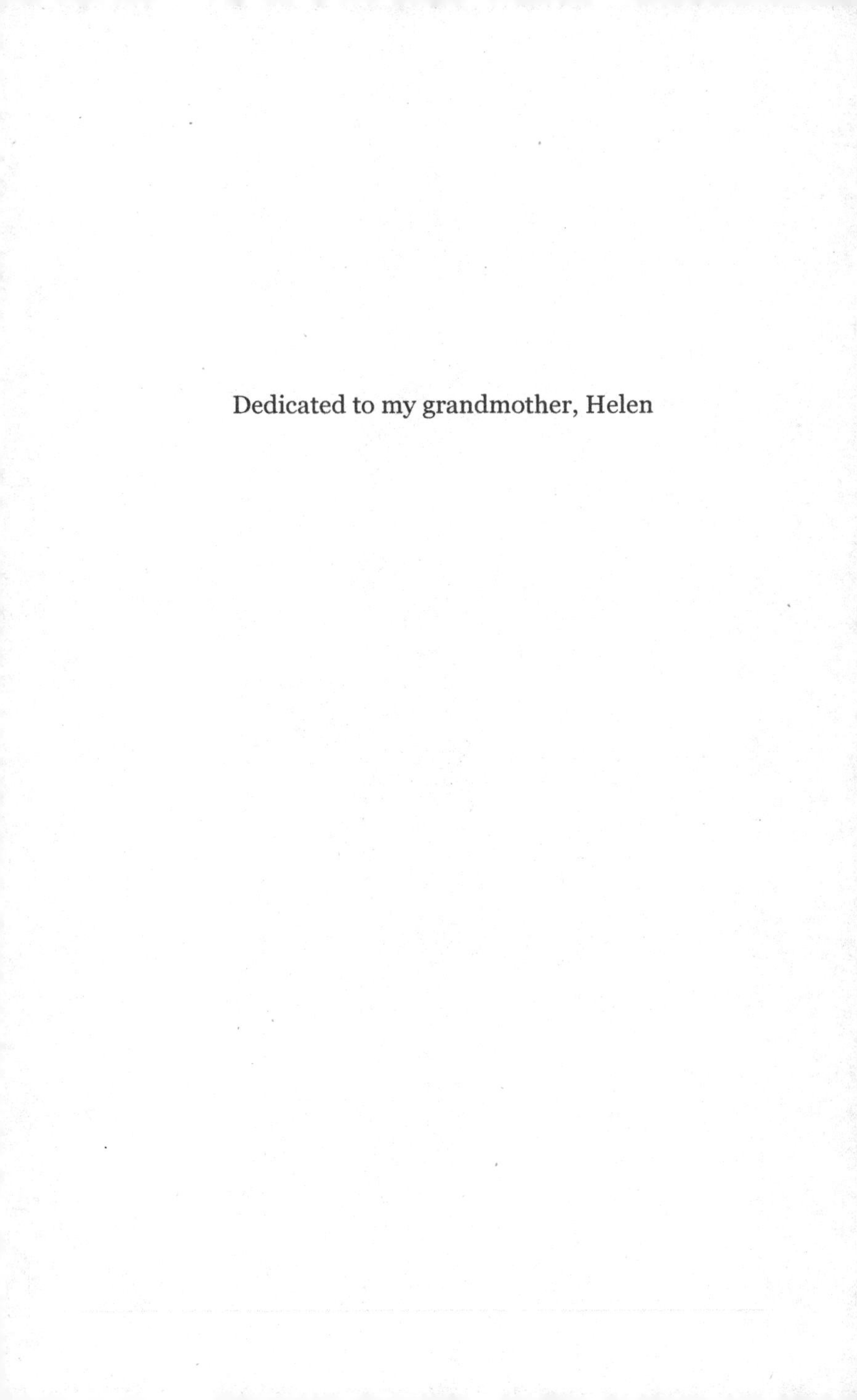

Dedicated to my grandmother, Helen

Lucy Saunders thought her bar days were long over. Yet, here she sat in a bar, scratch that, a *pub* somewhere in Dublin's city center. She had never dreamed at thirty-three, she would be a single mom. Despite all the crap Jeremy had put her through, Lucy honestly believed he would grow up and put a ring on it.

Ireland was never in the original plan, either. She was far from her home on the Oregon coast, eager to start a new life with her twelve-year-old daughter.

"I can't believe I let you drag me out here!" Lucy yelled toward her sister, Abbey, who sat on the stool beside her. "I'm tired. I'm jet-lagged. And I left Kaylee alone on our first night here."

Abbey rolled her eyes at her older sister. "It's not your first night here."

"Fine, second night, third night? I'm jet-lagged, remember? I should be unpacking and settling in. I'm not ready for all this." Lucy circled her hand over her head.

"For what? We're just having drinks." Abbey pushed a shot glass toward her sister. "You deserve the break. It's okay to take a little time for yourself."

Lucy ignored the shot in front of her. "I need to pee." She had already tossed back three of whatever liquor Abbey kept putting in front of her.

"Toilets are in the back." Abbey motioned with her head.

Lucy slid off the stool. The room tilted in front of her, causing her knees to buckle.

Abbey grabbed her sister's arm. "You ok?"

"I'm fine." Lucy laughed, releasing herself from Abbey's grip. "I wasn't expecting that."

"You sure you're okay?"

Lucy waved Abbey off but cautiously stepped away from the bar. The room straightened again as she made her way toward the back of the pub. Overhead, she saw a large sign reading "Toilets."

"Well, that's putting it bluntly," she muttered under her breath.

As she pushed open the door marked *Ladies*, Lucy felt she had stepped back in time. A wave of claustrophobia swept over her. The room hardly had enough space for the toilet and sink crammed inside. More shocking was the toilet's tank clinging to the wall above her, its long pull cord dangling down one side.

"What on earth?" Lucy felt uneasy about the tank's precarious attachment to the wall, half-convinced it would come crashing down at any moment.

Twisting around to the toilet, Lucy was annoyed that there were no toilet seat covers. With a deep sigh, she reluctantly hovered over the toilet, thankful to at least have toilet paper, even though it seemed extremely thin. When she finished, she cautiously pulled the cord, jumping back on the slight chance the entire thing would tumble down from the wall. Thankfully, everything held in place.

As if this experience couldn't get any stranger, Lucy was baffled by the sink; there were two separate faucets, neither marked hot nor cold. Had she fallen down a rabbit hole and ended up in Wonderland? She picked one faucet and yelped as water gushed out, burning her fingertips. Quickly, she turned on the second tap, which produced freezing water; this sink had no in-between. Drying her hands on a paper towel, she gave her distorted reflection one final glance before heading back toward Abbey.

"There you are." Abbey appeared in front of her, grabbing her arm. "Come on; we have to get a table."

"What for?"

"The whole reason I brought you here," Abbey laughed. "Well, besides the excellent drinks, you need the full Irish experience. The Trad band is setting up; you're going to love this."

Lucy scrunched her nose. "Never heard of them."

Abbey ignored the comment, half-dragging Lucy toward a table occupied by two other people.

"Can we join?" Abbey asked them.

The couple nodded, and Abbey plopped down, pulling Lucy into the seat next to her.

"Shouldn't we find our own table?" Lucy whispered.

"Don't be silly," Abbey said. "It's about to get very crowded in here. Table sharing is necessary."

"Why? Who is Chad Band?"

Abbey laughed. "Trad. Traditional Irish music. Everyone loves this stuff. Flutes, guitars, banjos, tin whistles, feet stomping, *Oh Danny Boy*?"

Lucy shook her head as if Abbey were speaking a foreign language.

"You've never heard of Trad music?" Abbey looked shocked. "It's one of the main attractions here, along with the Guinness. Tourists come from all over just to hear the Irish play while drinking a pint."

Lucy gave her a look, still shaking her head. "Did you know about the music before you moved here?"

"Actually, yes," Abbey said. "Shortly after you flew the coop, I went deep into an Irish obsession. I used to listen to loads of Irish, Celtic, and even some Sea Shanty music online. It drove Mom crazy, but I think those Celtic ladies started growing on her."

Lucy stared at her sister, intrigued. "I never knew you had a thing for Ireland. I thought you only moved here because of Rob."

"I probably fell for Rob *because* I was obsessed with everything Irish." Abbey smiled. "The minute he spoke with that Irish accent, I was smitten. But, I dreamt of living here long before I met Rob; he was the icing on the cake."

Lucy rolled her eyes. Abbey had always been a hopeless romantic. Lucy, unfortunately, knew better.

"You were only ever focused on leaving the house," Abbey continued. "I dreamt bigger. I wanted to leave the country."

Lucy stared down at her hands as memories washed over

her. Abbey had her pegged. As soon as she met Jeremy, she became laser-focused on getting the hell out of that house. At eighteen, she packed her bags and left home without a single goodbye. Unbeknownst to her, Lucy was about to learn a lifetime's worth of lessons in a short period of time. She had naively believed anywhere was better than living under the same roof as her mother but would quickly learn how wrong she had been.

"Here they are." Abbey touched her arm, drawing Lucy back into the present.

Lucy stole a glance at Abbey, who sat upright, her hands clasped together in eager anticipation, excitement dancing in her eyes, and a cheesy grin etched across her face. It was clear Abbey loved this band.

Three men and two women navigated through the mass of tables and people, moving toward a cluster of chairs arranged in a semi-circle in front of the crowd.

"Kenny, git us started!" One of the men shouted. He looked toward the crowd and, in his thick accent, yelled, "John in!"

Lucy leaned toward Abbey. "Whose John?"

Abbey gave her a strange look. "John? I don't know a John."

"He yelled for John to come in or something," Lucy said, brows furrowed.

Abbey chuckled. "Join. He said join in, not John."

Lucy felt her face flush. "How can you understand this accent?"

"You'll get used to it." Abby patted her hand. "Give it time. You'll be acclimated before you know it."

Lucy watched as the guy supposedly named Kenny put a flute to his lips and began to play.

"He's holding that wrong," Lucy said out the side of her mouth. "Aren't you supposed to hold a flute to the side, not straight down?"

"Oh, Lucy, you are soooo American." Abbey couldn't help laughing. "You have much to learn, my little Grasshopper."

Lucy gave a bewildered stare.

Abbey sighed. "That's a tin whistle. It's kind of like those plastic recorders we learned to play in school, but much cooler."

The tin whistle player ran his fingers through dark, wavy hair, glancing at the other band members as he tapped his foot, setting a steady rhythm.

The older man tucked the fiddle under his chin and joined in the upbeat tune. The crowd cheered and began clapping along to the beat. One of the women picked up an accordion, seamlessly pulling it in and out as she swayed to the music. The second woman strummed on the banjo while the third man played the guitar.

Lucy was quickly captivated, clapping her hands as she became swept up in the excitement surrounding her.

Lucy felt drawn to the man with the tin whistle. Every inch of his body seemed connected to the rhythm, as if lost in his own musical world. His dark hair swayed ever so slightly, as if it, too, couldn't resist dancing along with the melody. She couldn't take her eyes off him. Was it how he connected with the music that fascinated her or something else? It *had been* a while since she'd been with a man. Jeremy had always been in and out of her life, spending most of the past year on the latter. Although she wasn't actively looking to date, she could still appreciate a handsome face.

Their eyes met through the crowd; Lucy hadn't realized she was staring and quickly dropped her graze. When she dared look back up, the man was still gazing in her direction, and he offered her a small smile. Lucy's heart skipped a few beats as a tiny thrill rushed through her veins. Instantly, she felt like a schoolgirl with a crush on some unattainable heartthrob. At least it made the night all the more interesting as she allowed herself to be caught up in the moment.

The song ended, and the band carried straight into another upbeat melody. The older man set his fiddle across his knee and began to sing. Around the room, people joined in as if he sang a popular top 40s hit. Lucy could hardly understand the lyrics, but part of her wished she could sing along with the rest of the crowd.

When the music stopped, Lucy's disappointment surprised her. It had been nice allowing the music to distract her from her thoughts and fears surrounding this massive change her life had recently taken.

"We'll be takin' a wee break," the older band member announced. "Git some more of da black stuff— and git me a round too."

The older man laughed heartily as his bandmates slapped him on the shoulder.

"Shall we get more drinks?" Abbey wiggled her eyebrows. "I need to visit the ladies' room first."

"Apparently, the band does, too." Lucy made a sour expression. "Seems a weird thing to announce."

Abbey glanced at Lucy. "What are you on about?"

"They said they were taking a pee break," Lucy reminded her.

Abby chuckled. "I see where you went there. A *wee* break. That isn't what they mean; wee as in small, not pee."

Lucy rubbed a hand up and down her face, attempting to wipe away the flush growing across her cheeks. "Everything is different here. I thought this would be an easy transition. I mean, we speak the same language, but at the same time, we don't."

"It will get easier, I promise." Abbey placed a comforting hand on her shoulder. "To be fair, I had Rob and his Irish dialect for several years before we moved here. When I first met him, he was like you, completely thrown off by the way Americans spoke and how we did things. Being with him, I learned the Irish way of saying things; I suppose I knew what to expect when we moved here."

Lucy shrugged. "I hope it's just temporary. The last thing I want is to stick out like a sore thumb."

Abbey raised her brows. "Too late for that," she laughed again. "You get the drinks and I'll go to the toilets. I'll take a Guinness."

Lucy stood awkwardly at the crowded bar, contemplating how best to catch the bartender's attention. Finally, he made his way down to where she stood.

"You okay?" he asked hurriedly.

Lucy was unsure why he was making small talk at this busy time, but she had heard the Irish were a friendly bunch. "I'm okay, and you?"

The bartender furrowed his brows, looking her up and

down before moving on to the next customer.

Lucy opened her mouth to protest, but he had already turned his back to her.

"He was askin' for yar order," a deep voice informed her.

"Oh, I misunderstood." Lucy hung her head. "I thought he wanted to know how I was doing?"

The man chuckled as he squeezed into the spot next to her. "Hiya, Colin," he called toward the bartender.

Lucy glanced up at the man next to her. It was the tin whistle man from the band. She blushed as she took in his features. His cheeks dimpled when he smiled, and his blue eyes sparkled with a hint of mischief.

Leaning over the counter, he looked toward her. "What're ya havin?"

Lucy couldn't speak; she was captivated by those eyes, the bluest she had ever seen.

The bartender cleared his throat, thrumming impatiently on the counter.

Lucy quickly turned to face the bartender, somehow managing to find her voice. "One Guinness and a Jack and Coke."

The man next to her made a pfft sound. "No, no, Colin, this blow-in needs a right Irish drink."

"Excuse me?" Lucy wasn't sure whether to be offended or not.

"Ya visit Ireland; ya need the full experience," he said with a wink.

"I got Guinness," Lucy pointed out.

"That's for yer woman," the man said. "*You* ordered a 'Jack and Coke.'"

He said 'Jack and Coke' with a nasally American accent.

"First of all, she's my sister, not my woman," Lucy said defensively. "Second, what's wrong with a Jack and Coke?"

He laughed, a smirk playing on his lips. "Come 'ere, if it's a whiskey ya want, ya need the good stuff. Irish whiskey, forget that American shite," he turned back to the bartender. "We'll go easy on 'er. Git 'er an Old Fashion, with the good stuff, Connemara whiskey."

"I don't—."

"I'll buy. Ya don't like it, I'll drink it fer ya." He smiled, and Lucy felt her knees go weak. Ignoring any further protest, he turned back to the bartender. "Can I git a round for the band?"

"Yer bringing in the customers," the bartender said.

Tin whistle guy winked before heading down the bar to chat with another group of people. Lucy couldn't take her eyes off him. No matter how tempted she may be, there was no way she would be hitting on him or any other guy this evening. That wasn't what tonight was about. She was here with her sister, acclimating to a new country and, hopefully, a new life.

A high-pitched giggle came from down the bar. Lucy felt an unexpected tinge of jealousy coursed through her as she caught Kenny, if that was his name, chatting with a group of women. She couldn't help but notice the unmistakable desire flickering in their eyes as he leaned in a little too close. Not that it should matter much; it wasn't as if she had a shot with him, even if her brain was telling her to go for it.

"Got the drinks?" Abbey appeared beside her.

Lucy jumped, quickly focusing on her sister. "Yeah. He's

working on them."

"He's pretty hot," Abbey commented.

"The bartender?" Lucy asked.

Abbey tilted her head and glared at her sister. "Tin whistle guy. I saw you ogling him from a mile away. "

The bartender set the drinks on the counter.

"He bought our drinks," Lucy said, shrugging and picking up her glass. "I was being the typical foreigner, unable to communicate in my native English, and he helped me. I'm not even sure what's in this."

Lucy took a tentative sip.

Abbey watched her. "And?"

"It's good. Smooth," Lucy said, surprised. "It's an Old Fashioned? I've heard of it but never had one."

"Rob likes those," Abbey commented, then glanced down the bar. "That guy just picked it at random for you?"

Lucy put up her hand. "Don't read too much into it. I ordered a Jack and Coke; he made my drink more *Irish*. As you always say, the Irish are friendly."

"Not *buy you a drink* friendly." Abbey bumped her elbow playfully against Lucy's arm.

They walked back to their table and sat down. Lucy sipped on her drink and watched as tin whistle man rejoined the band, striking up a conversation with the pretty banjo player. He seemed like a real ladies' man, the way he was flirting with the women by the bar and now intimately touching the arm of the banjo player, laughing at something she said. Lucy couldn't tear her eyes away, even knowing she had no shot with him, not when he could have any woman in this pub. Not that it mattered; she wasn't looking for anything like that right now anyway.

"You like him," Abbey whispered, leaning into Lucy. "You should go for it."

Lucy stared into the drink in her hand. "Go for what? I'm intrigued, that's it. Besides, he clearly has a thing for his bandmate."

Abbey shrugged, taking a sip of her Guinness. "Maybe, but I didn't see him buy her a drink."

"He bought a round for the whole band." Lucy frowned.

"I'm pretty sure they get rounds for free," Abbey told her. "Their payment for bringing in customers."

Lucy hated how her stomach flip-flopped at the idea he had singled her out. Had he bought those other ladies drinks as well?

As much as she tried, she found it impossible to stop stealing glances his way. Something about him drew her in like a moth to a flame. A server weaved through the crowd, balancing a tray of glasses filled with dark liquid as she moved toward the band. Kenny smiled, saying a few words to the woman as he took the tray from her and set it on the table. The server beamed at him before returning to the bar.

The band members each grabbed a glass.

"To Kenny, our fearless leader."

Apparently, she had heard right; his name was Kenny. It was strange how the name didn't seem to fit the man.

Kenny raised his glass with the other band members; their pints clinked together in a cheer.

Kenny looked over at Lucy, his glass still raised in the air. He gestured to her, a pretend clanking of their glasses together.

Lucy quickly looked away, attempting to hide the blush creeping across her face.

"For you." Another server appeared next to Lucy, setting down a full glass. "From yer man over there."

"I don't have a man," Lucy snapped, swiveling her head back toward the band only to lock eyes with Kenny. He still held his glass raised as if proposing a second toast to only her.

When she made no reaction, Kenny nodded toward her drink. Despite her trembling hands, she somehow steeled her nerves, lifting the glass in a 'cheer' toward him, and took a sip with faux confidence. He nodded his approval before turning back to his bandmates.

"Looks like you do have a chance," Abbey whispered. "Take yer man home with you."

"He's not my man," Lucy protested again, her cheeks burning. "Why does everyone keep saying that? Earlier, he called *you* my woman; maybe he thinks we're together?"

Abbey laughed. "Yer man, yer woman; all typical Irish slang. It's what you say when you don't know someone's name or can't be bothered to remember a name. That guy, that girl, but they say, yer man or yer woman. You'll hear it a lot."

"Interesting," Lucy sighed. "I think his name is Kenny? Am I hearing that right?"

"Who cares, as long as he goes home with you." Abbey waggled her eyebrows.

"To your place?" Lucy teased. "Shall we do it right there on the couch? Or maybe in the room I share with my daughter? I know; I'll just bang that headboard all night, toss

Kaylee headphones, and ask her to keep her eyes closed."

Abbey rolled her eyes. "You could go to his place. A little action may do you good."

"I'm not going home with a stranger," Lucy said, taken aback, acting as if she had never done something so reckless in her life. Little did Abbey know, Lucy was no stranger to one-night stands, having had many in her days. "What about Kaylee? I can't just leave her alone."

"First of all, you know his name, and he bought you two drinks; you're friends." Abbey smiled. "I've got Kaylee; she'll be fine. She won't even notice you're gone."

The band started up again. Kenny had exchanged his tin whistle for the banjo; the woman playing it now held a tambourine. He counted off, tapping his foot in time with the beat. Lucy looked up, their eyes locked, and Kenny shot her a playful wink. Butterflies came to life in her stomach; maybe she did have a chance after all. She tried to push away those thoughts, but everything seemed to fade into the background, leaving only Kenny playing his song just for her.

2

One hour and four drinks later, Lucy managed to navigate her way back toward the bathroom, squinting in concentration and trying to appear more sober than she felt. The last thing she wanted was to completely humiliate herself by stumbling and staggering through the pub like the town drunk.

Once inside the cramped space, she plopped down on the toilet seat, forgetting her earlier disdain for the lack of toilet seat covers. At this point, the room was spinning, and she could not be bothered with hovering over the toilet. It had been so long since she had this many drinks, something she would surely regret in the morning.

The flirtation with Kenny continued as he repeatedly sent Lucy and Abbey drinks. Lucy, unable to hide her intrigue, blatantly stared at him as he switched from one instrument to another. He played to the room, but his gaze always returned to Lucy.

At some point over the last hour, Lucy bought a round for

the entire band. While it had earned her cheers and another free drink, Lucy wasn't sure how it would affect her wallet. Having only been in Dublin for two days, she hadn't changed her dollars to euros yet.

Lucy tried to remember the last time she had drunk this much. It had to have been before her pregnancy over twelve years ago. That was back when Jeremy took her out for wild all-night raves. Or the nights she drowned her sorrows in alcohol, waiting for him to come home. Whoa, this line of thinking needed to stop. Jeremy was the last person who should be occupying her thoughts right now.

Tonight was the night for fresh beginnings, a chance to start over. And there was a very handsome musician giving her most of his attention. Feeling confident, Lucy strutted out of the bathroom, only to trip over her own foot and tumble into the hallway. Strong hands gripped her shoulders, breaking her fall.

"Easy there," a deep voice said.

Lucy tried to stand upright, but the room tilted. Unable to regain her balance, she rested her head awkwardly against the stranger.

She could hear the chuckle deep in his chest. "You're a bit knackered; we better cut ya off."

Lucy laughed nervously, pressing a hand against his chest and straightening. Their eyes met, and she gasped.

Kenny.

Lucy dropped her gaze, feeling the heat course through the hand still pressed against his chest. "You're the one who keeps sending them," she said breathlessly.

"You kept drinking 'em," he replied, a playful grin

stretching across his face.

"It would be rude not to," Lucy teased, pushing the boundary of this flirtation.

Slowly, she raised her eyes and met his burning gaze. Her legs trembled, threatening to give out as she seductively ran her hand along his chest. In what felt like slow motion, he tilted his head and captured her lips with his own. Electricity shot through her entire body.

The kiss began lightly, but desire soon overcame them as the passion ignited. His arm encircled her waist, pulling her tightly against him. One hand slid behind her neck, fingers weaving through her hair.

Lucy casually slipped her arms over his shoulders. She sighed, parting her lips to allow his tongue to slide through. Lucy became lost in the moment, the alcohol numbing her brain, causing her to forget they were still in the hallway of the pub directly across from the toilets.

"Oh, sorry, I just need the toilet." A woman interrupted in her attempt to squeeze past.

Lucy pulled out of the embrace. Laughing nervously, she ducked her head and rushed back to the table. Plopping down beside Abbey, she gingerly touched the coy smile on her swollen lips.

Abbey examined her sister's face. "What on earth?" Glancing over her shoulder, she saw tin whistle man a few feet behind, the same sheepish grin across his face. "Did you? No—."

Lucy peered through her lashes at Abbey, keeping her chin down, as a childish laugh escaped her lips.

Abbey's eyes widened. "You did."

"It was just a kiss." Lucy struggled to stop smiling.

"Okay, then, on that note, I'm going home." Abbey began gathering her things.

Lucy grabbed her sister's arm. "Wait, what?"

"I'm going home," Abbey repeated, pushing up from the table. "You're staying here."

The smile faded. "I'm not staying here; how will I get home?"

Abbey placed a hand on her sister's shoulder and leaned in. "I'm hoping you don't come home."

Lucy grasped her sister's hand, feeling dizzy.

Abbey pulled her hand free. "Just have fun. Stay for one more song; if you want to come home, you can figure it out. You'll have to learn the way eventually." Abbey winked and walked away.

Lucy spun around in the chair to chase after her, but the quick movements caused an overwhelming sense of vertigo. All she could do was slump in the chair while figuring out the next course of action. She sat in a fog as the band began to play once again.

"Drink this."

Kenny placed a glass in front of her before taking his place with the band. He picked up the tin whistle and jumped back into the song without missing a beat.

Lucy sniffed the liquid in the glass.

Water.

Grateful, she downed the entire thing, hoping it would sober her up. She was convinced Abbey was playing a joke on her, but on further inspection, it became clear her sister was long gone.

"Is your friend coming back?"

Lucy jumped, too engrossed in her thoughts to notice Kenny's approach. The band was packing up, and the crowd was quickly dispersing. Was it closing time already?

"Umm—." She was at a loss for words.

"I can give ya a lift," he said.

She gave him a confused look, trying to register what he was offering.

Kenny held out a hand. "Come on, nothin' a cuppa wouldn't cure."

"Okay?" She wasn't quite sure what he was saying but wasn't ready to walk away from him yet.

Taking his hand, Lucy grabbed her coat and purse as he led them out the door. The air felt cool against her skin. She hadn't realized how warm the pub had been with all those bodies heating the room.

Kenny led her down the cobblestone street until they reached his car. He opened the driver's door and motioned her to enter.

"I can't drive. I been drinking," she said, slurring the words a little.

Confusion crossed his face, but then he cracked a smile. "Aye, American. Ya drive on the wrong side. Take a peek in; no steering wheel on this side."

"Oh." Lucy grinned sheepishly, collapsing into the passenger seat. "This car's backwards."

Chuckling, he closed the door, rounded the car, and slid into the driver's seat.

"Wait," Lucy said. "Should you be driving?"

He waved her comment off. "I only hada couple pints. I've

been drinkin' water fer the last hour. I'm grand."

Satisfied with that answer, she settled back against the seat. As they drove, it dawned on her that she was in a car with a complete stranger. She had no idea where they were, where he was taking her, or even how to get back to Abbey's place. The alcohol made her careless. But, then again, Abbey wouldn't have left her if she was in potential danger, would she?

Kenny pulled into an underground parking garage. Once parked, she blindly followed him toward an elevator. Inside, her heart raced as they stood inches apart, electricity filling the space between them. Her fingers itched to touch him, her lips quivering with anticipation, but he kept a respectable distance.

Once the doors reopened, he grabbed her hand and led the way down a long hallway and into a cozy apartment.

"This is me gaff," he said, dropping his coat over the back of the couch. "Make yourself comfortable. Can I git ya some water? Tea?"

Lucy stood awkwardly near the couch. For some reason, she had lost the ability to speak altogether, the opposite of her usual outgoing demeanor. It wasn't the first time she had gone home with a man she just met, and it certainly wasn't the first time she had drunk her weight in liquor. Her mind was whirling, and she forced herself to focus.

"This is a nice place," she said slowly, trying not to slur her words. She crossed the room and looked out the large sliding glass door into the darkness. "Not much of a view, huh?"

He laughed. "Not at this hour. During the day, it's

sound."

Sound? Did he mean loud? She couldn't be bothered to decipher words right now.

"Water? Tea?" he asked again.

Turning from the window, Lucy absently sat on the arm of the couch and looked toward the kitchen. "Tea, I guess?"

He pulled open the refrigerator door. "Do ya take milk in your tea?"

"No, ew." Lucy made a face. "Wait, that was rude, sorry. Umm, no milk, just a pinch of sugar, please."

With his back to her, he filled the kettle in the sink, his shoulders lightly shaking.

He could laugh all he wanted; milk in tea did not sound appealing. That being said, she didn't intend to insult anyone's choices.

He switched the kettle on and pulled two cups from the cupboard. "Most Americans have the same reaction. The perfect cuppa has to 'ave just the right amount of milk."

"Cuppa?"

"Cuppa tea." He tapped on one mug.

"How do you know I'm American?" Lucy asked.

"Accent." He placed tea bags in each cup.

"Accent? I don't have an accent." Lucy brought a hand to her chest dramatically. "You're the one with the accent."

He nodded at her, a sly smile playing across his lips.

"May I use your bathroom?" Lucy asked.

He pointed down the hallway. "First door on the left."

Lucy entered the bathroom. Now, this was more like the bathrooms she was used to. It wasn't huge, but at least there was space to move around. The toilet's tank was attached to its back rather than the wall, and the sink looked standard.

She took a moment to gather her thoughts, scanning the room in the process. One electric toothbrush stood on the back of the sink next to a tube of toothpaste lying on its side. In the mirror, she saw a single gray towel hanging on the back of the door.

"Definitely single and picks up his own towel," Lucy mumbled. "That's promising."

Proud of herself, she splashed cold water on her face and studied her reflection in the mirror. Why had she drank so much? Hadn't drinking been the reason she got pregnant with Kaylee in the first place? Well, it was a mix of binge drinking, late-night parties, and forgetting to take her birth control.

Birth control.

When was the last time she took the pill? How did one go about getting the pill here, anyway? Why was she hyper-focused on the pill right now? Hopefully, this guy had condoms.

Wait, maybe she was jumping the gun. Was she even getting sex tonight? She laughed at her reflection. Of course she was; why else would he bring her home? Lucy knew how this all worked. Surely, Kenny hadn't brought her home simply for a cup of tea and a friendly chat.

She gasped at her reflection. Her hair was ruffled, her lipstick smeared; she looked a little worse for wear. Perhaps sex was not on the table after all. Then again, when it comes to sex, isn't it more about opportunity than looks?

A mix of anxiety and excitement filled her with a giddy sense of euphoria. Although this wasn't how she planned the night to end, she enjoyed feeling somewhat unrestrained tonight. She was ready to throw caution to the wind and, as Abbey said, live a little. After all, when in Ireland—do the Irish, or however the saying went. It wasn't as if she would ever see this guy again. Maybe a one-night stand was just what she needed to kickstart her fresh beginning.

Turning the faucet back on, she did her best to smooth the stray baby hairs sticking up every which way along her forehead. She noticed a small streak of lipstick smeared on her chin and quickly rubbed that off. Her appearance was far from stellar, but it would have to do.

Lucy returned to the kitchen feeling a bit more steady on her feet, her buzz wearing down. Quietly, she sat at the kitchen table and took a moment to admire the backside of the Irish stranger moving about the kitchen.

"All good?" he asked, carrying the steaming mugs to the table.

"Yes, thank you," Lucy replied as he handed her a mug.

He turned back to the kitchen, opening and shutting several drawers until he finally returned with a small saucer and two spoons. Passing her a spoon, he sat down and gently stirred the brown liquid in the mug. Next, he removed the tea bag, allowing its contents to drip back into the cup, before guiding it with the spoon onto the waiting saucer.

Through lowered lashes, Lucy observed his movements, mirroring each step to give the impression that she was a tea connoisseur. In reality, she rarely drank tea and was a bit of a slob about the whole process. At home, she would have squeezed the tea bag dry and left it on the spoon to dribble onto the table.

Kenny took a careful sip of his tea and nodded in satisfaction. Lucy was fascinated by the entire production, feeling this was a posh guy full of culture. She had never seen a man enjoying tea quite this way. Jeremy certainly would never be caught dead drinking tea, preferring beer over what he called an *old lady drink*.

She let the name Kenny roll around in her head for a minute. It didn't suit the man seated across from her for some reason. The name felt too American for this somewhat exotic man. After all, he could play several instruments, had a great accent, and enjoyed a leisurely cup of tea.

He glanced across at her, abruptly interrupting her thoughts. She was instantly mesmerized by his eyes; their color reminded her of the deep waters in a raging ocean. Their shade invoked in her a sense of calm serenity mixed with the alluring mystique of uncharted waters. Lucy realized she was staring and quickly dropped her gaze, pretending to focus on her tea, silently praying her cheeks were not flaming pink with embarrassment.

She felt his gaze burning into her. Tightness grew in her belly as she raised her eyes to meet the storm of desire swirling in his eyes. Lucy swallowed hard, her tea forgotten, as he pushed off the chair and moved towards her, his eyes locked to hers. Without a thought, she rose to meet him. He stood only a few inches taller than her, slightly inclining his head to capture her lips with his own. Her hands tangled into the dark waves swirling around his head as she pressed her body against his. She enjoyed the feel of him. Although he wasn't hard and chiseled, he was fit, an average weight, which helped her feel comfortable about her own body.

His hands ran down the length of her back, resting for a moment on her hips before he dared to cup her buttocks in his hands. Flames ignited through her body as he passionately squeezed her cheeks. In one quick movement, he grabbed behind her thighs and lifted her; her legs reactively wrapped around his waist. The kiss deepened, desire and longing radiating through each stroke of his tongue.

He carried her down the hall, stumbling along the way, but his lips refused to part from hers. Lucy felt the room rotate when he dropped her on the bed, unsure if it was the alcohol or the kissing, leaving her light-headed. Closing her eyes, she waited for the feeling to pass. When she eventually opened them, Kenny stared down at her, concern etched across his face.

"All good?" he asked.

That accent made her toes curl. Damn, if she wasn't a sucker for an Irish accent.

"Yeah," she whispered, sitting on the edge of the bed.

He continued to study her face. Lucy bit her lower lip and caressed his cheek. Feeling the confidence would fade any minute, she pushed off the bed. Standing before him, she unzipped the dress, pulling gently at the sleeves as she shimmied her way free, kicking it off her foot and awkwardly, sending a shoe flying across the room.

Lucy laughed nervously, sliding her other shoe off with less bravado. A boyish grin crossed Kenny's face, amused at her carefree attitude. His eyes eagerly scanned the length of her body.

"Your turn," she teased, playing with the hem of his

sweater.

Submitting, he lifted his arms, allowing Lucy to pull the sweater over his head. She frowned at the t-shirt still shielding his chest.

A genuine laugh escaped his lips as he quickly removed the barrier.

Lucy hungrily caressed his skin, leaving a trail of goosebumps behind. Her fingers danced through the light patch of dark chest hair. While he didn't have six-pack abs, his stomach was flat and smooth.

Stepping closer, she planted kisses along his collarbone, lingering at the base of his neck. There was something about a neck she couldn't resist, and this man had a beautiful neck. Greedily, she brushed kisses up one side and down the other until his entire body quivered in response. Her hands slid over his shoulders and down to explore the muscles along his back.

Kenny cupped her face, greed, and lust brewing in his eyes. Taking her mouth with his own, he parted her lips, his tongue eager to explore. As the heat overcame her, Lucy bit back a moan.

Fire coursed through her veins; her need for him nearly consumed her. Suddenly, Lucy pushed against his chest, breaking the contact. His lips were swollen and slick. A coy smile played on her lips as she gently shoved him back onto the bed.

Kenny landed on his back, eyes widening when Lucy straddled his thighs. She gasped as his length poked into her bare leg.

The desire in his eyes gave Lucy more confidence.

Reaching behind her back, she unhooked her bra and tossed it over her shoulder. His gaze dropped to her bare breasts, the blue hue darkening like a stormy sky.

"Oh. My. Days," he whispered.

She smiled down at him coyly. He tightened his grip on her thighs.

"Touch me," she murmured.

Bit by bit, his hands traveled along her thighs, over her hips, and across the soft skin of her belly. She trembled as a shiver coursed through her, goosebumps dancing across delicate skin. Her head fell back when he finally covered both breasts, squeezing and caressing them lightly. Shifting into a sitting position, he feathered kisses along her neck while toying with her puffy nipples as they hardened between his fingers. Releasing her breasts, he grabbed her waist and pulled her tightly against him. Lucy gasped as she felt his stiff cock tease the crotch of her panties.

Leaning her back, he took one nipple between his teeth. Lucy gritted her teeth, unable to hold back a moan. Her panties dampened as her hips took on a life of their own, writhing and grinding in his lap.

He growled as he took her entire breast into his mouth. Lucy struggled to hold on, already feeling close to an orgasm, and they weren't naked yet.

He must have had the same thought. Releasing her breast, he flipped her onto the bed. His eyes smoldered as he pulled her panties down her legs and traced his gaze over her naked body.

Her desire grew as he studied her, seemingly unfazed by the scars, stretch marks, and flabby bits she hated.

"I can't wait anymore," he growled, pushing up from the bed.

Butterflies pounded inside her stomach. She was wet, aching, and throbbing; it had been so long since she felt a need this strong. He yanked off his boxers, standing gloriously naked in front of her. His cock thick, hard— and different. Where was the bright pink head? And why was there so much skin?

Lucy failed to hide her look of confusion. Something wasn't right. Maybe he wasn't erect after all.

Kenny's face fell.

"What? Is somethin' wrong? Should we stop?"

"No!" Lucy shouted. "It's—I—."

She was staring at his penis as if it were some foreign object.

"Sorry, it's just—."

Kenny cracked a smile. "Wait, have ya never seen an uncut penis before?"

"A what?"

"You Americans and your circumcised dicks," Kenny laughed. "This is what a real one looks like." He pointed down at the stiff shaft proudly.

Lucy's face turned bright red; she tried to bury her embarrassment in the pillows.

He continued laughing while reaching into the nightstand for a condom.

"Ya can look now," he teased. "All covered up."

Lucy opened her mouth to protest, but he was gliding a finger up and down the slippery opening between her thighs. Instead of words, moans escaped her lips.

"You okay?" he whispered.

"Yes," she murmured.

"Good."

Positioning his body between her open thighs, he took her lips once again. Automatically, her legs wrapped around his waist, ankles locking into place.

The length of his erection rubbed against her swollen lips. Lucy sucked in a breath as sensations tore through her. His tip teased against her opening as he nibbled on her ear.

"Let me show ya how a real cock works," he whispered, sliding inside her.

Pleasure shot through her veins as his length filled her.

"Oh, my days," he breathed in her ear.

Her back arched in response. "Great gravy and all that is holy," she muttered.

She moved her hips until they fell into a perfectly matched rhythm.

"Ya feel amazing," he moaned.

She felt beads of sweat form along his back as she grazed over the ridges and curves. His breathing became faster as he moved. Lucy closed her eyes, thoroughly enjoying the feel of him on top of her and inside her. She wanted him closer, deeper. Grasping his butt, she pulled him further into her depths. A low roar escaped his lips.

"Whatta ya doin' to me?" he panted.

Lucy couldn't answer as waves of pure ecstasy enveloped her. Her mind went blank. The orgasm began deep within her, coursing through every nerve before exploding in her brain. Sounds she couldn't control spewed from her mouth. Moans, groans, and a few incoherent words. The feeling intensified, her body releasing warm liquid as she came.

Kenny moaned and continued moving faster and harder, kissing her deeply; his tongue danced with hers as his body tensed. Ripping his mouth away, he threw his head back; his body tightened and stilled, a groan tearing from deep in his chest as an orgasm burst through his body.

Panting, he looked down at her with hooded eyes. "Oh. My. Days."

With a quick kiss, he untangled himself and fell back onto the bed. They lay in silence for a moment, staring at the ceiling and breathing hard.

"I've never rode an American," he said, reaching toward the nightstand for a tissue.

"What?" Lucy asked.

"American," he said, placing the used tissue back on the nightstand. "You're my first."

Lucy popped up on her elbows, mouth agape. "You're a virgin?"

Kenny laughed. "Feck no. I'm just saying I've never had sex with an American before."

"Oh." Lucy felt her cheeks flush. "How did I do? Would my country be proud?"

"So-so." He teased, a sly smile playing across his lips.

Lucy's jaw dropped in mock horror. "Well, so-so isn't good enough." She sat up and looked down at him, smiling once she noticed the laugh he struggled to hold back. "We'll have to do much better than that. So-so is the Bronze, and Americans like to be the best. It's go big or go home, baby. If it's not the Gold, I can never show my face in America again."

Lucy straddled his waist, lightly rubbing her still-swollen

lips along his shaft. She could feel his erection growing.

A dark look crossed his face as their eyes met. His hands skimmed along her sides until they cupped her breasts. Locking his gaze on hers, he sat up to tease her nipple with his tongue.

Lucy moaned. "Where are those condoms?"

"Top drawer," he said, his mouth full.

Grabbing a condom, Lucy glanced down at his cock, intrigued. Lightly, she rubbed the foreskin, exploring its texture. She wanted to take her time and investigate all aspects of this strange penis, but right now, she needed it back inside her.

Ripping the wrapper off, she took the condom and rolled it down his shaft. Playfully, Lucy pushed against his chest until he fell back, gazing up at her in amusement.

"Time to make my country proud," Lucy purred, positioning herself over him and sliding down his length. "Let's go for the Gold!"

3

The sun glared through a small gap in the curtains. Lucy groaned as she cracked one eye open, immediately regretting it when the blinding light smacked her squarely in the face. A faint throbbing began at the back of her head. All she wanted was to close her eyes and fall back to sleep.

Instead, she forced her body to uncurl and stretched out her legs, her bare foot rubbed against something hairy. Startled, she whipped her head to the side, only to have the room spin as her vision blurred.

Shutting her eyes, she leaned against the pillow while the vertigo passed. Memories of last night flooded her mind.

Sex. Really good sex. Keith? Kevin? Ken?

Squinting, she stole a glance in his direction. Thank goodness he still looked attractive in the daylight. In the past, there was more than one occasion when she hadn't been as lucky, as superficial as it may sound.

Kenny? Was that it?

Whatever his name was, currently lay on his back,

breathing deeply. The duvet covered the lower half of his body, exposing his chest, stomach, and one bare leg, which looped over the covers. One arm flung lazily across his chest while the other rested along his side.

Carefully, Lucy slid from under the sheets, doing her best not to tug on the covers and wake him. The morning after a drunken love fest always felt awkward, full of lies and empty promises. She knew what this was, a one-night stand, and she had no intention of seeing this man again. There was no point in small talk or exchanging phone numbers; it was best to cut out early and avoid confrontation.

Tiptoeing around the room, she managed to find all her discarded clothing from the previous night.

The man sighed.

The sheets rustled behind her, and she froze, feeling silly for her actions as if not moving would make her magically invisible. She imagined him smirking as she stood unmoving like a naked statue.

Her heart raced as she turned toward him, dreading the conversation that would surely follow. She sighed in relief when she realized he was still sound asleep but pleasantly surprised to see he had kicked off the duvet, exposing the full glory of his manhood.

Overcome with curiosity, she crept toward the bed to take a closer look at the foreskin hiding the tip of his penis. Covering her mouth, she stifled a nervous giggle, amused by her fascination with his uncut member.

"Some things aren't taught in school," she mumbled.

All she had ever known or seen was a perfectly cut penis. Her naughty side wanted nothing more than to climb back in bed and explore this phenomenon. Last night was great and some of the best sex of her life; would it be so bad to go one more round?

No, it was time to leave. Shaking the thought away, Lucy dashed into the bathroom and dressed quickly. Kaylee was probably wondering where her mother was.

Kaylee. A pang of guilt gnawed at her gut. Not only had she uprooted her only daughter and moved across the country, but last night, she had abandoned her with relatives they hadn't seen in years.

Padding down the hall, Lucy sighed, thankful her one-night stand hadn't woken up. She gathered the rest of her things, double-checking the purse for her phone and wallet. As quietly as possible, she unlatched the door and slid silently into the hallway.

Her head pounded, and her stomach felt queasy. It had been a long time since she'd had a hangover quite like this. Looking up and down the long corridor, she tried to recall exactly how they arrived at the apartment.

Ding.

An elevator. She vaguely remembered the ride up from the parking garage.

A man in a business suit came around the corner and rushed past her, mumbling a quick greeting. She nodded in return and hurried in the direction he had come, rounding the corner and catching the elevator just as the doors slid shut.

After pressing the button for the first floor, she dug into her purse, pulling out the phone. Thankfully, Rob had given her a new SIM card and already programmed Abbey's number into the phone.

"Morning, Sunshine." Abbey's cheery voice came on the line. "Don't tell me—you're running away with the mysterious Irish man? Yes, of course, I'll adopt Kaylee."

"Haha, funny. I *am* running away, but alone."

"You snuck out?"

"Yeah, I'm skipping out. I wouldn't have gone home with him if you hadn't abandoned me."

"I was helping you adjust to a new country," Abbey teased. "Are you not a fan of the full Irish experience?"

"Stop." Lucy cringed as the elevator doors slid open.

"What was that?"

"Elevator." Lucy stepped into a hallway similar to the one she just left.

"You haven't left the building yet?" Abbey laughed.

Lucy looked up and down the hall for an exit to the outside. "No, and I don't see an exit. This floor is just apartments. Shouldn't there be some sort of lobby or main entrance?"

"What floor are you on?"

Lucy popped her head back in the elevator. "I'm sure I pushed the button for the 1st floor."

"Get back in the elevator," Abbey said dryly.

"What? Why?"

"You aren't on the main floor yet," Abbey said. "Get in the elevator and look for the G or zero button."

"Okay?" Lucy replied, unsure. "There is a G, but won't that take me to the garage?"

"It stands for the ground floor, not garage," Abbey explained. "What we call the first floor is called the ground floor here. What we call the second floor, they call the first floor. Ground floor, first floor, second floor."

Lucy scrunched up her face and grunted. "That doesn't make any sense. I'm far too hung-over to process that right now."

"It makes sense if you think about it," Abbey said. "Oh, and the elevator is called a lift."

"I did know that one," Lucy said as the doors opened for the second time. Now, she was in a small lobby. "I see light and a way out. Free at last."

"Hallelujah," Abbey cheered. "Any idea where you are?"

"Not a clue."

Lucy scanned the busy street. Cars, buses, and bicycles zoomed past in both directions. Several shops and buildings lined the road.

"Pull up your location on your phone," Abbey suggested.

"Good idea, hold on." Lucy put the phone on speaker, pulled up the map, and zoomed in on her location. "There's a harbor, a huge harbor. I must be near the ocean?"

"Zoom out until you can see the town name."

"Oh, umm, Done Log Hairy?" Lucy struggled.

Abbey burst into laughter. "I've heard it called many things, but done log hairy is a new one. It's pronounced Done Leer ee."

"That is not how it looks at all."

"You have so much to learn," Abbey teased. "But I was in your shoes not too long ago; thankfully, I had a good teacher."

"At least you didn't have a sister making fun of you," Lucy said.

"Worse, I had an entire Irish family to do that. The Irish people love to give out to foreigners, especially to us Yanks, but it's all in good fun."

"Good to know. Now, how do I get home?"

"Can you see the DART station? It's a train; hopefully, you can see tracks or a sign nearby."

"I see it on the map; it's not too far."

"Perfect, head in that direction. There will be plenty of taxis out front. I'll text you the Eir Code for our house."

"The what?"

"Eir Code. It's like a zip code, only better," Abbey said. "Each house has its own Eir Code; give that to the driver, and it gives the exact location of our house."

"Seems complicated."

"It's not, trust me."

Lucy sighed, longing to snuggle under the covers of her own bed and sleep off this hangover. "Ok, well, text me the code. I'm ready to get back to bed."

"You should have stayed with your bed buddy," Abbey taunted. "You could have had breakfast and a ride; he may have driven you home too."

Abbey burst out laughing at her joke. Lucy hung up, too tired to listen to any more teasing. The area looked beautiful; she would need to remember to come back and explore when her head wasn't throbbing. Or maybe she should have stayed with Kenny. The guy had seemed nice enough; perhaps they could have walked along this harbor and found a cozy place to have breakfast.

Dangerous thinking. That sounded a bit too romantic; more relationship and less one-night stand kind of thinking.

The last thing Lucy needed was to rush mindlessly into a new relationship. Hadn't it been a toxic relationship that sent her running halfway around the world in the first place?

Last night was fun and a great way to blow off steam, but she had responsibilities and needed to get back to Kaylee. This move was supposed to benefit both of them, giving them a chance at a better, more stable life.

Settling into the taxi, Lucy planned the rest of her day. First, a hot shower, followed by coffee, and then a day spent snuggled up on the couch watching old movies with her daughter.

****

"I need every juicy detail." Abbey filled the kettle from the tap.

"The girls are in the next room," Lucy whispered, combing through her wet hair.

Abbey pulled two mugs from the cupboard, setting them down on the counter between them. "They can't hear us; they're deep in Minecraft mode."

Lucy watched Abbey set a tea bag into one of the cups and move the other under the Nespresso machine. With the seasoned moves of a professional, she picked up the kettle and poured boiling water over the tea bag while setting the coffee to brew.

Lucy stopped mid-comb. "Do you put milk in your tea?"

Abbey stuck out her tongue. "Ew, no."

"I had the same reaction last night. The Irish guy asked me. It sounds disgusting."

"I like sugar or honey," Abbey said, setting both items on the counter. "Sometimes both. Of course, I prefer coffee, but, shhh, don't let them hear you."

Abbey looked around the kitchen as if the tea mafia would come for her at any second.

"They don't drink coffee here?" Lucy scrunched up her face. "I love coffee. Will I be seen as a pariah?"

"You're American; they expect us to drink coffee," Abbey said, setting the steaming black liquid they spoke of in front of Lucy. "Most of them drink instant coffee." Abbey made a gagging noise. "My machine here makes me an outlier. I try to drink tea here and there; Rob loves it."

Lucy's face turned serious. "Are you happy here? Honestly."

Abbey raised an eyebrow. "I am. It's hard to explain, but I feel like I was always meant to come here. Are you wondering if *you'll* be happy here?"

Lucy shrugged. "It's been four days, and everything is so different. I feel out of sorts and discombobulated. I don't know if I'll ever adjust."

"It's been *four days*," Abbey repeated. "That's hardly enough time to figure anything out. Remember, you're also dealing with jet lag and a big time difference. Big changes need an adjustment period. I thought you loved change and spontaneity?"

Lucy stared down into her coffee. "That was before I had a child to think about. I have to factor Kaylee into the equation and make good decisions for her. What if I made the wrong choice? I'm forcing her into a new school and a new country; what if it's too much to ask?"

Abbey leaned across the counter to cover Lucy's hand with her own. "Kids are resilient; we know that better than anyone. Our mom is never going to get a Mother of the Year award. And, with all the crap between you and Jeremy, Kaylee turned out great. If you want my opinion, you've already done an amazing thing by escaping a very toxic situation. Mom isn't the best role model for either of our girls and Jeremy—well, you know how I feel about him.

"Kaylee has an amazing opportunity to experience something new, a chance to escape conflict and chaos. And this is selfish, but she has a chance to get to know Lola and me. We never had cousins when we were kids."

As if on cue, laughter erupted from the next room. Abbey raised an eyebrow as if that proved her point.

"Lola and Kaylee spent their first two years together," Lucy reminded her. "Then you left me."

"You left me first," Abbey accused. "You always went back to Jeremy. I honestly never thought you would cut ties completely; I'm still in shock that you're really here."

"I'm done with him. For good this time." Lucy made an X across her chest.

Abbey wiggled her eyebrows. "And you got yourself *under* a hot man. Isn't that the first step in getting over someone?"

Lucy scrunched her nose. "I have nothing to get over. Jeremy is in the past, and I'm moving on."

Abbey smiled as she added honey to her tea.

"He wasn't circumcised," Lucy stated, absently stirring her coffee.

Abbey dropped the spoon she was holding. "Excuse me?"

"Irish guy, his penis– was– different." Lucy couldn't hide a smile as her sister stood gaping at her.

"Oh my." Abbey's cheeks turned light pink. Her eyes darted around the room quickly before she propped on her elbows, ready to share some steamy gossip. "Now, this is the conversation I was hoping for. Did it feel different to you? You know, Rob isn't cut. I don't think most Europeans are."

Lucy giggled like a schoolgirl, speaking in hushed tones. "Rob isn't? I never knew that. Of course, why would I? It isn't something I've ever thought about, circumcised versus uncircumcised, that is, not Rob's junk. I've never thought about Rob's—you know."

Lucy turned beet red.

Abbey couldn't stop laughing. "Oh my gosh, I don't think I've ever talked to anyone about penises before. It's kind of refreshing but feels naughty at the same time."

"I was completely distracted and fascinated by the whole foreskin thing," Lucy admitted. "I still am."

"It's different but the same." Abbey looked down at her tea thoughtfully. "Not that I have much experience; I only slept with one guy before Rob, and he was circumcised. I have learned you can do more to turn a guy on, and everything is more sensitive."

The thought of turning Tin Whistle Man on made Lucy's face flush. She imagined bringing him to his knees, desire burning in his eyes as he begged for release.

"I can give you some tips," Abbey interrupted her daydream. "Help you get that Irish guy going, if you know what I mean."

Lucy felt her cheeks burn. "No," she said too quickly. "I

mean, I'm not going to see him again. It was a one-time thing."

Abbey straightened. "It wasn't good?"

Lucy blew out a breath. "Oh, it was good. Really good."

"Then what's the problem?"

Lucy took a long drink of coffee. "I'm not looking for a commitment right now. It was a night of great sex, but that's it. It was a standard one-night stand; we didn't exchange numbers, and I don't even know his last name."

"Great sex and no commitment sounds like just what you need." Abbey teased. "He wasn't bad on the eyes either."

"And that accent. Don't forget the accent." Lucy's stomach flipped.

"It is the best." Abbey rolled her eyes up to the sky. "I loooow-ve it. It sounds like you should find this guy and give it another go."

Lucy shook her head. "I'm not looking for that right now. I'm happy to call it what it was and live with the memories. Besides, even if I wanted to, as you say, give it another go, how would I find him? And would he even want to go another round? I think it's best to leave last night in the past and move on."

4

Lucy leaned against the counter, cradling a cup of steaming coffee. Nervous energy coursed through her. The adjustment phase had ended, and their new life would officially begin today. Kaylee prepared for her first day of school, and Lucy started her new job in the city center.

Kaylee sat at the table, silently eating a bowl of cereal. The apprehensive look on her daughter's face set Lucy on high alert. Her motherly instincts wanted to protect her child, but she needed to let her go and take on this new challenge alone.

"You're going to love this school," Lola said, plopping down next to her cousin and shoving her hand in the cereal box.

Well, she wouldn't be entirely alone. Lola would be there, maybe not in the same classroom, but at least in the same school.

"I hate being the new girl," Kaylee said. "It's so embarrassing, and everyone will stare at me."

Lola swallowed the mouthful of dry cereal. "Nah. They'll

be curious about you. Every time a class gets a new kid, everyone is excited, and they'll have a million questions for you. But, it's not a big deal "

"I hate first days, too," Lucy said from behind the counter. "I have mine today as well. I always find the first couple of days are the hardest, but after that, it's smooth sailing."

Kaylee rolled her eyes.

Abbey bounced into the kitchen. "Today's the big day. Are we all excited?"

Lucy glanced sideways at her sister, jealous of how much energy Abbey always radiated.

Abbey spoke in a high-pitched, sing-song voice. "Your first day at the office. Kaylee's first day at school. It's all so exciting."

"Whoa, Mom, tone it down," Lola grimaced. "No one is ever that excited for school."

"It's going to be great," Abbey continued. "You'll make new friends and learn some Irish."

Kaylee's face turned pale. "Irish? I thought they spoke English. Do they speak Irish all day?"

"Oh no," Lola said, shaking her head. "We have Irish lessons in school, but only for a little bit."

Kaylee pushed back from the table and, dragging her feet, carried her bowl to the sink.

"It's going to be fine," Lucy reassured her.

"Yeah," Kaylee muttered.

"Come on, I'll tell you about all the kids while we get dressed." Lola grabbed Kaylee by the arm and pulled her toward the stairs.

Abbey glanced toward Lucy. "She'll be fine, you know

that, right?"

Lucy nodded. "I do, but I still worry. Seeing her so anxious makes me feel guilty, especially because I'm the one forcing her to do this."

"We'll walk them to school, and you'll see," Abbey said, pulling two lunch boxes from the shelf. "She'll do great; it's an excellent school. I've met several parents from the PTA and their kids, and everyone is always very nice."

Lucy sighed. "I hated school."

"That's because you were always off alone," Abbey said. "I loved school."

"Well, I wasn't like you."

"And Kaylee isn't like you. She's friendly and approachable."

Lucy scoffed. "I'm not?"

Abbey lifted her eyes toward the ceiling. "Not back then."

Lucy grunted, accepting the truth in that statement.

"You get ready, and I'll make the lunches." Abbey dug through the fridge, tossing carrots and juice boxes onto the counter.

"Are you sure? I can make my own daughter's lunch."

Abbey smiled and waved her off. "I got this."

Lucy ascended the stairs deep in thought. Her mind flashed back to their school days. It was true; she had been a loner throughout high school, but that was a conscious choice. Abbey didn't know the entire story, primarily because Lucy had wanted her younger sister to experience a better childhood than her own.

Lucy spent her free time working odd jobs to put food on the table and keep the lights on, allowing Abbey to indulge in the whole high school experience. Abbey spent her evenings out with friends while Lucy washed dishes at a rundown diner off the highway. While Abbey went to the movies and on dates, Lucy skirted sexual advances by strange men knowing every butt grab, slap, and pinch earned her extra tips to fund Abbey's nights out.

All work and no play had been her mantra during those days. Their father had been nothing more than a sperm donor, and their mother, an alcoholic who spent the majority of their childhood incapable of getting out of bed.

Lucy had no desire to revisit those days.

"Today is the first day of the rest of your life," she confidently told her reflection. "Forget the past and focus on the future."

"Who are you talking to?" Kaylee asked, peering into the bathroom.

"Myself." Lucy pointed toward the mirror. "Just a little pep talk."

"Are you nervous, too?"

Lucy turned from the mirror to face her twelve-year-old daughter. "All the time. Ever since that plane landed last week, I've second-guessed everything."

"Don't," Kaylee said, her face solemn. "You made the right choice, and we're both going to be fine. Things just need to be uncomfortable for a little bit. Isn't that what you said when we decided to leave?"

Lucy smiled, pride welling inside her. "Sounds like me."

Kaylee took a deep breath. "This is the uncomfortable part. It will be over soon enough."

"I'm not going to cry," Lucy said, touching her heart. "I

just put on mascara, but you are so brave."

Kaylee beamed.

"Do I look okay?"

"You look fine, Mom. Hurry up, we have to go."

The walk to school was much quicker and easier than Lucy had imagined. Since first arriving, they hadn't ventured around the area, and other than the night out with Abbey and her one-night stand, they had hardly left the house. It was nice to get a glimpse of the neighborhood.

They passed a few small shops, similar to a 7-11 or Circle K, a café, a Pharmacy, and a small restaurant Abbey called "The Chipper." Lucy made a mental note to ask about that one later.

The morning was overcast, with a slight chill hanging in the air. As they rounded a corner, the landscape quickly changed from a commercial area to a residential one. Before them lay a vast green field, perfectly manicured with white goalposts set at each end. Across the field stood a white two-story building encircled by a thick black fence.

"That's it!" Lola screeched, excitement causing her voice to come out several octaves higher.

Kaylee fell silent as they entered through the gates and followed Lola around to the back of the building.

Lucy leaned toward her daughter. "You're going to do great."

Kaylee nodded.

They walked toward an enclosed courtyard, where children darted about, yelling and chasing one another. Adults lined the sidewalk outside the yard, gathering in small groups to chit-chat.

Longing passed over Lucy as she observed other people's lives playing out before her. What was it like to be greeted by name on the school grounds? She imagined the parents chatting about their morning struggle to get the kids out the door and then discussing their plans for the day ahead. It was hard to picture anyone wanting to engage in conversation with her or being interested in her daily life.

"Abbey, how are you?" A cheery woman stole her sister's attention away.

Lucy stood alone in this crowded space. Back in the States, she watched from her front window, drinking coffee while adorned in yoga pants and slippers, as Kaylee boarded the school bus. She hadn't known any of the kids in Kaylee's class, let alone the parents.

She would love to be one of those cool moms from the movies. The mom all the kids adored. The one who spent mornings at yoga or coffee with friends or arguing for change on the PTA. Being a primarily single parent crashed all those dreams straight into the mud; there was no time for personal activities when juggling a full-time job and parenting duties. By the time Kaylee started kindergarten, Jeremy was hardly around, and when he was with them, helping with Kaylee was never top on his list. Lucy worked a full-time job and came home to cook and clean for a child and a man who spent his days playing video games. It was exhausting; she would never have the energy for PTA meetings.

"Come on. I'll show you where to line up." Lola pulled Kaylee through the gate.

Kaylee glanced over her shoulder at Lucy. The look was a

cross between excitement and 'save me.'

"Good Luck." Lucy mouthed.

Kaylee hesitated briefly before quickly running off behind Lola.

Abbey returned, slinging an arm over Lucy's shoulder. "She'll be fine."

Lucy watched Lola lead Kaylee toward a group of kids and introduce everyone; it warmed her heart to know Lola would look over her cousin. The two of them had instantly clicked; they were kindred spirits like long-lost sisters finally reunited.

Abbey had begun a conversation with another parent, leaving Lucy on her own once again. She glanced back to Kaylee, wanting to wave one final farewell, but Kaylee had her back turned.

Then, she saw a vaguely familiar face.

No, it couldn't be him, she thought. *My eyes are playing tricks on me.*

Tin Whistle Man? Kenny?

It couldn't possibly be.

Lucy squinted, hoping he would magically morph into someone else. The trick didn't work, and, like a startled rabbit, she practically dove behind a car.

"What on earth are you doing?" Abbey looked down at her sister, perplexed.

"It's that guy," Lucy whispered harshly, popping her head up just enough to ensure he was actually there.

"What guy?" Abbey said, looking around.

"Shh." Lucy grabbed her sister and pulled her down behind the car. "The music man."

Abbey's mouth fell open. She jumped up and scanned the yard. "Oh wow, that is him. Does he have kids here?"

"I don't know," Lucy hissed through gritted teeth. "We didn't do a lot of talking."

Abbey burst out laughing.

Lucy smacked her sister on the arm. "Knock it off! I need to get out of here without him seeing me."

"You are such a chicken. You should go say hi."

"I can't do that. I ran out on him, remember?"

Abbey couldn't stop laughing.

Lucy glared at her sister as she slunk backward, hunched over, attempting to keep out of his line of sight should he happen to glance their way.

"I better take you home," Abbey said. "We can't have you getting lost. Lord knows you may end up at his house instead of mine."

"Ha ha." Lucy rushed out the gate and hurried away from the school.

Thirty minutes later, she tentatively boarded the LUAS, the tram that would take her into the city center. Rob had supplied her with a Leap card to pay for her journey and given her a quick rundown of how the tram worked and which stop to get off at.

Knowing she had about twenty minutes until her destination, she found an empty seat and sat down. Her mind instantly went back to the school sighting. What was *he* doing at school? Did he have a child or two? Thinking back to the apartment, she couldn't recall anything that shouted a child lived there. She distinctly remembered the bathroom having only one toothbrush. But that didn't rule out the possibility of him being a part-time dad.

She had only given their night together a passing thought, convinced they would never cross paths again. Out of the blue, bam, there he was, in the most unlikely place: her daughter's new school.

Even in the brief moment she noticed him, he somehow looked better today than she remembered. Of course, she had too many drinks that night and a banging hangover the following morning; her vision was a bit skewed.

The one-night stand rises again. She smiled at the pun, her mind returning to that night.

The sex had been very good.

Her stomach fluttered; she had to stop this line of thinking. It was a path leading to nowhere good. After all, this was her first day at a new job; the last thing she needed was to show up flustered and red in the face.

However, images continued to dance across her mind like a dirty slideshow; she felt helpless to stop them. The smooth feel of hands sliding over her body. His chest slick with sweat as he moved on top of her. Thighs clenched tightly around his waist, their bodies tangled together, moving in perfect rhythm. And, of course, the fascinating foreskin of his uncut penis.

Lucy shifted in the seat as arousal swam inside her, moisture threatening to pool between her legs. She had to think of something else, anything else, or she would need to change her underwear.

Turning her attention out the window, she tried focusing on the houses whizzing past. The lust slowly died away, replaced with a tinge of regret; maybe she had jumped the gun. She probably should have stuck around or, at the very least, exchanged numbers. Perhaps she needed one more night to flush him out of her system.

No. She needed to stop this self-inflicted torture; a one-night stand could only be one night. These feelings of regret most likely stemmed from the move; she was homesick and lonely. Her desire for connection fueled these impossible daydreams of a casual encounter becoming more serious. Starting a new life was a massive change, and while a small part of her missed the familiarity of her mom and Jeremy, she needed to escape the toxic hold they had on her life.

Then there was Kaylee. Did she miss her grandmother and father? Truthfully, Kaylee didn't need those two in her life. Despite what people may say, blood wasn't always thicker than water, especially when that family was unpredictable. Those two adults should have been someone Kaylee could rely on, but they had only failed her repeatedly. Lucy felt guilty for giving her daughter a deadbeat for a father. And her own mother, who spent the majority of her time with Kaylee, remained emotionally stunted, often acting like a child herself. Neither were ideal role models for a pre-teen.

On top of everything, Lucy's biggest fear was turning out exactly like her mother, miserable and bitter at the world. Her parents had never married, but her mother never lost hope her father would one day commit. Sadly, she wasted half her adult life waiting for a man only interested in easy, free sex. Her mother had convinced herself that was how love worked.

"He always comes back to me," her mother always said.

"No matter what, he always comes back."

Meanwhile, Lucy had no relationship with her father. The only times she saw him were the random days he showed up to screw her mom. He never acknowledged his two young daughters, focusing only on pulling their mother into the bedroom. Lucy would crank up the TV volume or take Abbey outside so they wouldn't hear the groans and grunts. Their father was always gone by morning, leaving their mom buried in blankets and snuggling a bottle of whiskey.

Lucy couldn't wrap her head around her mother's decision to continue the torturous cycle. At a young age, Lucy had fully understood her father never intended to stay, yet her adult mother refused to accept that truth. After all, he wasn't the father type; he never committed to anything and believed monogamy was for wimps.

Sometime in her early twenties, her father died. There may have been a funeral, but Lucy never asked; she wouldn't have attended anyway. Her father meant nothing to her.

The LUAS doors opened, and a man with a briefcase sat beside Lucy, pulling her back to the present.

"Oh, my stop," she mumbled, jolting from her seat, and rushed off the tram just as the doors slid shut behind her.

5

One week later, Lucy felt confident as she stood outside the four-story brick building housing the offices of *The IT Group*, the consulting company she worked for. The building was part of a cluster of rowhouses now converted into office buildings.

Last week, she had been a bundle of nerves, starting a new job while worrying her daughter would be miserable at her new school. Despite her angst, the first day had gone well for both of them. Lucy quickly found her groove at work, finding her co-workers easygoing and loving the laid-back atmosphere of the Irish work scene.

Kaylee's experience almost mirrored her mother's. She discovered the school environment to be relaxed and the kids eager to make a new friend.

Smoothing down her skirt, Lucy ascended the steps and opened the bright red door. She loved the brightly painted doors on these beautiful Georgian townhouse buildings. It was modern and mixed into the rich history of the city. From her desk by the window, she could hear the traffic along the road in her office; occasionally, there came the faint clip-clopping of the horse-drawn carriage tours, reminding her of how life must have been long ago.

Once inside the building, she dropped her coat and purse on the desk and walked into the small kitchen a co-worker had called *the canteen*. The kitchen had a coffee pod machine similar to the one Abbey owned; there was none of that instant coffee here. The coffee pods sat perfectly arranged in a revolving stand, adding to the organized and inviting vibe of the office. Rotating the stand, she examined each pod, settling on a vanilla-flavored one. She popped it into the machine, placed a mug underneath, and set it to brew.

While she waited, she busied herself by tidying up the counter. After tossing stray stir sticks and empty sugar packets into the garbage, she pulled a paper towel from the dispenser and wiped the counter clean.

Once the coffee finished brewing, she pulled a small carton of milk from the fridge, adding a splash to her cup, along with one sugar packet. She cleaned up her mess and carried the steaming cup back toward her desk.

"Saunders! Conference room."

Lucy jolted. Hot coffee spilled over the side of the cup, splashing onto her hand.

Lucy held back a curse. "Be right there!" She called through gritted teeth.

Backtracking to the kitchen, she set the cup down and ran her hand under cold water. Thankfully, the burn was minimal, but she had lost half her coffee. There was no time to make more.

With the mug wiped clean, she hurried toward the opposite side of the room, carefully navigating through the maze of cubicles. A knot of anxiety tightened in her stomach as the big corner office loomed before her. Her residency in Ireland depended on this job; she couldn't afford to make any mistakes. The man on the other side of the glass door could change her future with a snap of his fingers. Desmond O'Neill, President of *The IT Group*, was kind and generous while holding an air of serious professionalism.

Lucy took a deep breath, pushed the door open, and entered the room. Desmond sat hunched over his laptop and didn't look up when she walked in.

"Sit," he said, motioning toward the row of chairs across the table from him.

Lucy sat.

"We're moving half this office to the second floor," he said, jumping straight to the point while staring at the screen.

Lucy wasn't sure if she should respond as silence drug on for several minutes.

Finally, he glanced over at her and continued. "We've just finished installing a section of new servers downstairs, and we need to migrate the entire office to those servers." Desmond liked to move his hands when he spoke, flaying his wrists around in the air. "Bigger, faster, better. And then we'll need to move a few of our customers, but I'm getting ahead of myself."

Lucy frowned. Migration. Her worst nightmare.

"It's shite, but it's a big opportunity for you," he said, noticing the look on her face.

She raised a brow.

"I'm giving you the lead on this project."

"Me? But I'm the newbie," Lucy said.

"You came highly recommended." Desmond waved her words away and slid a plastic folder across the table. "Proposed plans. I've already assembled the team for you. You and your team will be moving upstairs today. There are a few desks and chairs, but all the computers are in boxes. I leave it to you to set the space up however your team suits. Prep the team, make a plan, do the work, and prepare for the migration as soon as possible."

Lucy leaned back, staring at the ceiling, her brain in full planning mode. "It's going to take some time. We don't have the office space set up; I'll need to consult with the server team, we need to test everything repeatedly, transfer data–."

"I don't need the specifics," Desmond cut her off. "I only need a timeline and assurance this is something *you* can do."

Lucy straightened in the chair. "I can do it."

"Good," Desmond continued. "I've emailed the team members, and they're ready on your command. I'll send up Rob to help configure the space. Necessary contacts are in the folders. I'll need the strategic plan in a fortnight."

Lucy furrowed her brows. "A what?"

"A fortnight," Desmond repeated, turning his attention back to his laptop. "This is a huge project; you'll be rewarded handsomely once it is completed."

Lucy leaned forward. "Rewarded?"

"A promotion," Desmond replied. "Systems Admin. Manager. Keep that in mind while setting up the office space."

Lucy's eyes widened. While it would be a massive project,

the opportunity to move up the ladder within a few weeks of starting a new job was mind-blowing.

Desmond studied the perplexed look on her face. "Your credentials are impeccable. You've proven to be a self-starter from day one. I've been bragging to the big bosses, so let's show them you deserve a promotion."

"Thank you," Lucy said, still in shock.

"Don't make me regret this." Desmond waved his hand in dismissal.

Twenty minutes later, Lucy stood alone in a large room with only two empty desks. It was hard to believe she was tasked with transforming this space into a bustling hub of activity. She placed her laptop and the folder on one desk and searched for a chair.

Once comfortable, she opened the file, curious about her new team.

"It's quiet up here."

Lucy jumped at the interruption. "You scared me."

Rob, her brother-in-law and co-worker, grinned. "Sorry."

Lucy set down the file. "It's a little eerie up here, to be honest."

Rob sat on the edge of the desk. "I had a quick debriefing with Des; this is a brilliant opportunity for you, Lucy."

Lucy blew out a breath. "I know, it really is. Of course, this project means longer hours for a few weeks, probably a few nights, and maybe some weekends. I'll have less time with Kaylee."

"Aye, but a big promotion once it's all done," Rob reminded her. "Don't forget you have a team; use them, delegate; no sense taking everything on yourself. Things are more laid back here; there are time constraints, but we like to be home for dinner; no one will expect you to burn the midnight oil. We work normal hours, with overtime only when it's essential. Remember that."

Lucy sighed. "Old habits are hard to kick. That reminds me, I have a dumb question for you. What is a fortnight?"

Rob chuckled. "Two weeks. You'll hear that a lot here. We get paid fortnightly, come back in a fortnight, finish this or that in a fortnight. It loosely means two weeks, but remember, we're relaxed here, so it could be three."

Lucy nodded. "Desmond wants the strategic plan in a fortnight."

"He's a good boss; he understands there is loads of work to be done, and he doesn't want a rush job." Rob jumped off the desk and studied the room. "Enough chit-chat; we best get started. We'll need to map out the room configuration and set up all these desks and computers."

***

Lucy rushed through the door, shaking out of her jacket. "I'm late, I know. I'm sorry."

Laughter drifted from the kitchen.

Lucy glanced behind her at Rob. "Sounds like they haven't even noticed we're late."

Rob shrugged. "Maybe we should sneak off to the pub to celebrate your victory."

"I'm not promoted yet," Lucy said, hanging her coat and heading into the kitchen.

Opening her mouth to issue another apology, she quickly

shut it as she entered the scene. Abbey, Kaylee, and Lola stood, covered in white powder, around a powder-coated counter. A bag of flour lay on its side, its contents spilling into a pile at their feet.

Abbey was laughing so hard that tears streamed down her face. "This is a failed attempt at biscuit-making," she said between breaths.

"Flour bombs," Kaylee added, brushing powder off her shirt.

"Never turn a fan on next to a pile of flour." Lola burst into a fit of giggles.

Lucy furrowed her brows. "A fan? Why would you have a fan on the counter?"

Rob glanced at the mess and frowned. "That's a loaded question." By the look on his face, he wasn't amused.

Abbey rolled her eyes at his comment and pulled a broom from the utility closet. "You girls tackle the counter; I'll get the floor."

Lola and Kaylee continued laughing as they scooped flour into the trash can.

Lucy set her laptop bag on the table and sat on a stool near the counter. "So, how was everyone's day?"

"Great," Lola replied. "We moved seats in class. I sit next to Julia, one of my best friends."

Abbey sighed. "Oh great. I hope you don't get in trouble for talking too much again this year."

Lola made a face at her mom.

"I think you two are making a bigger mess," Abbey protested. "Is any of that flour making it into the bin? It looks like half landed on the floor I just swept."

Lola shrugged. "Then, do this area last."

"Or, better yet, you two do it." Abbey leaned the broom against the counter. "I need to get these mangled biscuits in the oven and start dinner."

"And how was your day, Kaylee?" Lucy tried to sound nonchalant.

Kaylee grabbed the discarded broom. "It was good. I hung out with this girl Chloe in yard."

Lucy sighed with relief. "That's nice to hear. I'm glad you're not on your own. How is your teacher? What is her name?"

"Aidan. It's a man." Kaylee swept around Lola's feet. A pile of flour dropped off the counter, landing on the spot she had just cleaned. "Hey, watch it."

Lola laughed, mischievously sprinkling another handful of flour onto the floor. Kaylee shot her cousin an annoyed look but couldn't hide the smile tugging the corners of her mouth.

Abbey pushed the tray of biscuits into the oven. "This mess will never get cleaned with you two running things."

Lucy ignored the chaos. "I'm amused you call your teacher by his first name. We would never have gotten away with that in my day."

"It's a very laid-back school," Abbey commented, then pursed her lips in thought. "Aidan. I'm not familiar with that name. Is he new this year?"

Kaylee shrugged. "Everyone is new to me."

Abbey made a face. "Funny."

"I should help with dinner," Lucy said. "It's bad enough I'm late."

"No, no, you're grand; stay seated." Abbey waved her off. "The girls and I have dinner sorted."

"You're grand? Sorted?" Lucy was still getting used to the standard terms.

Abbey patted Lucy's hand. "Give it time, my dear sister; you'll speak like a true oy-rish person in no time."

"Spot on with that accent, Mom." Lola's voice oozed with sarcasm. She gave her mother an overly dramatic wink and formed the OK gesture with her fingers.

Abbey tousled her daughter's hair. "Are you the accent police?"

Lola shrugged and playfully stuck out her tongue while Kaylee dumped the last bits of flour into the trash.

"It's like nothing happened," Abbey marveled. "Dinner should be ready soon. Do you girls have homework?"

"Yeah, yeah," Lola grumbled. "We'll go work on it."

"And maybe put on some clean shirts," Abbey called. "Please don't drip flour all over the carpet."

Kaylee and Lola looked down at their flour-dusted clothes and burst into another fit of giggles as they hurried up the stairs.

"So, I have some big news," Lucy said once the girls were out of sight. "I got the lead on a big project at work."

"Oh, Lucy, that's great."

"I've been told it could lead to a big promotion."

Abbey looked impressed. "Wow, fair play to you, and you've only been there a few weeks."

Lucy's eyes widened. "I know. It's a huge and somewhat complicated project; lots of work. I see many late nights in my future, and I already feel guilty about it."

Abbey shrugged. "Don't. This is huge for you, and if it leads to a promotion, it will be worth all those extra hours."

"I feel like I'm pawning Kaylee off on you."

Abbey waved her off. "Please, Lola is over the moon to have Kaylee here every night. Most nights, it's me and her on our own. You probably see Rob more than I do."

Lucy smiled. "Funny you say that; I worked most of today with your husband. It's the most I've seen him around the office." Lucy spoke louder, intentionally tilting her head toward the living room. "I was beginning to doubt he actually worked there."

"Haha!" Rob called from the living room. "I'm so good they have me working in multiple departments."

"Maybe no one wants to work with you," Lucy teased. "They have no choice but to keep moving you."

Rob entered the room, grinning. "Funny. Just remember you're stuck with me all day tomorrow. Unlike me, the boss doesn't trust you to be on your own."

"You think I can't configure hard drives? You do know I'm heading up an entire migration project."

Abbey threw her head back. "Oh no! Not another one. Nerd talk alert."

Lucy laughed, giving Rob a friendly punch in the arm.

"You could talk nerdy too if you cared enough to learn some of the terms." Rob's playful tone evaporated.

"I've tried." Abbey shrugged. "I just don't understand computer talk. Besides, I convinced Lucy to move here so you would have someone to talk nerdy with."

Rob's eyes darkened; he opened his mouth as if to say something but instead pursed his lips together.

"You're stuck with me for the next few days." Lucy elbowed him playfully in the arm, turning back to Abbey. "We'll keep the tech talk for the office."

"I need to shower," Rob said gruffly, abruptly retreating up the stairs.

Abbey turned toward the sink and concentrated on scrubbing a mixing bowl.

Lucy had caught the glistening in her sister's eyes. "Is everything alright with you two?"

Abbey continued scrubbing, keeping her back to Lucy. "We're fine."

Lucy tilted her head to one side and raised her eyebrows.

Abbey stopped scrubbing, her back still turned. "He gets cranky sometimes. I feel like he's mad at me, but I don't know what I did."

"I'm the last person to ask for relationship advice."

"I'm not asking for advice," Abbey snapped, dropping the bowl and placing her hands on the edge of the sink. "I'm venting."

"Okay," Lucy mumbled.

Abby turned, drying her hands on a towel. Her tone turned soft. "Sometimes, I feel like I don't have anyone to talk to. I can't vent my frustration to Lola; she's eleven. And I can't complain to my husband about—my husband."

"Okay?"

"I want that kind of relationship with you." Abbey looked across the counter at Lucy. "A real sister-like relationship. The kind you see in movies, where we talk about everything, laugh, and cry together." Abbey sighed. "We used to be so close, and asking you to move here was selfish on my part.

Remember how things were when the girls were small? I cherished those days when we were close and building a good bond. But every time Jeremy came back into the picture, begging you to give him another chance, you tossed everything we had aside and ran off with him."

Lucy hung her head. "I know."

"Then, he would leave, and we would start building our relationship again, only to have you abandon me when he showed back up. Somehow, I'm always the one getting left behind, and I–please don't leave this time."

Lucy was speechless, surprised by the desperation and pain on Abbey's face. For years, all Lucy had wanted was to protect Abbey; she had worked endlessly so her little sister wouldn't see the hell they were both trapped in. When Rob entered the picture, Lucy saw him as Abbey's savior and felt she could finally let her sister go. At this moment, she realized Abbey's world wasn't as perfect as it had always seemed.

Lucy reached across for Abbey's hand. "I've always been here for you, but I'm not going anywhere this time. Besides, I don't have anywhere to go."

Abbey gave a small smile. "I want you to know how much I need you to be in my life. I think you need to know that, too."

"Thank you," Lucy whispered.

Abbey leaned back and blew out a breath. "I've been on an emotional roller coaster lately. I'm starting a new company, and the dynamic in our house is changing. Those changes seem to be affecting everyone."

Lucy nodded. "Oh, I know all about that."

"Rob isn't always the most understanding person," Abbey confessed. "We love each other but know how to push each other's buttons. He laughs and jokes with you so easily and then snaps at me. It hurts. I feel like a child watching my best friend run off to play with someone new."

"Are you jealous because I joke around with Rob?" Lucy asked. "I hope you know he's like a brother to me."

Abbey straightened. "I know. I'm not jealous you two will run off together or anything. I'm jealous of the connection the two of you have always had." Abbey's eyes glistened again. "I know he feels protective over you, and I think you need that. You need a man who watches out for you instead of using you. But I'm scared to be left behind. I'm scared you two will team up and tease me or look down on me because I'm not as smart as you are. I'm scared you'll always take his side."

Lucy met Abbey's tearful gaze. "Oh gosh, Abbey, I will always take your side. You're my sister; we're blood."

"That's all I need to know, then." Abbey shrugged, wiping at her eyes. "Sorry, I'm so hormonal right now. I need chocolate and a heating pad."

"After dinner, we'll drink wine, eat chocolate, and talk about boys." Lucy batted her lashes.

"I love all of that, except the boys part." Abbey turned toward the oven. "I would much rather hear about this new project you're in charge of. Maybe you can teach me a few techie terms."

"You're on!"

6

Two weeks later, Lucy breezed into the kitchen, wearing yoga pants, a t-shirt, and fuzzy slippers. She yawned, making a bee line for the coffee machine. "First day off in a fortnight."

Abbey was peeling and slicing carrots for the lunch boxes. "How long have you been waiting to use that word?"

Lucy laughed. "From the moment I first heard it."

"What are your plans for this day off?"

"For one, I'm taking a much-needed break from all electronics." Lucy set her cup under the coffee maker and popped a pod into the top. "No computers and no checking my email. I will, however, be watching loads of trashy television."

Over the past two weeks, Lucy dedicated every waking moment to planning, strategizing, and meticulously testing each aspect of her migration project. With the next four days off, she had a small window for recovery before spending the weekend diving into the actual migration.

"No social media?" Abbey's eyes widened. "Oh, that

reminds me, I wanted to set up your Flare account today."

"My what?" Lucy poured milk into her coffee, reaching around Abbey for a spoon.

Abbey threw up her hands. "It's the latest and greatest dating app. You work in tech, and you don't know what Flare is?"

Lucy rolled her eyes. "I've been locked in a tiny office for two weeks, testing—things." Lucy stopped herself before using technical terms Abbey wouldn't understand. "I don't pay any attention to dating apps; they change faster than the weather in Ireland."

Abbey grinned. "Good one."

Lucy may have been stuck inside an office most days, but she quickly adapted to Dublin's finicky weather. One minute, it was raining; the next, it was sunny and warm, and just as the jackets had been packed away, a hail storm would blow through.

"Anyway, you have a few days off; what better way to blow off some steam than by blowing—something." Abbey wiggled her eyebrows.

Lucy rolled her eyes and groaned. "I didn't move here to jump straight into the dating pool."

"Who said anything about dating? Just jump someone." Abbey smirked. "How about tin whistle guy? One more wild night. We could go back to that pub and find him. Or stake out the school and wait for him to reappear."

Red crept across Lucy's cheeks. "I think that bridge is still smoldering in ashes. I ghosted him. That's what the kids call it, right?"

"Sounds right."

"Speaking of school, I have a parent-teacher meeting with Kaylee's teacher this morning. What are those all about?"

Abbey zipped up the lunch boxes and set them aside. "It's what they call a parent/teacher conference here. You'll get a quick update on her progress, and you can discuss any concerns. I have Lola's tomorrow."

Lucy sat down at the bar and sipped her coffee. "It will be nice to get an insider's perspective. I hope she's doing good. How do you think she's adjusting?"

"She really likes school. I think she *has* adjusted." Abbey scratched her head absently. "On another note, I'm on the committee for the Halloween Disco, and we could use a few extra hands."

Lucy gave a curious look. "Disco? Like 70's music. Abba and *Stayin' Alive*?" She swayed her hips, pointing one finger at the ceiling before crossing it over her body to point at the floor like John Travolta.

Abbey laughed. "Disco means dance. It's next Friday in the hall, and all the kids get to come. There will be food and drinks, everyone dresses up, and it's great craic."

"Craic, I know that one," Lucy said proudly.

"She's learning, folks." Abbey tapped a finger to her nose. "We can dress up and supervise. You'll get a peek into the school, see some of their friends, and maybe your hunky dad will be there helping too."

"Hunky dad?" Kaylee entered the kitchen and made a face. "There's a hunky dad at my school?"

Lucy shook her head wildly. "No, I thought I saw a guy I met at the pub."

"Oh, the one you went home with," Kaylee said casually,

grabbing her lunch box and shoving it into her school bag.

Lucy's face turned red, and her jaw hit the counter.

Kaylee squished up her face. "What? I'm twelve, Mom, come on. Did you think I didn't know what was up when you didn't come home from the pub that night?"

Lucy glanced down at her watch. "Okay, then. I need to change. I'm walking you to school this morning. I have my parent-teacher meeting."

Without waiting for a response, Lucy ran up the stairs. While she never wanted Kaylee to be a prude and always tried to be open and honest with her daughter, Lucy couldn't help feeling a little ashamed of her actions. She thought the one-night stands were far behind her, especially since she hadn't had one since Kaylee turned double digits. Although they had "the talk" a few years ago, that didn't mean Lucy was comfortable sharing details of her sex life with a twelve-year-old.

Exchanging her loose pants for skinny jeans, she shimmied and shook her hips into them. Shuffling through the closet, she found a light blue shirt that accentuated the green in her eyes. In the bathroom, she swiftly ran a brush through her tangled hair and brushed her teeth. Not in the mood to fuss with makeup, she applied a touch of mascara and some light concealer to hide the dark circles under her eyes.

Although the migration project would help distinguish herself within the company, it came with a price. She had spent many sleepless nights staring at a computer screen. Rob had told her to delegate and use her team, but scars from the past still haunted her. The consequence of people repeatedly letting her down made it difficult to rely on others.

"Good enough," she muttered, heading back down the stairs.

"Ohh, you look fancy," Abbey said, leaning against the kitchen door frame.

"Fancy? This is casual," replied Lucy. "I feel like a mess."

Abbey shook her head. "You don't look like a mess. You look hot in those skinny jeans. Causal never looked so good."

"Are you hitting on me?" Lucy laughed.

"Are you hoping to run into a certain someone?" Abbey wiggled her brows.

Lucy glared. "I didn't even think about that—until now."

"Let's go, Mom," Kaylee called impatiently from the front door.

"Shall I walk a few feet behind you?" Lucy teased her daughter.

"No. I'm not embarrassed of you. I just don't want to be late." Kaylee looped her arm around her mother's. "I'm excited for you to meet Aidan; he's so cool. He might be the funnest teacher I've ever had."

"Really?"

Kaylee nodded, babbling with enthusiasm. "We're doing a bunch of different science experiments right now, and they are so fun. It doesn't feel like work; he makes learning fun."

Lucy's heart soared hearing the excitement and joy in her daughter's voice. Back in their hometown, Kaylee was a great student but never enjoyed school. Here, Kaylee couldn't get enough of school and dreaded the weekends, a huge turnaround.

Lucy relaxed on the walk to school, delighting in the extra time with Kaylee and Lola. Once the migration work was complete and she earned a promotion, she could work from home more and be present when Kaylee arrived from school.

"Aunt Abbey asked me to help at the Halloween Disco," Lucy said, testing the waters.

"Yes, you should; it's so much fun," Lola said. "Mom does it every year; she would love if you were there."

"How would you feel about that, Sweetie?" Lucy turned her attention to Kaylee. "I wouldn't do it if it made you uncomfortable."

Kaylee gave her mother a huge grin. "Why would you think that? When have I ever been embarrassed by you? If you want to help, you should. I don't care."

Lucy shrugged. "I guess the thought of my mother showing up at a school event would have horrified me."

Lucy couldn't help but project her past onto Kaylee. Back in high school, everyone called her mother a drunk and a whore. Lucy heard them whispering as she walked past; sometimes, those whispers turned into taunts yelled in her direction. That was a big part of why she was a loner in high school; kids were cruel.

"You're not as quirky as grandma," Kaylee told her.

Lucy laughed; she didn't have the heart to tell Kaylee her grandmother was far beyond quirky.

"You would want me there?" Lucy asked as they entered the front gates of the school.

"Of course," Kaylee said. "I can introduce you to some of my friends, and maybe you can meet some other parents."

Lucy's heart warmed; she didn't miss the subtle

encouragement in her daughter's words. "I'll talk to my boss."

Kaylee hugged her mom, and Lucy felt her heart soar; she wasn't an embarrassment after all.

Kaylee waved as she walked into the school. "Say hi to Aidan for me."

Lucy still found it strange hearing her daughter call the teacher by his first name; it seemed very informal. Dismissing the thought, she headed to the small counter belonging to the school secretary.

"Hi, you okay?"

"I'm Lucy Saunders."

"Oh, Kaylee's mum," the woman behind the counter said. "Such a lovely girl. How is she finding things?"

"Good, I think." Lucy suddenly felt shy. "I guess I'm about to find out."

The lady smiled warmly. "I'm Niamh. If you need anything or have any questions, give me a ring." She opened a notebook and set it on the counter. "You need to sign in here. Follow the signs up the stairs and to the left."

"Okay, thanks."

Lucy signed the book, repeating the directions as she climbed the stairs. Thankfully, at the top, a sign pointed toward the meeting rooms. Lucy followed the hall to the end, where a woman sat quietly on the couch.

"Hello," she said, sliding over to make room for Lucy. "I haven't seen you around here. Are you new to the school?"

"Yes. My daughter, Kaylee, is in sixth class."

"American?" the woman asked.

"How did you know?"

The woman smiled. "Accent. What part are you from?"

Lucy found her comment amusing. This was the second Irish person pointing out she was the one with an accent.

"Oregon, just outside of Portland."

The woman extended her hand. "I'm Sinéad."

"Lucy," she said, taking the hand. "Are you here to see Aidan?"

"No. My son is in fourth class. I'm here for Eiméar."

A door opened across from them, and a woman leaned out. "Sinéad?"

"Lovely to meet you," Sinéad said before entering the room, the door closing behind her.

Lucy stared at her hands. A few minutes later, a woman emerged from behind a different door. Their eyes met briefly, and Lucy gave a smile. The woman nodded in response before striding down the hallway, her fashionable high heels clicking along the tiled floor.

"Lucy?" A deep baritone called from inside the room. "Come on in."

Feeling nervous, she absently wiped her palms down her jeans before stepping into the room.

Kaylee's teacher, Aidan, sat hunched over a table, shuffling through papers. While straightening his tie, he pushed to a standing position and gestured to the chair in front of the table.

"Sorry, please have a—," his voice trailed off as their eyes met.

No, no, no! This was not happening.

She froze in place. Her legs suddenly turned to jelly, making it feel as if she had melted into this spot on the floor.

She struggled to say something, anything, but her brain seemed to have malfunctioned. She was a deer in the headlights.

Aidan's eyes grew wide as recognition crossed his face. A smile curved his lips, and he dropped down into his chair.

He ran a hand through his wavy hair. "Well, this is—unexpected."

Kenny. His name was Kenny. Was she in the wrong room?

Her heart was beating so fast she thought she would pass out. A rush of heat coursed through her entire body, and a deep shade of crimson crept up her neck. Blinking rapidly, Lucy begged her body to calm down.

Her brain kicked into overdrive; flashes of a night not too long ago played through her memories.

No, not here, she silently begged.

Too late. Dirty screenshots flew around her mind. Panting and heavy breathing echoed in her ears. Images of his uncut penis mocked her; this was not the time to picture everyone in the room naked.

Her throat went dry. Silently, she mouthed a greeting, but no words escaped her lips.

Awkwardly, she fumbled for the chair, tossing her body down onto it.

Aidan remained silent as he watched her, his gaze intense and unwavering. He covered his mouth with a hand, clearly attempting to conceal a smile and laughter at her expense.

Lucy's movements felt awkward as she tried to get comfortable in the chair, leaning forward and then sitting back, unable to hold still.

"All good there?" Aidan asked, trying to keep a straight face.

Lucy inwardly kicked herself. *"Pull it together, Lucy."*

Aidan's shoulders shook as he dropped his gaze and fiddled with the stack of papers in front of him. Grabbing a small pile, he lightly tapped the stack against the table, forcing them into perfect alignment.

Composing himself, he met her gaze again. "Lucy, is it?"

Amusement danced in those blue eyes. He seemed to be enjoying her discomfort a little too much.

Swallowing hard over the lump in her throat, she squeaked out, "Yes, Lucy."

Absently, she wiped a hand over her forehead several times, trying to regain composure. "I thought your name was Kenny?"

He placed his chin in his palm, resting an elbow on the desk. "Funny, I don't remember ya askin' me name?"

Lucy felt as if her face had just burst into flames. She narrowed her eyes, desperately trying to erase the memories flashing through her mind, but couldn't forget this man had seen her naked.

"You didn't ask my name, either," she said defensively. *Stop. Change the subject.*

Lucy wanted to run out the door.

Aidan looked toward the ceiling thoughtfully. "My surname is Kenny. My mates call me that."

Aidan Kenny. Now she knew Tin Whistle Man's name.

Aidan seemed unfazed. He glanced down at the papers in front of him. "How is Kaylee finding things? Is she settling in?"

Lucy bit her bottom lip. Oh geez, Kaylee. Her one-night stand had been with Kaylee's teacher. This was humiliating.

Words swirled around in her head, but she couldn't escape the gutter of dirty thoughts her brain seemed stuck in.

"Can I get ya some water?"

Maybe he could toss cold water in her face to help her snap out of this daze.

Lucy inhaled deeply and exhaled slowly. She had to pull it together and focus on Kaylee. "No, I'm fine. I think she's doing good."

"Grand," Aidan nodded. "I'm happy with her progress. She's kind, friendly, helpful, and fittin' in well."

Lucy could listen to his voice all day, not to mention that accent was an American's wet dream. Aidan's accent was thicker than Rob's and most of her colleagues; she would have to ask Rob about accents later.

As he continued to speak of Kaylee's progress, chills ran down her arms; she was grateful the jacket she wore hid them from view. Butterflies danced in her stomach as she watched his lips move. Dropping her gaze to his hands, she swallowed hard. Those hands had felt every part of her, gliding carelessly over every inch of her naked flesh.

Coughing to hide her arousal, she stared at the floor. She couldn't look at him without her body responding. Electricity sparked through her as the urge to touch him became more than she could take. She imagined swiping the papers off the desk and letting him take her right now.

Damn, stop that. Concentrate.

"She can be shy sometimes," Aidan continued talking. "Reluctant to raise her hand even when I'm positive she knows the answer."

Lucy nodded, trying to focus on the words instead of the man speaking them.

Kaylee. This was about Kaylee.

Her palms were slick with sweat, and she continually rubbed them up and down her jeans.

Aidan's gaze seemed to burn into her as he casually continued through the progress report.

How was he so calm when her every nerve was on edge?

"Are ya alright?" Aidan's tone turned serious.

Damn.

She was making a fool of herself. She may have thought she was being subtle, but instead, she acted like a toddler doing the pee-pee dance. She couldn't stop squirming and fidgeting.

"I'm sorry, I—it's just—." Lucy closed her eyes and raised a finger, indicating she needed a moment. Rubbing her hands over her face, she squared her shoulders and shifted her head from side to side as if working out a stiff neck muscle.

When she opened her eyes, Aidan was looking at her with an amused smile.

"Look, this is really awkward," she exclaimed. Pushing out of the chair, she paced the small room. "You surprised me. I didn't expect to see you again. Ever. Certainly, not here. Not now. My daughter's teacher? You. You're her teacher. What are the chances?"

Her tirade over, Lucy fell back into the chair, rubbing her temples. Aidan watched her intently but didn't respond.

Lucy took a deep breath and exhaled slowly. "Sorry, that was unprofessional," she said quietly. "Let's just focus on

Kaylee. You were saying she can be shy?"

"Right." Aidan said slowly, looking back down at the papers. "Kaylee is adjusting well. I would like ta see her engage more. My one concern is her Irish; she's far behind the other students. Is there anyone Irish in the home who can work with her?"

Her stupid heart skipped a few beats. Was he asking for himself or as a concerned teacher?

"No," Lucy answered quickly. "Well, my brother-in-law is Irish, but I've never heard him speak the language."

"Have you lived in Ireland long?"

Lucy blinked, confused as to why he was asking personal questions.

"I'm only askin' because some exemptions exist for children over twelve who have recently moved from abroad." Aidan went back to shuffling papers.

"Oh, umm yeah," Lucy sputtered. "We just moved here a few months ago."

"Ah, grand," Aidan said. "She can apply for an exemption if you wish. Niamh, at the front office, can help sort that for you."

"Ok, great," she responded.

"Do you have any concerns regarding Kaylee?"

Lucy shook her head; her only questions had nothing to do with Kaylee.

"Alright, well, it was good to officially meet ya," Aidan said, standing. "If anythin' does come up, feel free to email me."

"Ok." Lucy jumped out of the chair, knocking it over backward. "Oops."

Her stomach did flip-flops as an amused smile crossed his lips. As she approached the door, the air felt charged with tension and electricity. She hesitated, half convinced the door handle would shock her the moment she touched it.

The sound of a chair scraping against the floor sent a tingle up her spine. She sensed him standing behind her and could feel the heat from his body as he moved in closer. Her breath caught as he reached past to grasp the doorknob. Blood pounded in her ears. Once more, she was immobilized, unable to move. His breath tickled the nape of her neck, turning her legs to jelly.

"It was good to see ya again," he whispered dangerously close to her ear.

He pulled open the door, breaking the tension as a cold breeze snapped her out of her trance. The next parent looked up from the couch, and Lucy ducked her red face. Feeling as if everyone could see the lust overtaking her body, she hurried down the hall without looking back.

7

Lucy was amazed she managed to get back home. Her mind had been whirling as she rushed home in a daze.

Kenny was Aidan.

Aidan was Kaylee's teacher.

Her one-night stand, the man she slept with and ghosted, was her daughter's teacher! Of all the Irishmen in all of Ireland, why did it have to be this one? It boggled her mind. Ireland was small, but it couldn't be this tiny.

Bursting through the front door, Lucy kicked off her shoes frantically, leaving them haphazardly in the hallway.

"Abbey!" she yelled, making a beeline toward the kitchen while yanking on the arm of her sweatshirt. "Abbey!"

"What? What's wrong?" Abbey hurried into the kitchen from the living room, concern etched across her face.

"Abbey, oh my gosh, Abbey. It was him, it was him." Lucy's words tumbled out in breathless gasps.

Abbey looked her sister up and down, noting her disheveled appearance. "Good gravy, what happened to you?"

Lucy's face was red, and beads of sweat rolled down her forehead. Her hair was windblown and tangled. One arm hung out of the top of her zipped-up hoodie as she struggled to wriggle out of it.

"It was him!" Lucy's eyes were wide.

"Who?"

"Aidan. Aidan is the guy." Lucy continued to fight with her sweatshirt, pulling on the sleeve to free her arm. "Confounded thing."

"It helps if you unzip it first." Abbey shook her head, reaching out to pull down the zipper.

With her dangling arm finally freed, the sweatshirt swung to one side and hung off her shoulder. "Kaylee's teacher is the guy," Lucy said breathlessly.

Abbey squinted, her brows still furrowed. "You knew he was a guy."

"Not a guy, *the* guy." Lucy gripped her sister's shoulders and gave a slight shake. The sweatshirt slid onto the floor; Lucy glanced down, momentarily confused about how it ended up there. "Tin whistle man. Kenny is Aidan!"

Abbey's jaw dropped. "No!"

"Yes!"

"Hot, steamy, one-night stand guy is Kaylee's teacher?" Abbey couldn't hold back; she burst out laughing.

Lucy released her grip. Her face dropped, and she glared at her sister. "It's not funny."

"Oh, but it is." Abbey nodded, still laughing.

"This is a nightmare." Lucy leaned over and retrieved the sweatshirt, hanging it on the back of a chair before slumping down onto it. "I slept with my daughter's teacher."

"Today?"

"No, not today!" Lucy snarled, frowning.

Abbey shrugged. "You kinda look like you did."

"What?"

"Sorry, you look a little—rode hard and put away wet."

"I look what?" Lucy pushed up from the chair and rushed into the tiny bathroom under the stairs. "Oh my gosh!"

As Lucy cursed at her appearance, Abbey erupted into another fit of giggles. Lucy returned to the kitchen, slouching and shuffling her feet while running her fingers through unruly hair.

The coffee machine stuttered and sputtered before spewing hot coffee into a mug Abbey had set beneath it.

"All I know is you didn't look like that when you left," Abbey said, holding her hands up in defense. "You looked hot; maybe too hot."

Lucy sat down and dropped her head into her palms. "This is a nightmare. I mean, I couldn't even concentrate on what he was saying. All I could think the entire time—I tried not to—but–."

"You were picturing him naked!" Abbey bent over in laughter, tears running down her face.

"You aren't helping. This isn't funny." Lucy tried to keep a straight face but knew how humorous the situation was.

"This is making my day," Abbey gasped, trying to catch her breath. "Do you think he was picturing you naked?"

Lucy groaned. "I didn't even want to think about that. I hope not. Oh, this is so humiliating."

Abbey handed a steaming cup of coffee to Lucy and

began preparing another. "How did he act? He did remember you, right?"

Lucy scowled. "Of course he remembered me. Actually, he didn't seem very phased at all." A pensive look crossed Lucy's features. "I think he was shocked but recovered faster than I did. I was still processing things when he jumped right into talking about Kaylee."

"They have several meetings to get through; he was probably just short on time."

Lucy rolled her eyes. "Probably. I made a fool of myself. I was fidgeting like a child; I could not hold still for my life. If there was any chance for a second round, I screwed that up. I didn't just burn the bridge; I bombed the shite out of it."

"Wait! What are you saying?" Abbey stopped mid-sip of her coffee. "I thought it was one and done? Do you want a second go?"

"No," Lucy protested a little too harshly. "I feel guilty for running out on him. I made a fool of myself, so there is no chance at a second chance."

"You sound like you want there to be?" Abbey raised a brow.

Lucy forced a laugh. "It may have crossed my mind when I thought he was just another parent in the school. But not now, I'd say that line of thinking is off the table."

Abbey shrugged and sipped her coffee. "That's probably for the best. From how you describe his response, he probably feels the same way. It was just a one-night stand and something he doesn't intend to repeat."

Lucy's face fell.

Abbey didn't miss the gesture. "Ah-ha, so you do want

there to be something."

Lucy pursed her lips and sat back, crossing her arms over her chest. "No, that's not—I don't—."

Abbey arched her brows and silently drank her coffee, allowing Lucy space to sort through her thoughts.

Lucy couldn't put into words what she was feeling. The truth was Aidan had rattled her to the core, stirring up emotions she hadn't felt for so long. With Abbey grilling her, she was now unsure of her true feelings. She had wanted to believe it had only been a one-night stand, but the memories taunted her. Ever since the day she spotted him in the schoolyard, flashbacks from their night together played on constant repeat.

Why had she acted like a complete buffoon in his presence? That was not a reaction she usually had. As shocking as it had been to see him again, she had always been able to compartmentalize her sexcapades and laugh off awkward encounters. This wasn't Lucy's first time seeing a one-night stand in the real world, but it was the first time she reacted so strongly. Typically, encountering casual partners in places like the grocery store didn't faze her, and she had no problem acting as if they'd never met.

Aidan had thrown her off; he had been so calm and collected as if their night together had never happened. In contrast, Lucy froze up, feeling weak in the knees and losing all control simply by being in the same room as him. Her reaction was surprising.

Lucy waved a hand as if to wave off her thoughts altogether. "It doesn't matter. Now that I know he's Kaylee's teacher, he's off limits."

"Oh, don't say that," Abbey warned, a teasing tone to her voice. "Off limits might make you want him more. We always want what we can't have."

"I don't even think I can show my face at that school again," Lucy said, rubbing her eyes.

"What about the Halloween disco?" Abbey asked. "I was hoping you would help."

Lucy sat upright. "Oh, crap. Kaylee and Lola begged me to help. I think I said yes."

"You can't go back on your word."

"What am I going to do?" Lucy drank the coffee, enjoying the warmth as it slid down her throat.

"You're going to show up." Abbey gave her a stern look from across the counter. "No one knows about you and Aidan unless he spills to the other teachers."

A surprised gleam filled her eyes. "He wouldn't!"

Abbey laughed. "Your face is priceless!"

"You're cruel." Lucy scowled.

"You make it so easy." Abbey picked up a towel and began wiping down the counter. "Look, I've done this disco countless times. It's not a big deal. The hall will be so crowded, I doubt you'll see each other."

"I'll know he's there." Lucy cradled her mug. "I'll be self-conscious the entire time."

"It's Halloween. Wear a mask, and he'll never know you're there. You are not getting out of this."

Lucy sighed, knowing Abbey was right. Besides, she would never be able to tell Kaylee her reason for backing out. The last thing Kaylee needed to know was that her mom had seen her teacher naked.

8

"Oh, Lola, you look amazing!" Lucy leaned back against the counter as her niece entered the room the following morning.

Lola attempted to spin in her sleek, black gown that tapered down to the floor and clung snugly to her ankles, making turning and walking difficult. The dress's long sleeves cascaded down to her fingertips, stopping just shy of her perfectly polished black-colored nails. To complete the look, she wore a jet-black wig styled into straight, sleek strands that flowed down her back.

"Your Morticia Addams costume is class." Lucy gave a sheepish smile. "Did I use that right? Is that how you say it?"

Lola rolled her eyes and shrugged. "I've never heard anyone say that."

Lucy frowned. "I'm sure I've heard your dad say it multiple times."

"Not really," Lola said, reaching for an empty bowl.

"Maybe he spent too much time Stateside," Lucy said. "He must have lost some Irish lingo because he was too busy saying things like *dude* and *awesome*."

"You're so weird." Lola tried to hide a smile. "Where's Kaylee?"

"Right here." Kaylee jumped through the doorway, stretching her arms out to showcase her outfit. "Wednesday Addams has arrived."

"I love it!" Lucy clapped her hands excitedly. "You pull off the goth look really well."

Kaylee took a bow, casually flipping one of her black braids over her shoulder as she stood tall again.

Shopping the previous evening had led to the discovery of Kaylee's black dress with its stark white collar. Neither Lola nor Kaylee had any idea what costume they wanted for today's disco. However, as soon as Kaylee saw the dress, she knew instantly she had to be Wednesday Addams.

It became their mission to complete the outfit. Abbey suggested they go to the fancy dress shop in town. At first, Lucy scoffed at the idea, not interested in buying formal attire. Abbey explained that *fancy dress* was the Irish term for costumes.

The girls and their moms had so much fun going through all the different costumes and accessories. Lola, loving Kaylee's Wednesday outfit, decided to go as Morticia Addams. Abbey talked Lucy into matching theme-based costumes as well.

"We're helping at the disco," Abbey had reminded her. "We might as well have a bit of fun, too."

The coffee maker cranked to life, snapping Lucy back to the present.

Kaylee was staring at her mother with a look of confusion

on her face. "What is this all about?" Kaylee waved her finger up and down Lucy's costume. "Messy bride?"

Lucy's mouth dropped open in feigned insult. "What? Have you never heard of Madonna? *Like a Virgin*? MTV Music Video Awards, circa 1984. An iconic moment in music history?"

Kaylee and Lola exchanged bemused glances, silently conveying to each other that Lucy may be a little coo-coo. To them, 1984 might as well have been a hundred years ago.

"I've failed you!" Lucy cried, clasping her chest. "This costume represents a legendary performance, scandalous at the time, although now it would come across as tame. I can't believe I've never introduced you to this era. I. Have. Failed. You."

Lucy spun around dramatically as she spoke, her knee-length lacy wedding dress flaring as she turned. It was much more conservative than Madonna's original, which consisted of a corset and see-through lace. Lucy's dress was a safer *school* version; there was no corset, it was longer, and she wasn't showing off too much skin.

"I haven't even finished the look yet," Lucy added. "I have a wedding veil and need to tease up my hair a little."

"Okay," Kaylee said, rolling her eyes. "I still don't get it."

"We'll have to watch the video later." Lucy turned to the coffee maker, taking the mug from beneath it. "You will not be disappointed."

"Girls just wanna have fun!" Abbey belted out the song as she danced her way into the kitchen.

Lucy turned to face her sister. "Ah, you look amazing!"

Abbey continued to dance and sing her way through the

kitchen. Wearing a vibrant red dress with a flared skirt that swirled around her with each move, she radiated energy. The punk rock look was brought to life by her fishnet stockings and the rhythmic clicking of the collection of colorful bangles on her wrist. To complete the look, she wore a bright red, spiky cut wig similar to the style Cyndi Lauper had made famous in the '80s.

A wave of nostalgia washed over Lucy, reminding her of a simpler time.

"I will never understand that look," Lola commented; a slight look of disgust crossed her face as she waved a hand at her mom's outfit. "The high hair, the bright clothes that don't match at all, and the music."

Abbey whirled on her daughter, pointing a finger. "Don't you dare talk about the music! You goth kids will never understand." Abbey hid a smile as she poked fun at the girls' costumes.

Lucy pressed her lips together, holding back a laugh. Abbey had always had a theatrical side, having been in numerous school plays and even a few at their small town's local theater. It was a shame she never pursued an acting career; she would have shined.

Lola rolled her eyes. "We aren't even goth."

Kaylee nodded in agreement. "Were either of you even alive in 1980?"

Abbey gasped and slapped a hand over her mouth in mock shock. "Your grandmother is rolling over in her grave!"

"Grandma is still alive," Lola said flatly.

Abbey turned away, waving a hand in dismissal toward

the girls as she placed her head on the counter. "I can't look at you right now," she muttered.

"Oh, brother." Lola shook her head. "Kaylee, let's finish getting ready; these two are flying off the deep end."

Lucy laughed; she missed this side of Abbey. Her sister always had a charismatic side, and her vibrant energy drew people in.

Abbey winked at Lucy as their girls thundered up the stairs. Lucy took her coffee and followed behind them at a much slower pace.

In her bedroom, she began applying make-up as she allowed her memories to drift back to the days Madonna, Cyndi Lauper, and Blondie filled their house with music.

Kaylee had been right; Lucy and Abbey were not alive during most of the '80s, but their mother had been. Lucy loved flipping through her mother's old photo albums and seeing her in leg warmers, bright colors, and sky-high bangs. In the photos, her mother looked happy and carefree, which was a stark contrast to the woman Lucy knew.

As a child, Lucy loved the days when her mother danced around the house, blasting music and belting out the lyrics to her favorite songs. It was a sign her mother was happy, at least for that day. Often, her mother would pull Lucy and Abbey into the middle of the room and dance with them. Lucy would sing along, mesmerized by her mother's energy, the same energy Abbey possessed now.

As Lucy entered her teenage years, those happy moments all but disappeared. The music still played, but her mother no longer danced or sang. Instead, she turned to alcohol and tears, mourning the loss of a better life. Looking back, Lucy realized her mother blasted the music as a lifeline. The music had taken her mother back to a time when life was full of endless possibilities before everything spiraled out of control.

It was hard for Lucy to fathom why her mother had given up so easily. Or why her father had so much control over her mother's emotions. Her mother could be so fun, but she allowed depression and hopelessness to overtake her.

Today, Lucy wanted to channel the good times from her childhood. Maybe she could become that younger version of her mom, reviving that lost teenager's hopes and dreams.

Lucy's wedding dress costume was not an accident; she had put far too much thought into it. For one, Madonna's *Like a Virgin* performance had been scandalous at the time; it reminded Lucy of the judgment she received during her childhood. Part of her outfit today was to laugh in the face of that teased child.

Her ulterior motive behind wearing a wedding dress was to ward off extra attention from a particular guy. Men tended to fear the white gown and all it symbolized. Although sheer, the veil she intended to wear offered a semblance of anonymity; it would either hide her identity or help foster the illusion that's what it was doing. Ultimately, Lucy hoped the dress would cause Aidan to think twice before approaching her.

Her heart raced at the mere thought of Aidan. Memories and images once again danced through her mind, teasing and taunting her. She couldn't believe he still affected her like this. It had been one night, months ago. Sure, the sex had been great, but certainly, that had to be due to the fact she had gone so long without it. Or, perhaps, it was because she had endured so many years of unsatisfying sex with Jeremy. Aidan had been passionate, making her feel desired and wanted. Sex with Jeremy had revolved around his pleasure; it was always about him. Most times, she didn't finish before he moved off of her, panting and relishing in his release.

Her palms started to sweat as she compared the difference between the two men. In her limited time with Aidan, she had orgasmed more than she had during her entire relationship with Jeremy.

"Let's go, girls!" Abbey's cheerful words echoed up the stairwell. "Let's get this party started!"

Lucy's nerves were suddenly on edge. What was she doing? Suddenly, she was second-guessing everything. Her outfit was too much, and her hair was a disaster. Instead of hiding in the corner, she feared she would draw too much attention to herself. Maybe if she wore jeans and a T-shirt, no one would notice her.

No, she was acting like a child. There was a chance, a big chance, she wouldn't see Aidan at all.

"You okay?" Abbey slid her shoes on. "You look a little pale."

"I don't think I can do this," Lucy whispered, her throat dry.

Abbey grinned. "You got it so bad."

"No, I don't!" Lucy shot back. "I'm nervous. I want to make a good impression on the other parents, and I don't want to embarrass Kaylee."

"The lady doth protest too much." Abbey winked. "But whatever helps you get through this day. You're coming if I have to drag you kicking and screaming."

Lucy glared at the back of Abbey's head. Her sister was too perceptive; Lucy could lie and deceive herself, but Abbey saw right through her. In reality, Lucy never cared what other people thought of her. Growing up, she knew precisely what her small town thought of her, yet she always managed to hold her head high.

Her nerves today were solely based on Aidan. No matter how often she tried to convince herself otherwise, the mere thought of him ignited a fire within her. Since the parent-teacher meeting last week, she could not keep him out of her head.

"Okay, girls, have fun this morning, and we'll see you in a few hours," Abbey called as Lola and Kaylee headed toward their lines.

"Try not to embarrass me," Lola yelled over her shoulder. "No robot or chicken dances like last year."

Abbey laughed. "Your friends thought I was hilarious."

Lola groaned. "They were laughing at you, not with you."

"Rude," Abbey gasped, hiding a smile with her hand. Turning to Lucy, she said, "They were so laughing *with* me."

Lucy patted Abbey on the shoulder. "I'm sure they were."

"We're meeting the rest of the committee inside." Abbey led the way into the school. "We need to decorate the hall, set up the refreshments, and make sure everything is ready before the kids come in."

Lucy stared at the ground as she straightened her veil, fiddling with the lacy fabric.

Abbey reached for the door just as someone exited from the other side. "Oh, sorry."

"No worries," a male voice answered.

Lucy's head jerked up. Her eyes locked with Aidan's. The air left her lungs, catching in her throat. Rooted in place, her feet felt anchored to the hard cement, keeping her frozen in the moment.

"Lucy." Aidan broke the gaze, acknowledging her with a nod before striding towards the yard.

Abbey snickered. "Wow, you could cut the sexual tension with a butcher knife."

"Shut up," Lucy mumbled, playfully shoving her sister through the door.

"He's cute up close," Abbey commented. "And he called you by your name."

Lucy refrained from punching her sister in the arm, feeling frustrated by her reaction to Aidan. She couldn't understand why her body responded to him this way; he was just a one-night stand. It had meant nothing, but clearly, her body thought otherwise.

Goosebumps covered her arms as she imagined him whispering her name, his lips lightly grazing her ear. Her body trembled as she thought of his lips moving from her ear to her neck, causing more body parts to tingle, parts that were not supposed to be tingling on school grounds.

Lucy redirected her attention to the tasks before her, shaking her head to clear her thoughts. The hall was full of several parents already. A few ladies hung orange and black streamers along one wall while another group taped up ghosts and witches. A man and woman placed a pumpkin-covered tablecloth over a large folding table.

"Abbey!" One of the streamer women called out, sticking

a final piece of tape on the wall before hurrying over to them. "You look amazing. I love this get-up."

"You too," Abbey said, admiring the woman's witch costume. Black dress, dark hair, tall pointy hat, and fake nose, complete with a wart on the tip. "Jenny, this is my sister Lucy."

"We've heard so much about you," Jenny said, a warm smile crossing her lips. "I hear you'll be joining the PTA soon?"

Jenny winked and patted Lucy's arm.

"I'm still working on that," Abbey said. "I'll break her down, don't you worry."

"Come 'er, it's worth a shot," Jenny said, turning back toward the hall. "So, we have balloons that need inflating near the far wall. You two okay to work on that?"

"We're on it," Abbey replied, heading in the direction Jenny pointed.

"Thanks a mill."

"Mind if I start some music? Get the mood going?" A man called from across the room.

"That'd be grand, Stephen," Jenny replied.

Abbey found the balloons lying on the floor and ripped open the bag, littering the ground with orange and black balloons.

"Stephen over there, he always runs the sound and music for these events," Abbey said, picking up a balloon and stretching it. "His wife, Ciara, is working on the drinks table."

Lucy began blowing air into the first balloon. "Dang, I forgot how lightheaded this makes me."

"Careful, there," Abbey teased, then continued to point out each parent. "Jenny, she's the leader of this ragtag team. Chairperson of the PTA. Those two women over there are Áine and Siobhán."

Lucy tried to remember each name Abbey threw at her. "You know everyone."

"Not everyone, but most of these people," Abbey said.

"Hot water for tea and coffee in the kitchen!" Jenny yelled.

Abbey placed her palms together in prayer. "Oh, thank the stars. I'll get us some coffee. Milk and sugar?"

Lucy nodded, her cheeks puffed out as she inflated an orange balloon. Pinching the end, she tied it in a knot before setting it down and grabbing a black one. Four balloons later, the room started to spin.

"Don't pass out," Abbey laughed, handing her a mug of hot coffee.

Grateful for a caffeine hit, Lucy took a careful sip of the coffee and grimaced. "Oh, that's bitter."

"Instant coffee, an Irish specialty." Abbey held up her mug in a mock cheer.

"I might need more sugar." Lucy coughed. "A lot more sugar."

Abbey laughed. "You'll get used to it in time. Sugar and milk are in the kitchen over there."

Lucy made a beeline in the direction Abbey pointed. Pushing through the door, she was impressed by the quaint space, surprised to find a legitimate kitchenette. The room held a large sink, boiler for hot water, fridge, ample counter space, and even a dishwasher - not too shabby for a school.

On the counter, she spotted the sugar packets in a mug between a box of tea bags and a small container of instant coffee. Lucy grabbed two packs, tore off the tops, and poured them into her cup. Pulling open the fridge, she decided another splash of milk might help cut down on the bitter taste of this strong coffee. After mixing it, she tried a small sip. Not the best, but it would do. After replacing the milk, she took another drink.

"Hi."

With her mouth full, she turned towards the door, shocked to see Aidan standing behind her. She gasped, inhaling coffee. Coughing and sputtering, she spun toward the sink, spitting out the remaining coffee in her mouth.

"Ah Christ, are ya alright?" Aidan rushed up behind her.

Setting the mug on the counter, Lucy hung over the sink, coughing and waving him off, pretending she was okay.

She was far from fine.

This was a nightmare.

Her face turned multiple shades of red, and she couldn't stop coughing, finding it difficult to catch her breath.

"Here." Aidan moved around her, filling a cup with water. "Drink this."

Lucy shook her head. She didn't need to drink more; she needed to expel the current liquid from her lungs.

Her heart was racing; it was difficult to tell if it was due to the coughing or the mere presence of Aidan. Most likely, a mixture of both those things. At this moment, all she wanted was to sink right into the floor and disappear.

"I don't think you're okay." Aidan's voice filled with concern. "Should I get some help?"

Finally, the coughing began to calm down.

"Wrong hole," Lucy whispered hoarsely, avoiding eye contact. "I'm okay, thanks."

Still coughing, she moved around Aidan and rushed out the door.

Abbey glanced up, concern immediately crossing her face. "What on earth happened to you? You look—."

Lucy continued to cough but managed to get a few words out. "Choked. On. My. Coffee."

Abbey's brows furrowed as she looked toward the kitchen, surprised to see Aidan walking out. Her eyes widened as she looked between Lucy and Aidan, a silent question in her expression.

"What happened in there?" Abbey chuckled as she teased her sister.

Lucy buried her red face in her hands. "I humiliated myself. Please tell me he isn't walking over here."

Aidan took a few steps toward Abbey and Lucy but stopped when Abbey sent him the thumbs-up sign. After a brief hesitation, he walked out of the hall.

"He's gone." Abbey turned her attention back to Lucy. "Now, what on earth happened in there?"

"Nothing," she said, reaching down to grab a balloon and resume decorating. Lucy coughed a few more times, the taste of coffee filling her mouth.

Abbey took the balloon from her hand. "I don't think you should be blowing these up. You can start taping them to the wall while spilling the beans."

Lucy rolled her eyes in resignation. "I took a huge gulp of coffee, and when I turned around, he was standing there.

Caught off guard, I panicked a little, inhaled my mouthful of coffee, and choked. I was coughing and spitting coffee everywhere."

Abbey burst out laughing.

"Way to kick me while I'm down," Lucy mumbled. "I thought I was going to die in that kitchen, not only because I was choking but because I was humiliated."

"I'm sorry, but you have to admit it's funny," Abbey said, touching Lucy lightly on the arm. "I've always pictured you as cool, calm, and collected; nothing ever seemed to bother you, but now this man walks by, and you completely fall apart. It's amusing and fascinating. Kind of like watching a newborn deer learn to walk."

Lucy glared at her sister, grabbing the roll of tape and huffing toward the wall. Mentally, she berated herself for allowing Aidan to affect her behavior this way. She needed to pull it together and stop making a fool of herself whenever he was around. Abbey was right; usually, she would never act this way around men. It was as if he were a wizard casting a spell on her, one that caused her to lose her mind and freeze in place.

Her behavior had to be confusing to Aidan as well. Was he wondering what happened to the confident girl he had taken home from the bar? These past few encounters displayed an alternative side to her, indeed. She shuddered to think how different things would be if she had acted this way the night they first met.

"You like him." Abbey appeared beside her, interrupting her thoughts.

"He's seen me naked," Lucy whispered through clenched

teeth. "I'm a little self-conscious about that, that's all."

Not only had he seen her naked, but had also heard her moan while bouncing on top of him.

"It looks great in here." Jenny's voice echoed through the hall, making Lucy jump. "Fair play, the kids will love it. Everyone get to your assigned stations; the kids will be here any minute."

Lucy could feel her face heating up. Had she just been thinking about sex and picturing scenes from that night here, of all places? She had to put a lid on these thoughts. This was not the time or place to let her mind wander down that path.

Taking a deep breath, she turned her attention to the door as a class of chattering children entered the hall. Witches, ghosts, vampires, fairies, and pirates piled into the room, giddy with excitement as they marveled at its magical transformation.

Stephen blasted out *Monster Mash* as more classes filed in.

"Abbey, Lucy, you're on the refreshments table," Jenny reminded them in a rush. "One juice box per kid, and don't let them take too many sweets."

Thankful for the distraction, Lucy hightailed it to the table, grateful they would focus on the kids, not the teachers.

The volume rose as more kids streamed into the hall. Music pumped from the speakers, adding to the noise. The younger children danced and bounced around to the music while the older ones gathered in small groups along the walls and engaged in lively chatter.

"Looks good in here." Lola came up to the refreshment table and swiped a juice box. "You two aren't dancing? Isn't this one of those old people songs you love, Mom?"

Abbey narrowed her eyes. "*Thriller* is a classic, young lady. Michael Jackson is a pure icon."

Lola rolled her eyes, hiding a smile behind her juice box.

"You want to see some dancing?" Abbey teased. "This song has moves, you know. Trust me, this would have been a viral sensation if TikTok were around in the eighties. Grandma made sure we knew this song and dance."

"I'm pretty sure you can find the trend on TikTok," Lola muttered.

Abbey moved from behind the table. "Then, you should be a pro. Let's show them how it's done."

"Mom!" Lola protested.

Lucy couldn't help but laugh as Abbey practically dragged Lola into the middle of the room. Catching Lola's silent plea for help, Lucy shrugged, knowing, truthfully, Lola was enjoying herself.

"Hi, Mom." Kaylee appeared at the table. "This is so cool. I can't believe we get out of doing schoolwork for this."

Lucy's heart kicked into a gallop. If Kaylee was here, that meant Aidan was somewhere in the room.

Kaylee picked up a juice box and struggled to remove the straw from its packaging. "Aren't these costumes great? We haven't done any work today. Aidan is the coolest teacher."

Lucy could not focus on the tirade of information her daughter was spewing. Her thoughts focused only on Aidan. Nerves and anxiety rushed through her; she felt a desperate need to see him, regardless of the embarrassing choking scene from earlier.

"Lola looks so embarrassed right now." Kaylee was laughing.

Lucy tried to concentrate on her daughter. "I think it's all an act," she managed to say, her throat suddenly very dry.

"Well, you know, she has to act cool." Kaylee shrugged, taking a sip of her juice. "It looks like fun; I'm gonna go dance with them."

Kaylee set down her nearly full drink and disappeared into the crowd, leaving Lucy to fidget awkwardly with the juice boxes and popcorn bags.

Suddenly, the air felt charged with electricity. Lucy looked up and spotted a small group of what she assumed were teachers huddling together deep in conversation. Her gaze fell on the man dressed in black, a dark robe draped over his shoulders. Even with the white mask half-covering his face, she knew it was Aidan dressed as the Phantom of the Opera.

The pounding of her heart echoed in her ears as she watched him fully immersed in the conversation. His smile caused her legs to go weak. She couldn't hear the discussion from her place across the room, but Aidan's elaborate gestures drew her in as if he were sharing a thrilling story. She longed to be part of that group, if only to hear his voice and the lilt of his thick accent.

As he laughed, he turned to scan the room, his gaze locking onto hers, jerking her out of the daydream. In a panic, Lucy knocked over a row of juice boxes, attempting to appear busy. Hopefully, he hadn't noticed her staring.

"Do you have any sweets?" a little girl interrupted her internal berating.

Lucy focused on the young girl. "Sweets?"

"Chocolate or gummies? My friend said you had some."

Sweets, oh right, that's the word for candy.

"Yes." Lucy, grateful for the distraction, pulled a pumpkin-shaped bowl full of small packaged treats from behind the table. "You can have two things."

As the girl skipped away, Lucy glanced curiously across the room, but Aidan was gone.

A line quickly formed at the table as clusters of kids came to claim their juice boxes, popcorn, and candy. Aidan was momentarily forgotten as she got caught up in complimenting costumes and chatting with the children while pushing straws into juice boxes, opening popcorn bags, and discarding wrappers into the trash bin behind her. After each batch of kids left, Lucy would tidy up the table and set out more juice boxes.

She was halfway under the table, pulling out the last container of juice boxes, when she heard movement at the table.

"One second," she called, yanking the box open and grabbing a handful of juice.

"Can teachers have a juice box?" His voice sent fire through her veins.

Aidan.

Lucy jumped, bashing her head on the table and sending juice boxes flying.

"Ow," she said, gritting her teeth and rubbing her bruised head.

"Are ya okay?" Aidan asked. "Should I get some ice?"

Lucy drew in a deep breath, embarrassed and frustrated with herself. She felt a small knot forming on the back of her head. "I'm alright, just a bit of a klutz lately."

"I've noticed," he teased, a sly smile forming at the corners of his mouth. Casually, he picked up some of the fallen juice boxes and set them back on the table. "Not ta sound cocky, but do I make ya nervous?"

Lucy's heart dropped into her stomach. She opened her mouth to speak, but no words came out.

"I don't remember ya being so—skittish the first time we met."

Scorching hot blood raced through her veins. Did he just reference their hook-up? Her heart surged into overdrive, pounding a million miles a minute. The way he said it so calmly as if their first meeting had been in a grocery store and had not ended in hot sex.

"Ummmm, well." Lucy swallowed hard. Beads of sweat formed on her forehead, and it was getting hard to breathe. How was she supposed to respond to that? Honestly, she decided. "I wasn't expecting to see you—."

"Ever again," he finished for her.

She hung her head sheepishly. "Pretty much."

"I was surprised too," he confessed, lowering his voice. "I thought ya were a tourist headed back to the States. I was just as shocked ta see ya in the meetin' room."

"That was a surprise," she agreed, lifting her eyes to meet his gaze.

The intense look in his eyes was too much, and she glanced away, absently reaching to tidy the juice boxes on the table. Aidan grabbed for them at that exact moment. Electricity jolted through her as their hands touched. Pleasure, desire, and memories coursed through her brain. Neither broke the connection.

"I was disappointed when I woke up ta find ya gone," he whispered, lightly grazing the back of her hand with his fingers.

It was too much. Lucy swallowed hard, pulling her hand away. "I was avoiding the awkward morning after because I didn't think it meant anything. We were just two drunk singles having a good time."

"Is that all it was?" His voice was thick.

Lucy glanced up, a half-smile spreading across his lips. Was he teasing or flirting with her?

"Wasn't it?" she replied, over the lump in her throat. "You thought I was just passing through, remember?"

Aidan shrugged, his expression impossible to read.

"It doesn't matter anyway." Lucy went back to organizing the juice boxes, ensuring his hands were far away from hers. "You're Kaylee's teacher. That pretty much takes you off the table."

"Do ya want me—off the table?" He lowered his voice and leaned in closer. "Or would ya rather 'ave me—on the table?"

Lucy shuddered as a rush of tingles shot down her spine, prompting an unintentional but rather loud gulp. Aidan's eyes smoldered, and his lips curved suggestively, sending a thrill through her. The air between them crackled as Lucy licked her suddenly dry lips.

For an instant, everything around them faded into the background, leaving only Lucy and Aidan. Her fingers twitched with the urge to touch him, to feel the warmth of his skin.

"Mom, come dance with me." Kaylee pushed through the

crowd, bursting apart the tension between her mother and teacher. "Oh, hi, Aidan. You here for a juice box?" Can teachers have juice boxes?"

Lucy snapped back to reality. As if in slow motion, the music steadily became louder, the children's dancing came back into focus, and the chatter became nearly deafening. Lucy felt like a kid caught with her hand in the cookie jar, but Kaylee was oblivious to the situation she had interrupted.

Aidan seemed to bounce back quickly. "Of course, we can have a juice box. You think I'm too old for one of these?" He picked up a box for emphasis.

Kaylee raised a brow at him. "I mean—you're not a kid?"

"I'm a kid at heart." Aidan placed a hand on his chest.

Kaylee laughed and pulled Lucy into the crowd. Lucy gave Aidan a final glance as they settled near the center of the room.

"Aidan is so funny, don't you think?" Kaylee asked.

Lucy's cheeks flushed. "I don't know—I guess?"

Kaylee furrowed her brows. "Wait, I'm not in trouble, am I?"

"What? No!" Lucy looked alarmed. "You're not in trouble at all."

Kaylee shrugged, continuing her awkward dance movements. "Phew. You two looked serious when I walked up. I hope I didn't interrupt anything."

"He was only saying hello," Lucy said quickly. "Oh, there's Aunt Abbey." Thankful for the distraction, Lucy pulled Kaylee toward Abbey. "Dancing alone again?" Lucy teased her sister.

"What can I say? I love to dance," Abbey said, waving her

hands in the air and bobbing her head to the beat. "Lola abandoned me a while back. Apparently, I'm *super embarrassing* this year."

"The *Thriller* dance was cool," Kaylee said. "Everyone loved that."

Abbey frowned. "It went downhill from there. I peaked at *Thriller*."

Kaylee and Lucy laughed as the music died down.

"Thank you, everyone, for a great turnout," a voice cackled over the loudspeaker. "Unfortunately, we all need to get back to our classrooms. Please line up with your teachers."

A large groan rippled across the room.

"That went fast," Abbey said.

Kaylee gave Lucy a quick side hug. "See you after school. Thanks for coming today. It was fun."

Lucy smiled as she watched her daughter hurry toward her line, excitedly conversing with her classmates. Her eyes locked with Aidan's, the intensity of his stare stirring a surge of desire in her belly. He winked in her direction before turning his attention to the students. Lucy found it impossible to look away, standing frozen in place until the class had left the hall and he was no longer in view.

9

Abbey pulled the last of the streamers off the wall. "That was a lot of fun."

The other parent helpers had rushed off shortly after the students left the hall, citing work and childcare obligations as excuses. Lucy, Abbey, and Jenny were left to handle most of the clean-up.

"Thanks a mill for your help today," Jenny said, closing the box of decorations. "Fair play to everyone; I think the kids had a great time."

"Me too." Abbey laughed. "If you ask Lola, I probably had too much fun."

"Ah, sure, bless; I think they love having us here, even if they say otherwise." Jenny winked. "Listen, I gotta leg it to créche to collect Zoey. You can handle the final bits?"

"No worries. Lucy and I will finish up," Abbey replied.

"You're a star." Jenny grabbed her purse and jacket. "I've no doubt Lucy will be running events before we know it."

Lucy smiled but shook her head. "Don't count on it."

Jenny laughed and waved as she exited the hall.

"That wasn't so bad now, was it?" Abbey asked.

"It was fun," Lucy agreed. "I'm glad I came."

"Good." Abbey lifted the box of decorations. "I'll take this up to the store room. You can work on the kitchen. Pretty straightforward, the mugs go in the dishwasher, wipe down the counters, you know, act like you're at home."

Lucy raised an eyebrow in amusement as they parted ways.

In the kitchen, Lucy took in the chaos. Abbey was right; this was a familiar scene in their home lately. The mug she had abandoned earlier still sat on the counter, currently surrounded by several others that wouldn't fit in the crowded sink. Empty sugar packets lay discarded, their tiny, white granules scattered haphazardly across the counter. Milk droplets added to the disorder, along with several stray tea bags leaving stains that mingled with the milk and sugar remnants.

Lucy went to work, tossing the veil from her head onto a vacant chair. Aidan instantly filled her thoughts; it seemed that was the first place her mind wanted to go today, especially after two awkward encounters. Absently, she rubbed her head lightly, where a bruise was definitely developing.

She couldn't figure this man out. Was he being playful, flirting, or simply enjoying watching her squirm? There was no denying the chemistry between them; he had to feel it, too. However, he seemed to be able to turn his emotions on and off like a light switch. Despite the intensity of his gaze, he appeared utterly calm in her presence while she battled a storm of emotions raging inside her.

What would have happened if Kaylee hadn't interrupted their moment earlier? The tension had been so thick between them, or at least it had been for Lucy. Nothing *could* have happened, not with the room full of students. Even so, she couldn't shake the feeling of something brewing between them, although it might be a case of wishful thinking.

Her mind took a nosedive in the erotic direction as she ran a washcloth under the faucet. The rag's sweeping movement across the counter conjured an image of Aidan making the same motion across the refreshment table, little juice boxes crashing to the floor. Her imagination ran wild, picturing Aidan lifting her onto the table and kissing her deeply. Lucy wrapped her fingers around a mug, imagining how easily her legs curved around Aidan's waist.

Lust and desire burned through her veins. She wanted to laugh out loud as she conjured up scenes that were a mix of a cheesy romance movie and a bad porno. Her hands weren't the only body part getting wet as she rinsed the mugs and placed them neatly into the dishwasher.

Shaking her head to clear her mind, Lucy closed the dishwasher and squatted down, balancing on the balls of her feet, as she rummaged through a drawer searching for dishwashing tablets.

"I have one more."

Lucy jolted at the voice, losing her balance and somehow managing to topple backward, landing flat on her back.

"Sorry. I'm so sorry." Aidan set his cup on the counter and knelt next to her. "Are you okay? I didn't mean to startle you."

"Oh geesh," Lucy muttered, feeling absolutely mortified as she lay flat on the cold, hard floor. "I'm okay."

Aidan grabbed her arms and hoisted her up until they stood face-to-face. The quick movement caused Lucy's head to spin. A wave of dizziness washed over her, and she began to sway.

Aidan placed a hand on the small of her back, steadying her. "Whoa, easy there." He was so close she felt the warmth of his breath against her cheek.

Closing her eyes, she took a deep breath, hoping to steady herself. Instead, her legs felt like jelly. As she inhaled, she caught a whiff of soap and sandalwood. He smelled good. One arm tightened around her waist, and the other held her arm. Lucy's heart pounded against her chest as butterflies swarmed in her stomach. Again, time seemed to stand still; they were dangerously close.

"I'm okay now," she whispered after several silent seconds.

She rested her hand against his chest, fully intending to push away and stand on her own, but a momentary glance into his smoldering eyes caught her off guard. Unintentionally, she sucked in a breath at the intensity of his gaze. His breathing accelerated, and she could feel his heartbeat thundering beneath her palm.

As if in slow motion, Aidan released her arm, reaching up to gently caress her cheek with his thumb. Lucy thought her heart would pound right out of her chest. The pad of his thumb swiped across her lips as he studied her mouth. The wire of tension between them snapped as he bent his head and kissed her.

Electricity coursed through her body as their lips touched. Impulsively, he pulled her tight against his chest and deepened the kiss. Lucy's hand glided up his chest, sliding around to rest along the back of his neck. Her other arm encircled his waist, closing all distance between them.

Aidan groaned, sliding his hands down her back and over her butt to lift her from behind her thighs. Pushing his tongue between her parted lips, he carried her back, setting her down on the freshly scrubbed countertop.

Carnal need caused an ache to flood her body. Her legs, having a mind of their own, wrapped themselves around his waist. She tangled her hands into his hair, pulling him deeper into the kiss. Her desire for him overwhelmed all thought and reason. Neither was thinking straight, consumed by their desperate need for each other.

Lucy slid her hips to the edge of the counter to press firmly against him, feeling his desire rub against her crotch. A moan escaped his lips as she rubbed seductively against him. Aidan fingered the lacy trim of her dress, his knuckles lightly rubbing along the skin above her knees before slowly traveling up her thigh. She quivered at his touch, his fingertips leaving a fiery path along her flesh.

She sighed as he buried his face in her hair, kissing her neck as his fingers toyed with the lace of her panties. Lust pooled mere centimeters from his fingers; she knew he could feel the dampness and heat emanating from her core.

Aidan pulled away as if suddenly yanked by an invisible string attached to his back. Placing his hands on his knees, he panted. Lucy's lips were plump and red; she was breathing hard. Her body was ready for him. If he wanted her right here, right now, it would be nearly impossible to say no.

He took another step back. "Shite," he whispered breathlessly, running a hand through his messy hair. "I—class—damn—bye."

Before she could respond, he was gone. Her entire body felt numb; all she could do was continue to sit on the counter, staring after him, unfulfilled and way too turned on for the current setting.

Abbey walked in several minutes later to find Lucy breathing hard as she sat on the counter, her hair a tangled mess and her dress hiked up to her thighs.

Abbey's jaw nearly touched the floor. "What are you doing?"

Lucy jumped from the counter, her face crimson as she straightened her dress.

Abbey pointed at Lucy. "Did you just—? Were you—?" Abbey stuttered. "You didn't, you know?" Abbey gave her a quizzical look, putting two fingers together and moving them in a circular motion down toward her crotch.

Lucy looked horrified. "What? No!" Absently, she pulled at the hem of her dress. "I did not just pleasure myself on a counter in the middle of a school—on a school day!"

Abbey pretended to wipe sweat from her forehead. "Phew. No offense, but you sort of look—flustered. Your hair could use brushing, and your dress was—a bit provocative. Why were you sitting on the counter like that anyway?"

"Well, I understand why you would think I was—" Lucy mimicked her sister's movement with her fingers. "It was Aidan."

Abbey smirked. "Obviously; I figured you were thinking

about Aidan."

"No," Lucy whispered harshly. "Aidan was in here."

"What?" Abbey leaned back in surprise.

"Shh!" Lucy looked around as if someone would walk any minute. "Literally, just a few minutes before you walked in. Didn't you pass him?"

Abbey shook her head. "Not that I recall. What were you two doing in here?"

Lucy's face burned, and she stared at her feet. "We may have kissed a little."

"A little? Girl, you look like it was intense. You have sex hair."

Lucy playfully slapped her sister's arm. "Shut up."

"You like him," Abbey replied.

Lucy held up her hands. "You caught me; I'm a little infatuated."

"Oh, I think it's more than that. You two were getting hot and heavy *in the school kitchen*."

"Shh!" Lucy gritted her teeth. "I confess, I'm horny these days, but I promise you it's nothing more than that."

Abbey rolled her eyes. "If you say so."

Lucy turned back to the dishwasher. "Let's start this dishwasher so we can go home. Any idea where the soap for it is?"

Abbey opened a drawer above where Lucy had looked earlier and pulled out a tablet. Dropping it into the machine, she pressed a button and slammed it shut.

"That's that. We better hurry out of here. I don't want to be here if *you know who* walks in again." Abbey winked. "Things could get awkward."

Lucy glared at her sister as they shut off the lights and headed out the door.

Abbey waited until they were off school grounds to broach the subject again. "What are you going to do about Aidan?"

Lucy shuffled her feet. "What can I do?"

"Jump his bones again and again and again."

Lucy rolled her eyes. "You sound like a horny teenager."

"I wasn't the one getting hot and heavy on school grounds." Abbey poked Lucy's arm. "And I don't blame you; he's hot. If the sex is good, girl, get it while the getting is good."

Lucy tried to hide a smile. "But he's Kaylee's teacher. Aren't there rules or something?"

"Rules against sleeping with hot guys?"

Lucy sighed, raising her head to the sky. "Get serious for a minute. There has to be some rule against dating your child's teacher, even if it's unwritten. I wouldn't want to make him or Kaylee uncomfortable."

Abbey gasped. "Dating? Who said anything about dating? Is that what you want?"

"No!" Lucy replied forcefully. "I'm just saying there has to be a rule against teachers fraternizing with their students' parents, whether it be sex, dating, or whatever."

Abbey twisted the key in the lock. "Well, there must be some strong chemistry if you couldn't keep your hands off each other in the kitchenette."

"Making out is not dating." Lucy hung her jacket on the hook. "I am not going to deny the chemistry between us, but it's just lust. Of course, I can only speak for myself. I have no idea how he feels about me."

Abbey turned, her mouth agape. "Are you kidding me? Obviously, he's attracted to you. For goodness' sake, he practically had his way with you right there in the school kitchen *while* working."

Lucy unknowingly placed a hand over her stomach as it flip-flopped wildly.

"I forgot he was technically at work." Lucy scowled, picking up her laptop and settling down at the table. "That was pretty scandalous. Thankfully, we didn't get caught. He would probably get fired for something like that."

"His desire for you made him risk it all," Abbey said wistfully. "It's a little romantic."

Lucy narrowed her eyes. "Maybe in your weird dream world. That moment was pure animalistic desire. We've slept together, and both enjoyed it, so maybe we wouldn't mind doing it again. However, if I hadn't gone home with him that night, he wouldn't have even noticed me today."

"Deny, deny."

Lucy turned her attention toward the laptop. "It doesn't matter anyway. He's off-limits. We shouldn't have let things get out of hand like that. As they say, there are other fish in the sea. I just need to fish in another pond."

"If you say so," Abbey said, waving a hand in dismissal.

The rest of the afternoon whizzed by in a blur. Work was a mess, and Lucy became wrapped up in fixing issues and messaging the team. Aidan became a distant thought, momentarily shoved aside by the demands of her job.

Kaylee returned from school just as Lucy was wrapping up a case.

After tossing her school bag on the table, she picked through the fruit bowl. "Hey, Mom." She chose a shiny apple and ran it up and down her dress. "The disco was fun, right? We don't have anything like that back home."

"It was definitely interesting," Lucy sighed.

Kaylee took a bite of the apple and sat down across from her mother.

"Did you know Halloween originated in Ireland?" she asked between bites. "It has a funny name. I kept calling it Sam Hain in class because that's how it's spelled. The kids at my table think I'm funny because I can never pronounce Irish words. It's sort of my thing, I guess."

Lucy glanced at her daughter and couldn't help but smile. Kaylee's eyes sparkled, and her animated recount of the day confirmed everything Lucy needed to know; Kaylee was settling in, making friends, and happy.

Lucy leaned back and closed her laptop, giving Kaylee her full attention. "How is it pronounced?"

"I'm still not sure," Kaylee laughed. "Saw-win or sow-in; something like that. Anyway, Aidan told us about different festivals and traditions; it was a fun day. And next week, we're on break."

"Sounds like a great day," Lucy said. "I know you were worried about this move. It's not easy starting a new school and making new friends, but I'm so proud of you for trying your hardest every day."

Kaylee shrugged. "I was nervous, but everyone here is so nice. They ask me all kinds of questions about America. I've even made some friends. In fact, Chloe invited me for a sleepover during the break."

"That's great." Lucy stretched her back out. "I would move back to America in a heartbeat if you told me you were unhappy."

"No!" Kaylee looked horrified. "I'm happy here. I love living here. I love having Lola around. She's like a sister to me, and I finally have someone my age to hang out with. Plus, you have your sister again. We finally have a real family."

Lucy smiled. "We had a family. Your dad and grandma."

"Pfft, I'd hardly call that family. Grandma spent time with me, but you and her can't stand each other. And dad——well, he has never lived up to that title."

Lucy frowned. "I'm sorry."

Kaylee waved the apology away. "You're happier here, too. I haven't seen you smile or laugh this much in a long time. And you don't look worried all the time anymore."

"You aren't supposed to notice those things."

Kaylee turned the apple in her hand. "Kids notice a lot of things."

Lucy nodded; she knew from experience how true that statement was.

"Do you miss Grandma?" Lucy asked.

Kaylee looked up thoughtfully. "I thought I would, and I do, but—." Kaylee's voice dropped off, and she concentrated on her apple.

"What?" Lucy urged. "You can tell me."

Kaylee blew out a breath. "It's just, I realize now how awful Grandma was to you. I didn't notice then, but looking back, she always made digs at you, mainly about Dad. She thought he was the most amazing person in the world and blamed you for him not wanting to be around us. She constantly told me if you tried harder, Dad would stay."

Lucy felt as if she had been punched in the gut. "And did you believe her?"

Kaylee shrugged. "At first, but Dad's kind of an asshole."

Lucy couldn't help but laugh.

"Grandma would say if you tried harder, I would have a family, maybe even a brother or sister." Kaylee's voice dropped. "It made me sad because I wanted those things, and I think you did, too. But I realize it was Dad who didn't want us."

"He didn't want me." Lucy reached across the table and took her daughter's hand.

"You don't have to protect him," Kaylee said quietly, squeezing her mom's hand. "He didn't want a family. He didn't want either of us. I heard all those fights."

"Oh, Kaylee, he doesn't deserve you." Lucy felt tears stinging the back of her eyes.

Kaylee stuck out her chin. "He doesn't deserve either of us."

"I wish I would have picked a better dad for you," Lucy said.

Kaylee lifted a shoulder. "It's okay. I don't need a dad; I have you. And, who knows, maybe while we're changing our lives, we can find a new dad." Kaylee smiled and wiggled her eyebrows at Lucy.

"I don't know about that." She released her daughter's hand and stood up. "I've had some bad experiences with men. I should probably take a break."

Kaylee sucked air through her teeth. "True, you aren't the

best picker. Maybe someone else should pick for you."

"Maybe." Lucy picked up her water glass and took a sip.

Kaylee's eyes lit up. "I have the best idea. I'll set you up with my teacher, Aidan. He's okay looking and really nice."

Lucy choked on the water she was drinking, spilling some on her shirt.

"You okay?"

"Wrong hole," Lucy whispered, which seemed to be a common theme when it came to Aidan. His name alone caused her to forget how to use basic motor functions.

"You remember Aidan?" Kaylee continued, unaware of the effect this conversation had on her mother. "You know, the one you were talking with at the refreshment table today? What do you think? Is he cute?"

I think I just about ripped off his clothes in the kitchen, Lucy thought.

Turning quickly, she hurried toward the sink, grabbing the towel and wiping her shirt as she searched her brain for some sort of reply.

What *did* she think? That was a loaded question. Certainly, not one she could answer without turning twenty shades of red.

"He was nice."

"Really nice." Kaylee nodded enthusiastically. Pushing up from the table, she approached the counter and faced her mom. "He isn't my type, but I guess he's good-looking, right?"

Lucy laughed. "Not your type? He's a little old for you." Lucy mused, realizing she had no idea how old he was. "How do you know he's even single? Maybe he's married?"

Lucy continued facing the sink, not wanting Kaylee to see how interested she was.

"I didn't see a ring." Kaylee shook her left hand. "Besides, he's never mentioned a wife, and there are no pictures of females on his desk."

Lucy turned around, leaning her back against the sink. "He has pictures on his desk?"

"Just a few of his mates," Kaylee replied. "That's what he called them, mates, isn't that funny? They were at some match, curling or hurling, or some odd Irish sport I've never heard of."

"Does he share a lot with the class?" Lucy asked.

Kaylee shrugged. "We played a getting-to-know-you game on the first day. That was one of his facts. Anyway, think about it; he could be a good catch."

"You wouldn't feel weird about that." Lucy absently bit her lip, knowing she was walking a fine line.

Kaylee laughed. "I don't know. I just thought about it now."

Lucy finished wiping off her shirt and hung the towel on its hook. She wanted to press the issue further, but she stopped herself. There was nothing between her and Aidan, so why continue to foster these thoughts? Sure, they had a lust-infused make-out session today, but it meant nothing.

"Give it some thought." Kaylee winked as she left the room.

That was precisely the problem; Lucy couldn't stop thinking about Aidan. And no matter which way she looked at it, she couldn't shake the gnawing sensation that if she pursued him, things would only end badly.

10

Lucy carefully applied a thick layer of mascara to her eyelashes. Somehow, Abbey managed to talk her into a night out in the city, not that she had put up much of a fight. Her stomach was already in knots, especially considering what had happened during their last pub outing and all the events that had unfolded these past few weeks directly related to that adventure. Even so, she looked forward to unwinding with a fruity drink and some greasy pub food.

Of course, as much as she tried to deny it, deep down, she secretly hoped they would run into Aidan. The thought alone sent butterflies dancing in her stomach. Fluffing her hair, she gave one last glance in the full-length mirror; the skinny jeans really did make her butt look good. Feeling confident and sexy, she headed down the stairs. Kaylee and Lola sat side by side at the counter, eating pizza straight from the box while watching videos on their tablets.

Lucy kissed Kaylee on the forehead. "Don't stay up too late."

"You either," Kaylee said, then after some thought added, "or, you know, stay out all night again."

Abbey burst out laughing as Lucy turned several shades of red.

"I'll be back tonight," Lucy said firmly.

"Should we place bets?" Abbey teased.

Kaylee and Lola smiled and wagged their eyebrows at Lucy.

Abbey put an arm around both girls' shoulders. "If she comes home, I'll take everyone out tomorrow night for ice cream."

"No one is betting anything," Lucy hissed, pulling on Abbey's arm. "We should leave before I call this whole thing off."

She could hear Kaylee and Lola laughing as they walked out the door.

"I'm not planning on any hookups tonight," Lucy said. "Just so we're clear."

Abbey rolled her eyes. "Oh, relax. I'm taking you to a completely different pub than last time. Just keep an open mind; whatever happens, happens."

Lucy stayed silent as they made their way toward the LUAS. A hint of disappointment passed through her; there would be no run-ins with Aidan tonight. But, perhaps now she could relax knowing another awkward meeting was off the table. A blush rose along her neck as she remembered the "off the table" comment from the Halloween disco. Had he really asked if she wanted him *on the table*? Yes. The answer was a hard yes.

"What's with the goofy grin?" Abbey asked as they

boarded the tram into the city.

Lucy snapped out of her daze and attempted to hide her smile. "I can't believe I'm letting you drag me out again."

Abbey gave her a sideways glance. "Oh, stop. Last time, you had a brilliant night. And sure, your casual hook-up led to a bit of an awkward situation, but at least you got some action. Tonight, you can find another uncircumcised cock to occupy your mind."

Lucy laughed. "I don't know about that. I'd probably end up screwing the principal or worse."

"A long-lost brother we never knew we had," Abbey suggested.

Lucy slapped Abbey's arm. "Gross. I hope we don't have any of those."

"I would say the odds are against us," Abbey said. "Dad was out there sowing his seed all around the town. I would bet we have a few siblings out there somewhere; however, I highly doubt they would end up in Ireland."

The LUAS came to a stop at St. Stephen's Green. Abbey grabbed Lucy's hand and pulled her into the brisk night air. Their heels clicked along the concrete as they headed down the infamous Grafton Street. Lucy was instantly distracted, admiring all the shops along the pedestrian-only footpath.

"This place is cool," she commented. "I'll have to bring Kaylee here one day and do some serious shopping."

Abbey grimaced. "It's fun to look at, but this area is very touristy. Shopping is expensive here; you can get the same things in Dundrum or anyplace further out of the city center."

"Well, we can come act like tourists." Lucy smiled, then

stopped walking and sucked in a breath. "Oh my gosh, what is this?"

"This is the famous Brown and Thomas Christmas window display." Abbey spread her arms wide.

"Kaylee would love this!"

Lucy was fascinated by the elaborate display across several windows. It appeared to be a train theme, and each window displayed a different car. The details were impressive. In one window, a mother and her children decorated a tree. Another window showcased a bustling bar with passengers celebrating the season. In yet another window, a woman sat dressed to the nines, using a vanity to apply make-up. The details in every window brought each scene to life.

"We'll come back later," Abbey said, pulling Lucy away from the magical display.

Abbey turned and led them up another street lined with more shops. Even at this hour, the city was lit up. The brick buildings looked old and antique, with apartments on the top floors and shopping at ground level. An enormous church stood out between a few of the brick buildings. In contrast to its red-bricked neighbors, the church was grey with ornate windows, turrets along the roof, and a large cross planted firmly to the top.

Lucy loved how this part of the city had a mix of modern and historical buildings. She had to get off her computer and explore more with Kaylee.

They rounded another corner and arrived in front of a bright red building. A group of smokers currently occupied a small sitting area covered by a black awning. Inside, the pub buzzed with noise, but it wasn't so packed they needed to push through a crowd to enter.

Traditional Irish music filled the air.

Lucy felt her heart kick into high gear.

Looking deeper into the pub, Lucy released a sigh of relief when she saw two unfamiliar men playing a banjo and fiddle.

"Disappointed?"

Busted. Abbey saw right through the façade Lucy tried to maintain.

"You are smitten," Abbey teased. "You're hoping he'll show up tonight, aren't you?"

Lucy frowned. "The opposite, actually. I'm hoping *not* to see him tonight."

"Hm-mm." Abbey cast her sister a sideward glance. "Look, there's an empty table. Quick, grab it."

Lucy tossed her jacket over the back of a chair.

"I'll get this round. You look like you need a minute."

Abbey flashed a smirk before turning to maneuver through the crowd toward the bar.

Lucy didn't protest; she was fully aware of how on edge she felt. Nervous energy tingled through her as her eyes darted back and forth across the room. She tried to be inconspicuous but failed miserably. It was obvious to anyone watching that she was searching for someone. She had to force herself to tone it down; otherwise, people may think she was high, or paranoid.

A game of tug of war was taking place between her heart and her head. Lucy couldn't deny her desire to see Aidan here tonight, even though she knew it was a horrible idea.

Her logical head told her he was off limits, that she would only hurt herself and Kaylee if she pursued him. Her heart, and other body parts, weren't quite prepared to let him go just yet.

While Aidan wasn't her first one-night stand, he was the first one she couldn't seem to get off her mind. Every other man had been easy to forget the next day. Some men were co-workers or people she encountered daily; however, none triggered the same reaction from her as Aidan did. Being in his presence caused her entire body to shut down, leaving her speechless.

Why was she even thinking about him right now? Would she ever be able to enter a pub without scanning the place for him? Would Trad music forever be wrapped up in images of him?

"Two tables down, red shirt."

Lucy jumped as Abbey set two glasses on the table.

"Huh?" Lucy looked up.

"I've been scanning the room for you." Abbey pulled out her chair and sat down, pushing a glass toward Lucy. "It's a great excuse to check out the men. So, red shirt guy. Take a look."

Lucy shook her head. "I just came for drinks."

"Just look," Abbey hissed. "He's looking over here."

"I'm not interested." Lucy stared at her orange-colored drink. "What is this?"

"Pornstar martini." Abbey smiled. "For my little porn star."

Lucy rolled her eyes.

"Come on, live a little," Abbey said lightly. "Or at least

give this old married woman the pleasure of living vicariously through you. You're in a new city, making a fresh start. Where's my wild big sister, the Lucy who didn't give a flying feck."

"She grew up," Lucy said solemnly, shaking her head. "Being that wild child left me brokenhearted. It's the entire reason I need to make this fresh start. I messed it up so badly the first time around.

"You're so lucky to have found Rob when you did. The perfect knight in shining armor, swooping in to save the princess from the burning tower. All I ever wanted was to be loved like you are."

The smile left Abbey's face. She fiddled with the stem of her glass and took a shaky drink. Swallowing hard, she seemed to regain her composure. "I just want you to be happy."

"I don't need a man to be happy." Lucy reached across to touch her sister's hand. "I'm perfectly happy."

"No, you aren't." Abbey narrowed her eyes. "You haven't been happy for a long time. I get that Jeremy was a grade-A asshole, and he sucked all the happiness out of you. You thought he was your savior, a chance to escape, but he turned out to be the devil hauling you straight down the road to hell."

"Well, that's a depressing analogy." Lucy frowned. "But, you're not wrong either. I swear I will never need a man to save me again."

"You don't need saving." Abbey took another sip. "You already saved yourself and Kaylee. You left that dead-end situation and moved halfway across the world. You have an amazing daughter, a great career, and a fabulous sister. But even a badass girl needs a partner. You can still ride off into the sunset with a great guy, and it doesn't have to be about rescuing anyone."

"You watch too many romance movies."

"Probably." Abbey shrugged. "I like living vicariously, remember? Now, let's get back to Mr. Red Shirt over there; he can't seem to take his eyes off you."

Lucy laughed. "I'm not ready for another one-night stand. Let's call Aidan a lesson learned the hard way."

Abbey's face turned serious. "I think you like him more than you're willing to admit."

Lucy shook her head. "Perhaps, but I'm a bit broken, and I need to heal before I jump into anything, serious or not. Aidan was a wild card, that's all. I had a fling with a man I never expected to see again. When I saw him at the parent-teacher meeting, I panicked."

"And when you made out with him in the kitchen? What was that?"

Lucy shrugged. "Physical attraction?"

The band began to play, making it impossible to discuss things further. Lucy was grateful for the distraction and the abrupt end of this conversation. Tracing her fingertip along the rim of her glass, she became lost in her thoughts.

Try as she might, Lucy couldn't hide her true feelings. Abbey was right; she was infatuated with Aidan. This man was consuming her thoughts lately. His face drifted through her mind all day and haunted her dreams at night, causing her to wake up in a cold sweat. No matter how hard she tried, she could not shake the intensity of her attraction.

It was true; she felt broken as if carrying deep scars from her past mistakes and childhood trauma. What scared her the most about Aidan was the last time she became consumed by a man; he nearly destroyed her.

Jeremy swore he would free her from the constant pain and disappointment she felt daily. Lucy believed he would, so much so, that she set him high on a pedestal he never deserved. She imagined a life straight from a book or a movie, the one that ended in happiness. For a short time, they had their happy ending, but it was merely a mirage, a false reality she clung to for survival.

They were both young, and Lucy was naïve when they ran off into the proverbial sunset. Jeremy had nothing to his name, but neither did she. He struggled to keep a job, his car barely ran, and he lived in a tiny trailer on the back of his uncle's property. But, to Lucy, he had all the riches in the world.

Lucy lacked attention from both her parents and was forced to grow up without a childhood. As long as Lucy could remember, her mother was useless. Their house was always in disarray, and food was scarce. At a young age, she learned to grocery shop and pay bills online with the money their absent father directly deposited each month for child support. As a teen, her afternoons consisted of chores and homework. Besides attending school, she rarely left the house. Making friends was deliberately avoided, as she didn't want to answer the endless questions regarding her home life.

Although only three years apart, Lucy was Abbey's primary caretaker. In between binge drinking, their mother somehow made it to work each day at the local bar, staying until long after closing and stumbling home to pass out in bed. There was no time left to care for her children.

Her mother was fired a few months before Lucy turned sixteen. The child support from their father dwindled off at about the same time. Lucy had no choice but to beg for a job at the local diner.

Leaving Abbey had been a difficult decision. After spending the bulk of her childhood raising her sister and the last two years working her fingers to the bone, she could no longer shoulder the responsibility. Of course, that meant Abbey would need to fend for herself for the first time in her life. Lucy had tried countless times to teach her sister simple things such as cooking pasta, scrubbing a bathroom, and using the washing machine. Still, Abbey had zero interest in learning life skills, and Lucy never pushed hard enough.

She had big dreams when it came to Jeremy, confident everything would be different. Finally, she would be free. Leaving home felt selfish, but Lucy had always put everyone else's needs before her own. She had wanted to bring Abbey, but Jeremy refused. It was difficult to know whether Abbey would have come; Lucy had ensured her sister had a decent childhood, not one full of struggles and hard work like hers.

Jeremy was a dreamer and a free spirit who wanted to spread his wings and fly, going where the wind led him. Initially, the adventure was exhilarating; every day was full of new experiences and endless possibilities.

They traveled the country, sleeping wherever they found space: friend's couches, in their car, seedy hotels, or the occasional park bench. Lucy didn't care where they ended up as long as she had Jeremy. It was all about the adventure.

She fell hard for Jeremy and would have done anything to keep him happy. While she wasn't a virgin when they met, her experience was on the conservative side. Jeremy lit a fire in her, igniting a raging passion, and she was desperate to please him. Like a drug addict, Lucy became addicted to him; she couldn't break the hold he had on her, even while he slowly destroyed every part of her. The day she boarded the plane to Ireland, she swore she would never let a man consume her that way again. Not even a man as good-looking and charming as Aidan Kenny.

"Lucy, what's wrong?" Abbey's voice was full of concern.

Lucy looked up at the napkin Abbey held out to her. Touching her cheek, she was surprised to find them wet. Had she been crying?

"Jeremy." Lucy released a sigh. "I let my mind wander to Jeremy."

"That asshole. I never liked him, you know," Abbey sneered. "And not only because he stole you from me, but because he was—."

"A devil," Lucy finished. "I know. You never believed he was the hero I built him up to be, dragging me down that dark path and all."

"Look at you now, you broke free," Abbey reminded her. "In the end, he threw you directly back to me."

Lucy let out a huff and smiled. "That's one way to look at it." She grabbed the menu lying on the table and scanned it. "No more talk of men. I need another drink, and I've been dying to try one of these toasties. Have you had one before? They sound delicious."

"They're like grilled cheese sandwiches," Abbey said. "They taste way better than the ones Mom used to make."

"Hey," Lucy squealed. "I'm the one who made those."

Abbey ducked her head. "Sorry."

Lucy laughed. "I always managed to burn the toast, didn't I?"

Abbey nodded.

"Let's see." Lucy ran her finger down the list of toastie options. "I'm a simple girl; I'll try the ham, cheese, and tomato."

"I'll take one, too," Abbey said, pulling out her wallet.

Lucy placed a hand over Abbey's wallet. "This one is on me."

Abbey gave a strange look. "It's fine. You should stay here and clean your face up."

Lucy's mouth dropped open. "Wow, do I look that bad?"

"Just some mascara smudge." Abbey pulled a compact from her purse and handed it to Lucy. "Thankfully, you don't have dark streaks running down your face."

Lucy gasped as she looked at her reflection in the mirror.

Abbey raised her eyebrows and disappeared into the crowd.

Lucy grabbed another napkin and dipped the edge into her drink before running it under her eyelids to wipe the mascara bits. She snapped the compact closed just as a glass appeared over her shoulder.

"That was fast."

"That's what she said." An Irish brogue tickled her ear.

Her heart hammered through her chest at the sound of his voice. Their eyes locked as he rounded the table. Her mouth went dry, and every word in the English language vacated her brain.

Casually, he sat down in Abbey's vacant seat. "How ya been keeping?"

Lucy looked around wildly, like a rabbit caught with a predator. What was she looking for? An escape hatch? A hole in the wall? A phone booth so she could change into a superhero capable of holding a normal conversation with this guy?

"I can go if I'm makin' ya uncomfortable," Aidan said suddenly. The chair scraped along the floor as he pushed back from the table.

"No! Stay." Her hand shot out, grabbing him by the wrist. A jolt of electricity surged up her arm, catching her off guard, and she immediately released her grip. "You can stay."

Attempting to mask the quiver in her voice, she lifted the martini glass and gulped down the final sip.

Aidan's eyes burned into her as she tried to swallow what felt like a burning lump in her throat.

"That's not your usual." He glanced at the empty glass. "What is it, or— was it?"

Lucy swallowed hard before attempting to speak. "How do you know what my usual is?" she asked, her chin jutting out.

Aidan straightened, his mouth slightly agape. "'Scuse me. I thought you liked a Jack and Coke."

Lucy glanced at her empty glass. "This is a Pornstar Martini."

Resting his elbows on the table, he leaned forward. "Interesting."

"My sister picked it out, so don't get any ideas," Lucy said.

"Too late." He winked. Then, his smile faded. "I 'aven't seen ya at school."

Lucy felt her heart jackhammer in her chest. Had he been looking for her?

Lucy smiled shyly. "I don't usually go there."

"That's unfortunate," he said, the sly smile returning to his lips. "I was hopin' to catch ya alone. In the canteen, perhaps, or some other darkened room."

Her breath caught. "That's probably not a good idea." Her voice sounded breathless. "Especially after last time."

"Aye, exactly what I was hopin' for."

Red crawled up her neck. Lucy dropped her gaze, afraid he would see the desire dancing in her eyes.

"You know that can't happen," Lucy whispered, staring into her empty glass.

"Oh?" Aidan leaned forward, pushing the drink he had brought toward her. "Do tell me more."

"Stop." Lucy peeked up at him through her lashes. "You're Kaylee's teacher."

"I'm not *your* teacher." Aidan picked up his glass of whiskey and drank.

Lucy watched his Adam's apple move rhythmically, remembering her lips caressing up and down the soft skin of his neck. She swallowed hard, her mouth suddenly overcome with moisture. "There has to be rules against it," she said thickly.

Aidan shook his head and lifted one brow. "I've read the handbook. Several times. Nothin' against it."

"Surely, we're talking about a conflict of interest at the very least?"

He made an X across his chest. "I promise to treat Kaylee horribly."

"Don't you dare!" Lucy's mouth fell open. "She really likes you."

His eyes darkened. "And her mom? Does she fancy me, too?"

Her heart raced. Did she fancy him? Yes, she probably did. But did he fancy her in return or simply enjoy the flirty banter?

Lucy tried to calm her breathing, opening her mouth to speak.

"Oh, hey there." Abbey returned, sounding surprised.

Carefully, she set the drinks and sandwiches on the table, looking from Lucy to Aidan. Lucy suddenly began digging through her purse, knowingly avoiding her sister's gaze.

Abbey had her hand on the back of a chair, about to pull it out, but changed her mind. Instead, she retrieved her cell phone from her back pocket and stared at the screen. "Oh, shoot, I need to go. It's Lola. I'm so sorry."

Abbey grabbed her jacket.

Lucy looked up. "Kaylee? Is she alright?"

Abbey waved her question off. "Kaylee is fine. It's nothing serious, just—girl stuff."

"I can come."

"No, no, you stay." Abbey tucked her wrapped toastie in her bag and slung it over her shoulder. "Someone needs to finish these drinks, and you have your toastie to try."

Lucy's eyes widened; her sister would not abandon her

again. "I can just take it with me."

Abbey finished pulling on her jacket. "Sure, I'm just going to clear out the tab. Finish your drink. I'll be right back."

Lucy opened her mouth to protest, but Abbey had disappeared into the crowd.

"She's not coming back, is she?" She asked, slumping in her chair.

Aidan shook his head. "She's sneaking out the door."

Lucy whirled around to catch Abbey leaving the pub. "I'll be sure to kill her later."

Aidan shrugged, happy to change the subject. "A toastie?"

"I've never had one," Lucy said. "Drinking gives me the munchies, and I've always wanted to try one of these."

"Never had a toastie?" Aidan raised his eyebrows. "My mum used to make them for us, but I haven't had a toastie in donkey's years."

Lucy burst out laughing. "What? Donkey ears?"

Aidan chuckled. "Donkey's years, come 'ere ya never heard that?"

Lucy couldn't stop laughing. "That's not a real phrase."

"You've loads to learn, little lass." Aidan winked. "I haven't had a toastie in a long time; is that American enough for ya?"

"I like donkey ears better."

Aidan's smile lit up his eyes. Man, he looked so sexy right now.

"What kinda toastie ya get?" Aidan took another sip of the drink.

Lucy pulled the sandwich toward her, examining the

layers. "Ham, cheese, and tomato."

"Class," Aidan said. "Come 'ere, I can give ya a lift if you need."

"I can take the LUAS," Lucy said quickly. "It's easy enough to get home from there."

The sly smile was back. "I wasn't plannin' on taking ya home."

"I don't think that's a good idea," Lucy replied, staring at the foil-wrapped sandwich.

"Ah, worth a try," he said, winking as he pushed back from the table. He downed the last of the whiskey and set the empty glass down. "Me mates are about to play. Maybe I'll see ya around."

She fought the urge to call him back as he weaved through the crowd closer to the stage. Clearly, he was itching for another night with her, but it wasn't a good idea despite how her body was currently reacting.

Abandoned by her sister and Aidan, she sat alone in this crowded pub. Slowly, she unwrapped the sandwich and took a bite. It tasted good, but she had lost her appetite. Wrapping the toastie back up, she glanced at the makeshift stage as the band began to play.

Why was she still sitting here? In front of her sat the two drinks Abbey had bought for them; leaving them would be a waste of money. Besides, a small part of her hoped Aidan would come back; maybe this time, she would take him up on his offer.

Across the room, Aidan jumped up onto the stage. A huge smile crossed his face as he took the banjo from his friend. Stomping his foot to the beat, he began to play. Heat rushed through Lucy as she watched him. He radiated pure joy, his love for music shining through.

The music reeled her in, and soon, she lost track of time, mesmerized by Aidan's performance. He was a born performer. She wondered if he was this passionate about teaching. Maybe teaching only paid the bills, but music was his real dream. Would he quit teaching if he could make a career out of playing music? These were great questions to ask if she wanted to get to know him on a deeper level.

Did she want to know him on a deeper level? That didn't fit well with her "stay away from him" mission. But he was a nice guy; maybe they could be friends.

Friends with benefits.

No!

Why did she allow her brain to keep going there? A friendship with Aidan wouldn't be possible, not when her body reacted every time she thought about him. It was best to avoid him; the only way to do that was to walk away now.

While the band began a new song, Lucy stood up and pulled on her jacket. Finishing her drink, she placed the wrapped toastie in her purse and zipped it closed. Fighting the urge to look back toward the stage, she focused on the tiled flooring and rushed out the door.

11

A gentle breeze tousled Lucy's hair as she lazily strolled along Grafton Street. After some wrong turns, she consulted the map on her phone to help navigate back to this street. She wanted to check out the Brown and Thomas window display again and resisted the urge to snap pictures, wanting to save that for when she could bring Kaylee.

During her short time in Dublin, she had hardly walked this popular pathway. Those few previous visits had consisted of battling the tourist crowds as she hurried toward a restaurant or pub. With the city winding down and without Abbey hurrying her along, she took the opportunity to take in all the area had to offer.

There was no rush to get home, and she took her time admiring the different shops and buildings along the way. She was fascinated by the Georgian-style buildings, with their box-like shape mixed in with Victorian-style buildings, with high arched roofs and bay windows protruding outward, all sitting atop contemporary stores.

Overhead, Christmas lights and decorations hung, ready to light up the street for the holiday season. Kaylee would love this. Christmas was their favorite holiday; the lights, the ornaments, the music, the shopping, baking cookies, and even wrapping presents were things they both enjoyed. Grafton Street would need to be added to their holiday tradition this year: a day of shopping followed by dinner as they watched the Christmas lights illuminate the streets.

Lucy made it to the end of Grafton Street and crossed over the tracks to her LUAS stop. The platform was already crowded. Although it wasn't quite midnight, many pubs and restaurants had closed for the night. Partygoers, pub explorers, and a few obnoxiously drunk travelers rushed the doors when the LUAS pulled in, pushing and shoving their way inside the already crowded tram.

Lucy quickly tapped her card on the validator and rushed toward the middle of the tram before the doors closed. Passengers occupied all the seats, and she struggled to find a place to stand out of the way. Her stop was near the end of the line; the tram would empty considerably by then. Wiggling toward the opposite doors, she squished into a tiny spot against the window and tried not to feel claustrophobic.

Two stops later, Lucy could hardly move as more people continued crowding inside the tram. The smell of alcohol mixed with the chatter made her head spin. It wasn't until now that she realized how buzzed she was from those extra drinks and wished she had finished that toasty in the pub. Maybe she could jump off this tram and catch the next one, although it would probably be just as crowded. Not to mention, it would be challenging to maneuver out of her current position crammed in the corner.

At the next stop, more people boarded. Lucy wondered when people would begin leaving instead of entering; surely, they weren't all getting off at her stop.

At this point, she could hardly move and felt the cold glass of the doors pushing into her back. With great effort, she managed to pull her phone from the purse wedged tight against her chest. Abbey would be disappointed to know she was heading home.

As the LUAS jerked to another halt, the man beside Lucy fell against her arm, knocking the phone from her grasp.

"Surry," he slurred, his friends laughing at his struggle to stand upright.

Lucy grimaced; the man smelt of stale alcohol and old cigars. Sliding down the wall, she felt around the floor for her phone, trying not to touch the other passengers inappropriately while avoiding the sticky floor. Finally, her fingers felt the hard edge of the phone, grabbing it just as a stranger's fingers grazed her hand. Through the maze of legs, she locked eyes with Aidan.

Startled, Lucy jumped, nearly smacking her head against a low handrail as she stood up quickly. A wave of dizziness came over her, and she swayed lightly.

"Careful." Aidan's eyes sparked as he watched her frowning at the row of frat boys unknowingly keeping them apart.

Lucy couldn't focus as she dropped her phone back into the purse. Was she imagining things?

The LUAS lurched forward, and the drunk man stumbled, shoving Lucy against the doors.

"Easy now," Aidan said sternly.

In one swift motion, Aidan pulled the man away from Lucy, positioning himself protectively in front of her, leaving barely an inch between them.

"Yer man's a bit well-oiled, ya know?"

"Huh?" Lucy was still trying to comprehend Aidan's unexpected appearance on the tram; she couldn't wrap her brain around his slang right now.

Aidan nodded toward the swaying passenger. "He's wasted."

"Yeah," Lucy managed to whisper, her ability to speak waning.

Each beat of her heart reverberated through her body. Aidan was too close; she could feel the heat radiating off his body. Her back pressed against the doors, knuckles white as they tightened their hold around the purse against her chest.

The tram jolted as it stopped. The drunk man lost his balance and slammed into Aidan. Tingles ran through her body as Aidan was pressed against her. Somehow, more people wedged into the tram, making moving impossible.

Aidan repositioned himself so his thigh rested between her legs, his chest pressed against the back of her hand. His fingertips grasped her waist, sending goosebumps down her arms. She could feel the stiff bulge in his crotch against her leg. Lucy could hardly catch her breath as the tram continued down the tracks.

Aidan's body kept her hidden from the other passengers, and his eyes burned with this knowledge; no one could see what he was doing to her. She gasped as he took her ear lobe in his mouth, sucking lightly. The thrill of getting caught, mixed with her desire for him, was almost too much; she bit her lip to keep from calling out. Aidan planted kisses along her neck.

A few passengers stepped off at the next stop, finally allowing more space. Aidan didn't move; he stayed pressed against her, eyes blazing. Of course, if he stepped back now, she would instantly fall to the floor; her legs felt like jelly.

While it was still too crowded for anyone to see what they were doing, Lucy felt shy. The other passengers would probably think they were a couple having a tender moment and not two horny adults holding back the desire to rip each other's clothes off. That was assuming anyone was even paying attention; most passengers were intoxicated or worn out, only thinking about getting home and sleeping.

"Oh, Lucy," he breathed in her ear.

She thought she would collapse right then and there. The way he said her name and with that accent made her legs, and the area around them, tingle with delight.

Lucy released the purse; it swung loosely from her shoulder and freed her hands. Looking up at him with hooded eyes, she slid her arms around his neck. Her lips felt dry as she met his gaze, licking her lips as his hand played with the hem of her shirt. He reached under the shirt to lazily run his fingertips against her stomach's soft, sensitive skin. At his touch, her insides flipped, and the other passengers faded into oblivion until they were the only two people in the entire world.

Aidan leaned his forehead against hers as he traced the underwire of her bra, sending shivers of desire down her spine. Blinded by lust, all her excuses vanished into thin air.

Reason had disembarked at the previous stop.

Again, the tram jolted. Aidan pitched forward, his hand sliding beneath her bra and covering a breast. Lucy inhaled sharply. Lightly, he toyed with her nipple, running the pad of his thumb back and forth before gently pinching it.

Lucy closed her eyes, allowing her head to fall against the doors, automatically arching her back and pushing her breast deeper into his palm.

"What're ya doin' to me?" He groaned, biting his lip and squeezing her breast.

Clamping her lips tightly, she forced back the moan threatening to escape.

"Look at me," he whispered in her ear. "Open your eyes and look at me."

Lucy shook her head, eyes and lips fused shut. Every nerve screamed for him. If she looked at him right now, all reason and logic would be gone. She would shove him into the nearest seat and ride him right here in the middle of this busy tram.

"I want you too much," she panted the words, fingers clawing at his shoulders.

Aidan growled as the tram came to a stop. Releasing her breast, he grabbed her arm and pulled her through the open doors. The cold breeze startled her out of her dreamy daze.

"This isn't my stop," Lucy said, struggling to catch her breath.

"'Tis tonight," Aidan spoke through gritted teeth. "You're comin' home wit' me."

Lucy's legs wobbled, and she felt dizzy. Aidan's arms circled her waist for support as he half-carried her through the parking lot to a taxi idling near the road. Aidan yanked open the door and mumbled his name to the driver before following Lucy into the back.

Lucy looked at him in confusion.

"I ordered a cab from the LUAS," he said quickly. "I saw ya leaving the pub and followed ya. I figured this would give me enough stops to try and change your mind."

"How did you know I would come with you?" Lucy asked, fumbling with her seat belt.

"I didn't." Aidan smiled. "But I had to try. This would've been my stop either way, although I hoped to convince ya to come wit' me."

"It worked," Lucy sighed, licking her lips.

"Thank God." Aidan turned to her and, finally, took her mouth with his own.

Lucy suddenly felt like a horny teenager, making out in the back of a taxi, but she didn't care. From the moment she saw him on the tram, all she could think about was how much she wanted to kiss him. Her body was on fire, burning for him and aching for him to touch her intimately.

The taxi ride felt like forever. Lucy was taken aback when Aidan got out of the taxi and walked away without paying. Even more shocking, the cab left.

"Are taxis free?" She felt foolish for having to ask.

"I wish," he said, waving his phone. "Paid on the app."

Aidan typed a code into the keypad, and the security door clicked. Lucy watched as he pulled the keys from his pocket with shaky hands. She had painted a picture of him as cool, calm, and collected, but perhaps he harbored her same fears and doubts.

In the elevator, he impatiently pressed the floor button repeatedly before dropping his hand and drumming fingertips against his leg. Lucy smiled, enjoying this new side of him. His nervousness somehow helped calm her racing heart.

Aidan ran a hand through his messy hair. "Ima bleedin' eejit, right?"

Lucy smiled, having no idea what he just said. It was interesting to watch him bumble like a fool. The tables had turned; he was the one squirming for once.

"She thinks I'm funny." Aidan raised an eyebrow, rubbing his hand over his stubble.

"I think you're cute," Lucy said, surprising herself.

Aidan gave her a smile that could melt the polar ice caps. The door slid open, and she followed him down the hall. Cursing, he fumbled to get the key into the lock.

"Well, that's a bad sign," Lucy teased. "You want to make sure to get it in the hole."

Aidan laughed. "Oh, I can get it in the hole, alright. Trust me."

Finally, he twisted the key and pushed open the door. Following Lucy inside, he kicked the door shut behind them and, wasting no time, pulled her into him.

"I'll get it in any hole you'd like."

Lucy melted; her legs gave out at the sulky tone in his voice.

Tightening his grip, he whirled her around, pressing her against the door. Their mouths smashed together in a kiss full of lust and pent-up desire. Her hands tangled into his hair while he desperately pulled at the hem of her shirt. They broke apart long enough for him to peel off her top and toss it over his head. Tongues glided together as he flicked open the clasp of her bra, flinging it away to reveal her breasts.

"Oh, my days," he sighed, taking in the sight of her topless. "Better than I remember."

"You think of them often?" she asked coyly.

He gave her a sly smile, then turned his attention toward her bare chest. Caressing one breast lightly, he ducked his head and devoured the other, his tongue flicking over the hardened nipple. Lucy moaned, her fingers intertwining deeper into his hair.

Aidan released her breast and returned to ravage her mouth. Why had she been depriving herself for so long? The carnal need between them was strong, and the way he made her feel was beyond anything she had experienced before.

Lucy seductively traced a finger along the waistline of his track pants. She felt his stomach quiver at her touch, and the tiny hairs along his navel stood on end.

"Oh, Lucy," he moaned. "You're drivin' me crazy."

"Good." She covered his neck with kisses and lifted his shirt.

Helping her out, he practically ripped the shirt off, tossing it toward the other clothes strewn haphazardly around the living room. Hungrily, her hands roamed the ripples of his chest and stomach.

"I can't wait anymore," he groaned, lifting her and turning toward the couch.

He continued to kiss her as he set her gently on the arm of the sofa. A look of uncertainty crossed his face. Lucy couldn't hold out much longer; she would let him ravage her anywhere. Biting her lip, she gripped the waistband of his pants, making sure to include his boxers, and eagerly yanked them down. He released a moan as his cock sprung free.

His reaction boosted her confidence, and she lightly grazed her fingertips along his length. The intact foreskin drew her in; she gently toyed with the folds, feeling the hidden tip buried inside.

Aidan responded with a series of pants.

"I can't think straight when you do that."

Passion blazed in his eyes.

Playfully, he grabbed her legs and flipped her over the couch's arm. Desperately clawing at the fly of her jeans, he yanked them, along with her panties, down in one movement, adding them to the heap on the floor.

"I can't wait a second longer," he growled, kicking out of his pants and boxers.

Lucy was breathless; her head spun as the anticipation grew, but she had one clear thought. She did not want to have sex on a couch like a horny teenager.

Pressing her hand against his chest, she pushed him back, pointing toward his erection. "Shouldn't we cover—"

"Feck," he muttered under his breath.

Taking her hand, he pulled her off the couch and dragged her toward the bedroom. Without a word, he pointed at the bed while he rummaged through his nightstand for a condom.

Lucy leaned against the pillows and watched him fumble with the foil packet.

Sparks flew throughout her body as he straddled her waist and kissed her. Gently, he parted her legs with one knee until they were on either side of his hips and ran a hand along the tender skin of her thigh. Fingertips brushed swollen, wet lips; her back arched as she moaned in pleasure.

"Tell me ya want me," he breathed in her ear.

Lucy's eyes closed as she tried to form words. Two fingers slid inside her, making it impossible to think; she dug fingers into his shoulders, feeling the pleasure begin to build as he stroked her.

"Tell me," he groaned.

"I–want–you," Lucy moaned.

Aidan's eyes smoldered as he pulled his fingers from her folds, replacing them with the tip of his cock. Lucy wrapped her legs around his waist as he teased her opening, bringing her to the edge.

Grabbing his butt, she coerced him deeper. Waves of pleasure took over all thought and reason as he slipped inside her.

"I want you all the time," she mumbled breathlessly, overtaken in the heat of the moment and hardly aware of the confession leaving her lips.

Aidan groaned, kissing her deeply. Lucy bucked her hips and matched his pace until they moved together in perfect rhythm. She lightly scratched along his back and shoulders, arching her spine as the storm swirled within. Sweat slicked their bodies as they moved together faster and faster, racing toward release.

She felt herself climbing closer to the edge, grasping onto Aidan like a life raft. His lips grazed against hers as he moved; they were both breathing hard. Lucy couldn't hold back anymore. Fireworks exploded, and she cried out as the orgasm slammed through her body. Her arms and legs felt like rubber as she struggled to reel it in until he could finish.

Aidan groaned at the sight of her pleasure, moving faster and harder. His face contorted as he threw back his head, eyes closed tightly. He went still, his muscles taut, as if suspended in time; a low growl tore from deep in his chest as his orgasm rocked through his body.

Breathing hard, he pulled out and dropped down on the bed next to her.

"Oh. My. Days." Lucy panted.

Aidan laughed as he struggled to catch his breath. "That's my line."

Lucy stared at the ceiling, a cheesy grin plastered on her face. "That was—."

"Deadly," Aidan whispered.

"Is that good?" she asked, turning her head toward him.

"Really good." His eyes were closed, and a silly smile spread across his face.

Lucy closed her eyes, basking in the post-coital euphoria. Damn, he was so good at pleasing her. They hardly knew each other, yet he brought her more pleasure than any man ever had. There was lust and desire, but, at the same time, he was sensitive to her needs, ensuring they both ended satisfied.

Aidan was the only one-night stand she couldn't seem to get over. All the other men had hardly crossed her mind once their night had ended. It scared her how much her body craved him. From that first night, once had not been enough; they had gone at least three rounds before both falling asleep from the exertion and ecstasy. Lucy spent too many nights hoping she would find herself naked in his bed again, and no matter how hard she tried to fight it, in this moment, she was exactly where she wanted to be.

She felt giddy. There was little doubt that before the sun rose, they would be taking part in several more rounds of pleasure-filled sex. Butterflies danced in her stomach at the thought.

"You okay?" Aidan stood next to the bed, looking down at her. A sexy smile curved his lips. His uncut cock, bare, glistening, and taunting her. "Not goin' run off again, are ya?"

Damn, he looked sexy.

Lucy pushed up on her elbows, the sheet slipping down to expose her naked breasts. Aidan licked his lips, drinking in the sight of her plump nipples.

"I'm starving," Lucy said.

Aidan kept his eyes on her nipples. "Me too."

A quiver of desire tickled her stomach. Heat raged between her legs. No one had ever looked at her with such intense desire before.

"I was thinking about my toastie," she whispered.

Aidan blew out a breath. "Not what I was thinkin' 'bout at all."

Lucy laughed and shook her head. "I never had a chance to eat it, and I've worked up quite an appetite."

"Well, we best get ya fed; you'll need your energy for what I have planned."

Lucy slid off the bed. Aidan's eyes darkened as he scanned the length of her bare body.

Shyly, she rushed past him and into the bathroom. When

she came back into the bedroom, Aidan was gone. Looking around the room, she searched for something to put on; their clothes were scattered in the living room, and she suddenly felt self-conscious.

She spied a sweatshirt on the back of the door and pulled it over her head. It barely covered her butt, but it was warm and smelled like Aidan.

In the kitchen, the air smelled of toast, ham, and cheese.

"You warmed up my sandwich?"

His back was to her. "Sorry, I promise I wasn't searchin' through your purse." He turned around and sucked in a breath. "Well, that old hoodie has never looked so good on someone, no doubt about it."

Lucy ducked her head, embarrassed. Spotting her purse on the counter, she picked it up.

A warm hand cupped her exposed butt cheek. "I can see just enough of your arse to drive meself crazy picturin' the rest."

He released her and stepped back, whistling as he admired her backside. Lucy purposely dropped her purse onto the ground, making a production of bending over to retrieve it, exposing more than just her bare butt.

"Have mercy! Are ya tryin' to kill me, woman?" he growled.

Laughing, she carried her purse to the table and sat down, pulling out her cell phone.

Hope you went home with Tin Whistle Hottie and aren't dead in a ditch.

Lucy chuckled at Abbey's text message.

Yeah, yeah, so you were right. Be home after a few more rounds.

"I hope ya aren't callin' a cab?" Aidan set a plate with her sandwich in front of her.

Lucy set the phone down. "Letting my sister know I'm not dead."

Aidan raised an eyebrow. "Did she honestly think ya were?"

Lucy picked up her sandwich. "Oh, she knew where I was."

Aidan cracked a sly smile.

"Oh, this is good." Lucy wiped some melted cheese from her lip. "Want a bite?"

Aidan took the sandwich she held out. "So, what brings ya to this fair country?"

"My sister." Lucy swallowed. "She's been bugging me to move here for a few years."

"And Kaylee's dad? He's okay with this arrangement." Aidan concentrated on a fingernail, picking away imaginary dirt.

Lucy studied the toastie in her hand. "He doesn't know. And he doesn't care. He isn't very invested in Kaylee's life or mine."

"Aye, a bit of a gobshite, is he?" Aidan reached over and took the sandwich from her.

"A what?"

"A piece of shit," Aidan beamed. "Gobshite."

"Sounds right." Lucy looked around the room. "What about you? Share this flat with anyone?"

Aidan nodded. "Actually, I do. I share this place with a pretty special lady."

Lucy's jaw dropped, unsure what to say.

Aidan laughed. "Me granny. This is me granny's place."

"Oh." Lucy pulled at the sweatshirt as if it would somehow cover her exposed skin.

"She isn't here." Amusement danced in his eyes. "We share this place. I moved in years ago while attending uni, the housing market being what it was at the time and still is. Anyway, 'bout two years ago, she bought a nice vacation home in Spain and spends most of her time there."

Lucy sighed in relief.

Taking the final bite of her sandwich, she dabbed a napkin along her lips. "That was delicious."

Aidan glanced at her. "Satisfied?"

A flirty smile curved her lips as she pushed up from her chair. Gripping the hem of the sweatshirt, she slowly lifted it, exposing the most private parts of her body inch by inch until finally pulling it over her head.

Walking naked toward him, she shook her head. "Oh, I'm far from satisfied."

12

Lucy stirred slowly, blissfully satisfied and a tiny bit achy, but in a good way. She lay on her side, pressed against Aidan, his arm draped lazily over her waist. Stretching out, careful not to disturb the man still sleeping beside her, she managed to steal a glance at the only thing she still wore, her watch. It was nearly eight o'clock.

Ugh. The very thought of moving from this cozy bed and warm embrace made her curse the rising sun. A lazy morning would be heavenly. Shutting her eyes, she imagined lounging in bed all day, eating takeout and, of course, several more rounds of lovemaking.

At this point, there was no sense rushing home. Abbey and the girls would be awake before she could make it back. Once they discovered Lucy's absence, there would be no denying she had spent the night with a man. So, she may as well bask in the afterglow for a while longer.

Aidan's breathing was steady, and she wondered how long he usually slept in on the weekends. Even while he slept, his cock was stiff against her bare butt. Something about morning wood, she figured, but the feel of it pushing into her buttock ignited a fire between her legs.

Tingles ran down her spine as desire took over her. Feeling flirty, she pushed her butt into his erection and rubbed along his length in slow circles.

Aidan groaned. "I would stop if I were you."

Smiling devilishly, she continued to move against him.

Aidan released a soft moan as his fingertips pressed into her hip. If it was possible, she felt him grow even harder. A nervous laugh bubbled in her throat.

"You're a tease." He whispered, nibbling on her ear.

He tightened his grip around her waist, thwarting her attempt to squirm away.

"Oh, no! I warned ya." Aidan pressed his stiffness against the soft skin of her bare butt. "Now, you have to pay the consequences."

Kissing her neck, he skimmed the delicate skin of her stomach, leaving behind a trail of goosebumps. Lucy shivered in delight as he swirled a finger in the manicured nest of hair between her thighs, inching down to tease the slick folds of her plump lips. She bucked forward as he gently caressed her swollen nub with the pad of his thumb, sliding a finger deeper into her core until she moaned in pleasure. Lucy stopped squirming, arching her back against him as his fingers moved inside her.

"This is punishment?" she moaned, reaching back to grip his thigh and opening herself to him. "I could be punished all day."

Aidan groaned in response. Nibbling her ear, his hand ran

down her thigh to pull her leg over his own, teasing her opening with his tip. Lucy sucked in a breath as he rubbed against her, releasing her just long enough to wrap up his cock. With an almost inaudible grunt, he drove inside her, his breath coming out in slow pants.

Lucy sighed, twisting her neck to kiss him once before leaning against the pillows. As he moved, he ripped back the sheet, exposing her body entirely. Gliding a hand over her hips and stomach, he greedily cupped her breast, squeezing playfully. His breath was hot in her ear; she could hear the pleasure mounting as his breathing became more rapid, and moans tickled her eardrums.

Every sound and touch increased her pleasure. The pressure built like a rollercoaster, climbing higher and higher, knowing she would burst over the top at any moment. Aidan must have sensed her climax; he reached down to, again, toy with her swollen clit. At his intimate touch, Lucy threw her head back, gripping the sheet with one hand and his thigh with the other as the orgasm ripped through her. Aidan continued to play with her enlarged nub. Shocked, Lucy felt the waves of pleasure building again. Fireworks exploded as she came once more. Never before had she experienced multiple orgasms.

As she struggled to focus, Aidan grabbed her hip, digging his fingers into its soft skin, and called her name as he released himself.

Breathing hard, he pulled out and fell to his back. Lucy's eyes were closed, her cheeks flushed, and a stupid grin sat on her face.

"That was a great way to wake up," Aidan mumbled.

Lucy's entire body felt like jelly; she could hardly move.

Aidan rolled off his side of the bed. "Give me two minutes; then we can go again."

Lucy gasped, watching as he disappeared into the bathroom, unable to gauge how serious he was being.

"Maybe you can go again," she called to him, pushing to a sitting position. "I'm not sure I have the energy. Besides, I have to get home. I can't stay in this pleasure den all day."

Aidan reappeared, drying his hands with a towel. "Pleasure den? I like the sound of that." He came toward the bed and handed her the towel. "Why don't we do that? We could stay here, in bed, all day. It would be great craic, the best craic in town."

Lucy smiled as butterflies danced in her belly. That was the most Irish thing he could have said at that moment, making it all the more difficult to say no.

"I have a daughter, remember?" Lucy raised her eyebrows at him as she stood up. "I need to get back to my motherly duties."

Aidan sighed, dropping his head in disappointment. "Okay, at least let me make ya breakfast before ya go."

Lucy's stomach betrayed her with a growl.

"Just breakfast." She pointed at him seriously. "Then, I have to go home."

"I'll be on me best behavior." Aidan bowed, then turned on his heels and sauntered out of the room, still naked.

Lucy shook her head and tried to ignore the tingles she felt whenever he looked at her. Their sexual chemistry was like nothing she had felt before. It had been foolish to think that after a long night of sex, she would finally be able to move on from him. Instead, she found leaving difficult, especially knowing this would have to be their last time.

She walked into the living room fully naked and searched out her discarded clothes. Aidan stood over the stovetop, his back to her. She quickly located the heap of last night's clothes and slipped into her panties and jeans. She was holding her bra when Aidan turned around, a white chef's apron covering the front of his body, leaving his buttocks bare.

His eyes fell onto her exposed breasts, and he stammered. "Eggs?"

Lucy's face burned as his eyes continued to feast on her breasts, not the slightest bit embarrassed she'd caught him staring.

Lucy swallowed hard. "Eggs are fine."

"Good." Aidan turned back to the stove. "They're nearly done. Be tragic if ya didn't eat eggs."

With her bra securely back in place, she quickly found her shirt and pulled it on. Walking into the kitchen, she heard the pan sizzling as he stirred the eggs with a spatula. Four slices of bread popped up from the toaster as he pulled two plates from the cupboard.

"I suppose you'd be wantin' coffee?" He turned toward her, lips twisted with disgust. "You Americans love yar mornin' coffee, right?"

Lucy leaned against the countertop, feeling ten times more confident and less vulnerable with clothes on.

"Oh, it's a must in the morning; otherwise, we turn back into ogres."

Aidan's eyes sparkled. "I may have liked ya more when

ya couldn't talk 'round me."

Lucy dropped her gaze, attempting to hide the scarlet dotting her cheeks.

Aidan returned to the cabinets, opening and closing them until he found what he was searching for. He retrieved a glass carafe and a long rod attached to a circular mesh-covered disk, placing both on the counter.

"I've no idea how this thing works." He frowned, flicking on the kettle.

Lucy walked to his side of the counter. "What is it?"

Aidan smirked. "The coffee guru isn't familiar with a French Press?"

He feigned surprise, placing a palm to his chest.

"Sounds familiar." Lucy lifted the canister and examined it. "I've never used one before. I'm lazy; I like a coffee machine that does everything for me."

"Don't those machines clutter up the counter?"

Lucy rolled her eyes. "Worth it. Do you have coffee grounds?"

Aidan scooped eggs onto the plates with the spatula. He nodded toward a high cupboard. "Try there."

Lucy found a small, black, vacuum-sealed bag and pulled it out. Scanning the contents, she read the words *ground coffee* and nodded to herself.

Aidan handed her a pair of scissors and turned off the kettle.

"Me sister bought all this coffee stuff as a gift," Aidan told her. "She said maybe I could become more sophisticated if I switched to coffee. Hoped it would help get me a proper woman and all that." Aidan stuck out his tongue in disgust.

"I like your sister." Lucy cut along the top of the bag, releasing the air. "She sounds smart."

"Don't tell her that." Aidan rolled his eyes. "She believes herself to be 'well-traveled.'" He used air quotes on the last part. "I told her I would never change me ways. Kat is a bit of a spitfire, though, and controlling. She tossed me instant coffee out and ordered me *never to stock that shite again.*"

Lucy laughed. "She's got that right. What is the deal with instant coffee in this country? If that's all I had to use, I wouldn't drink coffee either; it's horrible."

"What's the deal with Americans being obsessed with coffee?" Aidan used his best Valley Girl accent.

"What's your obsession with tea?" Lucy shot back without missing a beat. "Great accent, by the way, nailed those California girls."

"Don't you come for me, tea!" Aidan warned, pointing a finger and shaking his head.

Lucy couldn't stop laughing. Her heart melted. Handsome, funny, sexy, fantastic accent, great butt, and mind-blowing in bed; could he get any more perfect?

She poured a generous amount of coffee grounds into the bottom of the French Press and filled it with the boiling water from the kettle. Lightly, she placed the plunger on top.

"Let's give this a try," she muttered, unsure of what she was doing. "Give it a few minutes, I guess."

Aidan shrugged. "You could be doing it arse ways, and I wouldn't know or care."

He had pulled out the toast and generously buttered each piece, placing them on the plates.

"I got the plates; you get your witch's brew." Aidan

winked as he placed the plates on the small table in the center of the room.

Lucy set the French Press on the table and sat. Aidan was back in the kitchen, retrieving two mugs from the cabinet: one for her and one for his tea.

"This looks great," Lucy gushed. "He teaches and cooks? You're just the whole package, aren't you?"

"Does that turn ya on?" Aidan wiggled his brows, pouring hot water over his tea bag.

Lucy smiled but didn't answer. Instead, she cut into her breakfast and took a bite.

"Wow, this is good." Lucy was impressed. "You know, everything tastes better here. Better eggs, better bread, and this butter——I don't think I can ever go back."

"Were ya considering going back?" he asked, staring into his tea as he stirred.

"Oh goodness, no," Lucy replied as if he had burned her. She pulled the French Press toward her and pressed the plunger down. "Here goes nothing."

Aidan grimaced as she poured the hot, brown liquid into her mug.

"Not a big coffee fan, are you?" Lucy teased.

"No. Not at all. I can't stomach the taste."

"Well, you need to add milk and sugar," Lucy said, pushing her chair back. "The trick is to make it sweet, mask the coffee taste."

Aidan raised an eyebrow. "So, you like coffee that doesn't taste like coffee? Maybe you should try tea." He stood up. "Sit, eat, I'll get the milk and sugar. I've got sausage in the pan I've to grab anyway."

"Let me help," Lucy protested. "As much as I love the service here, I'm already up."

She followed him into the small kitchen area. He set a sugar container on the counter while she pulled milk from the fridge. Steam escaped the pan as he lifted the lid.

"That smells amazing. It's not blood anything, is it?"

"You mean blood pudding?" Aidan laughed.

Lucy cringed.

"No worries, this is just regular sausage."

Carrying everything back to the table, they returned to their seats. Aidan placed two sausage links on her plate as Lucy poured milk into her coffee.

"So, you have a sister. Any other siblings?" Lucy stirred the coffee with her fork.

"Ah, I shoulda grabbed a spoon," Aidan apologized, but Lucy waved him off. "I've also an older brother. How about you?"

"Just Abbey and I, as far as I know," Lucy said, wiping the handle of her fork on a napkin. "We could have more out there somewhere."

Aidan raised his brow.

"Our dad was absent most of our lives," Lucy explained, taking a slow sip of coffee. "We only saw him once a month or so. Abbey and I just assumed he was out whoring around the neighborhood like a tomcat. For all we know, he has several other abandoned children out there somewhere."

She bit her lip. "That was probably TMI," she muttered, picking up her toast.

Aidan swallowed the food in his mouth. "Well, my parents met in primary school; they lived in the same housing estate. It wasn't until after uni they got together. And after thirty-seven blissful years, they're still going strong.

"My older brother, Niall, is married, and they have twins, Cillian and Cian. My sister, Kat, writes a travel blog and spends her days galavantin' around the globe. While my parents hate her being away most of the time, it helps keep their little secret from comin' to light."

A devious expression crossed his face, and he leaned forward, dropping his voice to a low whisper. "Kat's a lesbian." He placed a finger to his lips.

Lucy frowned. "You have a problem with that?"

Aidan laughed. "Of course not, come 'ere, no one cares about that anymore. We've moved into a more accepting society. Me parents, though, are stuck in the old ways, or at least in appearing as good ole Catholic folk. I don't think they're bothered much, but they can pretend it's not real if they don't talk about it. That's the Irish way."

Lucy sighed. "I guess my family is the only one with problems."

Aidan shrugged. "No family is perfect, Lucy. We all have baggage; some might seem heavier than others, but it's still there."

She offered a soft smile. It was the perfect response to her confession. Glancing at her watch, she took a final drink of her coffee and pushed back from the table.

"I should go. It's getting late."

"We aren't finished with breakfast yet," Aidan protested, scooting back his chair.

Lucy looked down at her empty plate, confused. "I can

help you clean?"

Aidan stepped toward her. "I was hoping to make *you* part of my breakfast."

Lucy stepped back, throwing out her hands to push him away. "No! No, I can't."

Aidan stopped moving, but his eyes burned with desire. "You can stay."

Her heart kicked into overdrive as her body betrayed her, responding to the lust in his eyes. Every inch of her reacted, all but one tiny brain cell that was screaming for her to stop. That brain cell knew she wasn't ready for something serious or intense, and the way Aidan made her feel was leading straight down that road.

Jeremy had betrayed her and left her heart in pieces; she needed to heal before opening herself up again. Then, there was Kaylee. Her daughter was also healing while settling into this new life. Lucy could not, would not, risk everything for a brief love affair.

Swallowing the lump forming in her throat, she exhaled. "Last night was great. This morning was great. You're great."

She trailed off, staring at her feet.

Aidan's shoulders slumped forward. "I don't like where this is headin'."

Biting her lip, she met his gaze. "We can't keep doing this."

Aidan's smile faded. "Doing what? Avoiding each other 'til we both nearly explode? I agree."

Lucy blew out a puff of air. "I'm serious." She waved her hand between them. "This. You and me. Sleeping together."

"Are ya not havin' fun?" Aidan couldn't hide the hurt in

his voice.

"I did. Last night was amazing."

"Then, what's the issue?"

"Kaylee, for one," she replied, nervously running a finger over the back of the chair.

"Kaylee? What does she have to do with anything?" Aidan asked. "Are ya afraid I'll treat her differently? I'm a grown man; I can separate my work and personal life."

Now, he sounded insulted.

"I know that," she said defensively. "But, I have to think about her, and if things between us go sideways, she could end up hurt."

Aidan rubbed the back of his neck. "I'll never involve her."

Lucy nodded. "I appreciate that, but I'm also not looking for anything serious. I just got out of a crappy relationship, and I'm still–."

"Whoa, whoa." Aidan held up his hands, interrupting her. "Hold everything. I'm not proposing marriage; we're just havin' fun."

Lucy stared down at the floor, feeling foolish.

Aidan stepped forward, taking her hands in his. "I like ya. I think ya like me. There's no denyin' the chemistry between us, and the sex is deadly. It's been a long time since I've connected with someone this way, and I'd like to keep it goin'."

He stroked his hands up and down her arms.

"I'm not looking for anything serious either. There's no need to put labels on things."

Softly, he traced the outline of her jaw with his fingertips.

She trembled, his touch igniting a fire through her veins.

"I like you." Aidan's voice softened as he glided his hands into her hair. "There's no need to complicate things. Let's be friends, with benefits. Isn't that what Americans call it? No pressure, just sex." He dipped his head, lips grazing her ear. "I really like sex with ya. If that's all ya want, I'm happy to oblige."

Lucy giggled like a schoolgirl; his breath tickled her ear. With each touch, her body responded. Breathing became difficult as her heart raced. Her attraction to him was magnetic, pulling her under.

"Is that okay?" He nibbled her ear lobe.

Lucy's eyes slid shut, and she fought to hold back a moan.

A dark shadow crossed his face. The apron covering his crotch tented upward, grazing against her leg.

"I enjoyed the feel of ya next to me," he whispered, kissing her neck. "I *really* enjoyed the way ya woke me up."

Lucy leaned her head back, exposing her neck and allowing him to flutter kisses along her collarbone. The temptation to follow him back into his bedroom was strong; she wanted nothing more than to spend the rest of the day wrapped up in each other.

His erection dug into her thigh as he continued kissing her neck. Her thoughts drifted to his uncut penis. It was all new to her; she wanted to touch and play with it and learn what made him shiver and squirm until he couldn't hold back anymore. She pictured running her tongue under the sensitive foreskin, his fingers twisting in her hair, groaning while she pleasured him.

One more round wouldn't hurt.

With a devious gleam in her eye, Lucy pushed aside the apron and stroked his stiff cock. Aidan groaned. Still holding his length in her hand, she guided him toward the bedroom.

13

"Well, well, look what the cat dragged in." Abbey pounced the minute Lucy walked through the door. "It's pretty late. Did you get detention? Did Teacher need to spank you?"

"Shhh," Lucy whispered harshly. "For goodness sake, Abbey."

Abbey chuckled, waving the comment off. "The girls aren't here. Rob took them to Dundrum for shopping and lunch. Now, get in the kitchen and tell me everything."

Abbey's eyes were bright as she pulled Lucy impatiently toward the kitchen.

Lucy set her purse on the island and fiddled with the strap. "What's to tell?"

"What do you mean? Everything." Abbey looked her up and down. "Let's start with that silly grin you're trying to hide."

Abbey leaned on the opposite side of the kitchen island, not taking her eyes off Lucy, who continued staring at her purse.

"What do you want to know," she said quietly.

Abbey dipped her head and frowned. "Oh, will you stop acting so modest? I want to know everything. Let's start with how long you stayed after I left. I imagine it wasn't long at all."

Lucy glanced up. "You're wrong about that. And actually, we didn't leave together. We kind of—connected on the LUAS."

Abbey straightened. "I've got chills."

Lucy smiled at her sister's enthusiasm and recounted her stroll along Grafton Street, followed by the steamy LUAS ride.

Abbey's jaw practically hit the counter at the tale. "Oh, dang. That is so hot." She pretended to fan her face.

Lucy leaned in. "I was so turned on. I thought for sure he was going to do me right there in the tram, and I was all for it."

Abbey punched the air. "Yes, yes, yes! This is what I need to hear: all the hot and juicy details."

A cheesy grin crossed Lucy's face. She lifted her eyes toward the ceiling as if coaxing the memory back. "It was so good. He took me places, Abbs. I promise you; I have never had sex like that before."

"How many times? And don't you dare tell me I'm being too personal? One? Three?" Abbey thrust her hips back and forth.

"You are so immature." Lucy shook her head but held up her palm proudly and mouthed *five*.

"Five!" Abbey shouted, her mouth a gape. "You're a minx!"

Lucy held up her hands, acting coy. "What can I say, when it's good, it's good. We couldn't get enough of each other."

"That's a lot of sex."

"I'll definitely be sore for a few days," Lucy giggled. "Worth it."

Abbey made a face. "You dog."

"That man does things to me." Lucy sounded wistful. Her expression turned serious. "Do you think it's my age? I read we hit our peak in our thirties; something about losing our inhibitions because we're more secure in ourselves."

"Oh, forget all that mumbo jumbo," Abbey chortled. "You like him. You are head over heels for this guy, and that's what makes the sex so great."

Lucy grimaced. "I hardly know him. We just have this magnetic chemistry. It's all about the lust and nothing to do with feelings."

"Oh, please. You obviously have feelings; you can't keep your hands off each other."

Lucy shook her head. "It's just sex, Abbey. I'm telling you, it's possible to connect with someone on a purely physical level and nothing more. Simply because we're compatible in bed doesn't mean we'll make good life partners."

Abbey furrowed her brows, skeptical.

"Do you remember Norbert?"

"Norbert? Your weird friend in high school?" Abbey scrunched up her nose. "I remember that guy. What was his first name again?"

Lucy pursed her lips. "Ummm, Tony. Tony Norbert."

Abbey nodded. "Oh yeah, he used to get picked on a lot."

"So did I." Lucy rolled her eyes. "Anyway, I lost my virginity to him."

Abbey jumped back in shock. "What? No! He was—I mean, no offense, but—"

Lucy released an embarrassed laugh. "Yeah, I know; he was strange."

"Strange is not the word I would use."

Lucy lifted her shoulder. "Ok, so he wasn't great looking, and his personality was a bit—stale. But, in his defense, that man gave me my first orgasm."

"Ew!" Abbey stuck out her tongue, feigning a gag.

"I know, I know." Lucy shook her head. "I wouldn't have believed it either."

Abbey's eyes suddenly grew wide. "Is that why he came over so often? I thought you were studying."

"Studying human anatomy." Lucy cracked up at her joke. "The first few times he came over was to study. Then, after one particular grueling study session for finals, he asked if he could kiss me. Neither of us had ever kissed anyone before; we figured it would take the pressure off if we just got it over with. Surprisingly, he was an excellent kisser. Well, not the first kiss; it was pretty sloppy and awkward. But, we tried again, and it was good."

"Oh my goodness! Lucy Saunders, I don't know you at all." Abbey placed a hand on her chest. "This all happened at our house? How did I not notice?"

Lucy shrugged. "You were out with your friends, and Mom was either at work or passed out. It wasn't difficult. Anyway, making out soon turned into sex. I know it sounds a little ridiculous, but we had the opportunity to experiment, and we went for it. There was no pressure, and because we were friends, without feelings, it was easy to explore a little."

Abbey mimed an explosion coming from her head. "Mind blown. This is not a revelation I expected this morning."

"Anyway, the point of this– revelation, as you call it, is that good sex doesn't equal good relationships. Outside the bedroom, Norbert and I had no chemistry. We were both outcasts and became friends because no one else could stand us. There was no physical attraction between us."

Abbey pursed her lips. "Are you sure about that? I believe *you* felt nothing toward him, but I always thought he was smitten with you."

Lucy looked surprised. "Really? If he was, he never said anything."

"Why would he?" Abbey asked. "And risk ruining a good thing, like sex with the girl of his dreams."

Lucy scowled. "I don't think he felt that way."

"You didn't see what I saw." Abbey raised her shoulders. "So, how long did your little experiment go on?"

Lucy thought for a minute. "Maybe a year."

"A year!" Abbey gasped. "Geesh, Lucy, he must have felt like the luckiest guy in the world. Why did you stop? And let me guess, it was you who put a stop to things, right?"

Lucy nodded. "Actually, we made the decision together. We learned all we could, and things started getting stale."

Abbey chuckled. "Wow, did you tell him you were bored? Geesh, Lucy, you must have broken that poor boy's heart."

"It wasn't like that," Lucy protested. "He agreed with me."

"So it *was* your decision," Abbey said, pointing a finger accusingly. "You flat out told him he was boring. What other choice did he have but to agree? It was the only way to walk away with his head held high."

"He didn't seem that bothered," Lucy muttered, pangs of guilt clutching her chest. "I don't think it was like that. A few months later, he was dating someone, and I met Jeremy."

"And the sex was never good again." Abbey could hardly get the words out before bursting into laughter.

"You aren't wrong." Lucy lifted her brows. "It was never quite as good as it had been with Norbert. But Jeremy and I had chemistry and a strong attraction to each other. That made it—"

"Tolerable," Abbey blurted out.

"You really don't like Jeremy," Lucy said, not the least bit surprised.

"Not even the slightest. He was a snake, and he stole you from me."

"He also brought us back together, eventually," Lucy said. "And he gave me Kaylee."

Abbey moved toward the fridge, opening the door and retrieving a water bottle. "Ok, so you had great sex with Norbert but no attraction. Then, with Jeremy, the attraction was there, but the sex was so-so."

Lucy nodded in agreement.

"Water?"

"Sure."

Abbey removed a second water bottle and carried both over to the island, placing one in front of Lucy.

"Now, you have great chemistry with Aidan and great

sex. I don't see the problem here." Abbey twisted the top off her water and took a sip. "He sounds like the perfect match."

Lucy nodded, turning the water bottle in her hands. "While both statements are true, I hardly know Aidan. He could be a horrible partner. I thought Jeremy was amazing at first."

Abbey sighed, lifting her eyes. "For goodness sake, Lucy, are you going to compare every man to Jeremy for the rest of your life? I'm sorry he turned out to be such a loser, but—"

Lucy slammed her water bottle down, startling Abbey into silence. "This is not about Jeremy!" She inhaled deeply, forcing herself to calm down. Softly, she said, "It's about me."

Abbey calmly took another sip of water. "Everyone is afraid of getting hurt."

"There's much more at stake here." Lucy absently picked at the wrapper on the bottle. "Aidan is my daughter's teacher; I'm afraid of Kaylee getting hurt."

They stayed in silence for several minutes. Lucy continued to pick at the label, leaving tiny scraps of paper on the countertop.

"None of this matters," Lucy finally said quietly. "Neither of us are looking for a relationship."

Abbey furrowed her brows. "He said that?"

"He practically laughed in my face when I said I wasn't ready for anything serious." Lucy brushed the scraps into a little pile, refusing to meet her sister's gaze. "I felt stupid for even mentioning it, but I didn't want to lead him on. At the end of the day, it was just great sex, two consenting adults blowing off some steam."

"I don't believe that for a minute," Abbey said. "I've seen

the way he looks at you."

"Lust and desire; that's what you saw." Lucy feigned a smile. "Anyway, he offered me a friends-with-benefits situation."

"Norbert 2.0?" Abbey teased. "I think that sounds like a horrible idea."

"I thought you loved my sexcapades?"

"Oh, I do," Abbey agreed. "But I also like happy endings. That idea sounds like a fast train to hurt feelings and a broken heart."

"We've laid our cards on the table," Lucy said. "As you said, it would be like the *Norbert* experience."

Abbey scowled. "Except, you're Norbert in this situation."

Lucy's mouth fell open.

"Not in the weird, unattractive way," Abbey quickly corrected. "In the other way."

"I don't understand."

"Come on, Lucy, you can lie to yourself all you want." Abbey's tone was condescending. "But not me. You obviously don't want to be *just* friends with this guy."

"I don't want a relationship with him either," Lucy objected, irritation bubbling within her.

Abbey ran a hand over her face. "Okay. Let the record show, that I think a casual sex situation is a bad idea. You should either jump in with both feet or walk away completely; any other option will end badly."

"Noted." Lucy yawned and rubbed her eyes, exhausted from this conversation. "I'm tired. I'm going to nap before the girls come home."

Annoyed and frustrated, she grabbed the water bottle roughly from the counter. Abbey's eyes bore into her back as she headed up the stairs. She could no longer take Abbey's opinions and judgments, even if they weren't entirely off base. A casual affair with Aidan was probably a bad idea, especially since their attraction was so strong. But it couldn't last; even the most intense fires die out eventually.

Shutting the door to the small room she shared with Kaylee, Lucy set her purse on the dresser and collapsed onto the bed. This whole Aidan ordeal was too much drama. It should have ended after one night; instead, she felt like a teenager, conflicted and frustrated by a stupid boy. Of course, life was easier at that age, back when lust, desire, and stolen glances across the room were everything a girl believed she needed to find true happiness.

Perhaps Lucy's problem had been that despite watching her parents' roller coaster ride relationship, she had naïvely clung to the hope that lasting love was possible. While teenage Lucy believed in love, adult Lucy lost her faith long ago.

She was only seventeen when she met a rebellious twenty-one-year-old named Jeremy. Their meeting had been random, a simple case of being in the right place at the right time. Fate, or so she had once believed.

Lucy took a part-time job at the local gas station in addition to working at the diner. Her mother lost her job, and someone needed to pay the bills. Things with Norbert had ended, leaving Lucy desperate for a connection aside from her moody fifteen-year-old sister and alcoholic mother. She found that with Sherry, her nineteen-year-old co-worker.

Sherry was the polar opposite of Lucy, with her spiky purple hair, heavy eyeliner, netted tights, lacy gloves, and clunky black combat boots.

Sherry and her friends used to sneak into the local drive-in movie theater most weekends. No one drove or had a car, but they crawled through a hole in the fence and gathered on the hill behind the parked cars. Although they could watch the movie, without a car's speaker system, they couldn't hear anything.

None of that mattered because no one came to watch the movie. What they came for were the trucks full of teenage boys. They rolled in, parked in front of the hill, and blasted their speakers for all the girls to hear. Each truck bed held a mattress along with blankets and pillows. The boys would invite the girls to climb in the back and join them for movie-watching, or so they called it.

Sherry was always the first to hop in a truck, eager to share snacks and flirt with the boy who gave her the most attention. Things always started innocent, but after ten minutes, Sherry and her friends were making out with the boys, complete with heavy petting and dry humping. Often the dry humping led to real humping, and no one was hiding much under those thin blankets.

Lucy cringed at the thought of making out with random teenage boys every week. She knew how good sex could be and had no desire to be awkwardly dry-humped or fondled by inexperienced boys. She was not interested in doing it in the back of a truck, with everyone pretending not to watch.

In the beginning, before she knew what was expected of her, she climbed in with everyone else. As soon as they began partnering up, she returned to sitting on the hillside, pretending to be fascinated by the movie. Although she didn't often have fun, anything was better than being at home.

Everything changed when she met Jeremy.

From the moment he climbed out of his truck, flicking a cigarette from his fingers like a scene from a movie, she was hooked. Something about him caught her attention; she couldn't tear her eyes away from him. For a brief moment, their gazes locked. His eyes ran the length of her, licking his lips while he lingered on her breasts. She should have felt disgusted, but instead, her body reacted, disappointed when he turned back to his friends.

Behind her, the giggling group of girls were already piling into the bed of his truck. Finding her target early, Sherry climbed right onto the lap of a boy. Lucy felt she would be alone again tonight as everyone quickly partnered up.

Without glancing at the group, she plopped down in the grass and searched for the cute driver. He was strolling off toward the concession stand, and she felt restless, anticipating his return.

Nearly giving up hope he would come back, she turned her attention to her fingers, picking at some dead skin along the nails. A shadow crossed above her. Surprise widened her eyes when she realized the mystery boy standing over her. Without uttering a word, he handed her a red and white striped bag of popcorn, winking before strutting back to the truck.

Somehow, Sherry had witnessed the exchange while

tonguing her boy toy. "Go talk to him, idiot."

The other girls join the chant. "Talk. To. Him."

All eyes were on her. Deep down, she had that adolescent need to be accepted by the older girls, and wanted to impress them. With a deep sigh, Lucy made a show of rolling her eyes as if the entire ordeal was beneath her and stood, wiping dirt and grass off her butt.

He sat behind the steering wheel, his elbow resting in the open window. A cocky smile curved his lips as he stared out the windshield, tapping his fingers against the outside car door.

Lucy cleared her throat. "May I have a sip of your coke?"

"Cock!" The boy sitting in the passenger seat thought he was being clever with his play on words. "You can sip his cock, anytime."

Red crept up her neck; mortified, she turned away.

"Shut up, Carl!" The driver's door opened behind her; a hand encircled her arm. "Ignore that putz. I'll share my coke if you come and sit with me."

Lucy's heart thundered in her chest. Looking to the girls for reassurance, she was disappointed to find they had lost all interest and were back to making out. A knot formed in her stomach as logic and reason kicked into overdrive. Why was she trying so hard to impress these girls? They were nothing but playthings for those boys who would toss them out with the garbage in the morning. As harsh as that sounded, it was the reality of these weekend outings and the reason Lucy never wanted to partake. No matter how attractive this boy was, she wasn't in the market for a random hookup in his truck.

Nervously, she looked from the boy to the passenger seat, where Carl still chuckled at his pathetic joke.

"No thanks," she muttered.

He released her arm and held up his hands in surrender. "I'll be on my best behavior, I swear. I won't even touch you." He leaned into the car. "Carl, get out!"

Carl stopped laughing and looked insulted. The boy gave him a stern look and a grumbling Carl moved to the back of the truck.

"M'lady." He waved his hand toward the passenger side.

Lucy slid onto the seat, rubbing her sweaty hands on her jeans.

"I'm Jeremy."

"Lucy," she replied quietly.

"Lucy. I like that."

In those early days, Jeremy was always a perfect gentleman. That night, he almost kept his promise. At least halfway through the movie, the first touch was by accident. They both reached for the soda; their fingers grazed, and their eyes met. He smiled, intertwining his fingers with hers and holding onto them until the night ended.

For the next several weekends, she met him at the drive-in. Jeremy was careful. Eagar, to keep up his gentlemanly façade, he never pushed for too much. Their first kiss was gentle, not the clumsy and sloppy kiss of desperation, but sweet and patient. She felt protected and safe with him.

He asked her questions about her life, and she did the same. One night, she surprised herself by confessing what a disappointment her mother was and how much she resented her father for never showing an interest in her life. Jeremy was a good listener, and he responded with all the encouraging words she needed to hear. He held her while she cried, gently kissing away her tears.

By the third week, he confessed his love for her.

"Lucy, from that first second I saw you, I was beyond smitten," he murmured in her ear. "You are the most beautiful girl I've ever seen. How did I get so lucky? Why did you choose a troll like me? I love you so much. All I want is to be with you."

He never pushed or pressured, and he said all the things a woman wants to hear. Like a spider weaving its web while sweet-talking the fly, Lucy allowed Jeremy to create a false sense of security around her.

After a month, she gave herself to him.

They left the drive-in theater for the first time, parking in a secluded area beside the lake. Lucy had thought he was the most romantic man in the world. The truck bed was filled with blankets and pillows; they snuggled under the stars. Moonlight danced across the lake, creating the perfect backdrop.

As he whispered words of endearment, they made love for the first time. Again, he was slow and gentle; nothing was frenzied or rushed that night. Although it wasn't her first time, her body shook and trembled with each touch. Her nerves were on end, and she worried he wouldn't be satisfied when they finished. When he called her name at his climax, all her fears vanished.

They stayed together all night, wrapped in a blanket and each other, the stars blazing above them. At that moment, Jeremy was perfect. He devised a plan for them: a future full of adventure, travel, and conquering the world side-by-side.

In reality, Jeremy was a master manipulator, and Lucy the perfect victim. She was a broken girl longing for someone to save her. Jeremy saw her as an opportunity to create his ideal partner, one who would bend to his every whim and one he could train to please him in every way. He was a narcissist, and she was a puppet on a string.

There are moments when choices are made, each leading to separate outcomes. If Lucy's mom weren't the alcoholic, depressed shell of a human she turned out to be, then Lucy wouldn't have needed that job at the gas station. Without that job, she would never have met Sherry and, in turn, never would have met Jeremy that fateful night. Likewise, if her father hadn't been such a deadbeat, Lucy wouldn't have desperately needed male attention or been drawn to a bad boy. If only– if only– if only.

On the flip side, without Jeremy, there would be no Kaylee. And without Kaylee, Lucy's life would feel empty. Kaylee was the sunshine in the storm of her life: the angel who rescued a broken woman. And Kaylee deserved a better life than the one Lucy had.

Even though she finally broke away from Jeremy, her heart was still healing. And hadn't it been Abbey who suggested the best way to mend a broken heart was with sex? Or something like that. So, why wasn't casual sex with Aidan the perfect arrangement? Neither wanted a relationship or commitment, so what could go wrong?

He sent her hormones into overdrive, and it was embarrassing how turned on she got merely in his presence. Put those things together, and they were bound to have astronomical sex. Their chemistry was the driving force behind the unstoppable need to get naked, so what was the big deal? Friends with benefits sounded like a win-win situation for everyone involved.

Lucy didn't want a relationship; she was far from ready to give anyone her heart. But Aidan had been upfront and honest, revealing he wasn't looking for any of those things. If they could continue being honest with each other, then maybe it could work.

She pulled a pillow over her face, screaming into it. Why was this so complicated? A casual relationship is supposed to be easy, fun, and fancy-free, not a constant back and forth like a game of tug-of-war between her head and her heart. Simply because she didn't want a relationship didn't mean she wasn't a woman with needs. Needs Aidan was a pro at fulfilling. Was she willing to give up great sex simply because things might get awkward?

The body wanted what the body wanted, and her body definitely wanted Aidan. Screw it all. He promised Kaylee wouldn't be affected by their arrangement, and she wouldn't need to know anyway. What she decided to do with her personal time was nobody's business. Her only concern now would be, when things ended, could both walk away with their hearts still intact.

14

November passed in a blur. Lucy was living a double life; one she displayed to her family, and the other she hid from everyone. At work, she took on large corporate accounts and spent her days tackling their complicated issues. Her evenings were spent with Kaylee, helping with homework, or simply enjoying quality time together. The nights belonged to Aidan. As much as she hated the lying and sneaking around, she loved that those wee hours belonged to only them.

During the day, she mainly worked from home, wanting to be present when Kaylee returned from school. After dinner, homework, and sending Kaylee to bed, Lucy headed to the office, claiming to work on things she couldn't do from home. It was the perfect cover.

Deciding to take Aidan up on his friends-with-benefits offer, Lucy had to figure out clever ways to meet without getting caught. Abbey would never understand this arrangement, and Lucy was too old and stubborn for more lectures. One evening, her boss asked her to come into the office after hours; he needed her to set up and train the small overnight crew they had recently hired. This request led to her visiting the office several times a week to liaise on various projects and monitor accounts. What Abbey didn't know was that Lucy could, and did, accomplish those extra tasks online. Her office quickly became code for Aidan's place. As far as Lucy could tell, Abbey bought the story hook, line, and sinker.

Rob, whom Abbey playfully called Big Foot because his sightings were rare these days, had taken a work promotion. He was now the Senior Consultant for their company, and his job consisted of traveling several times a week. For Lucy, his absence helped sell her story. In fact, the one time Abbey questioned Lucy, who was running to the office for another late night, Rob quickly pointed out that their company ran 24/7 and had customers worldwide.

"Our midnight is someone else's morning," he chastised.

The lying and running around were exhausting. Lucy was burning the candle at both ends, and she was physically tired due to lack of sleep and emotionally drained from the façade. She was unsure how long she could carry on this way. Although she spent several nights with Aidan, their time together was limited. Fueled mainly by their desire for each other, the visit consisted of frenzied love-making before Lucy rushed home to catch a few hours of sleep.

"I think you killed them." Abbey touched Lucy's shoulder.

Lucy jumped and chuckled with embarrassment, switching off the electric mixer she used to mash potatoes in a large bowl.

"Drifted off there for a minute," she muttered.

"You've been doing that a lot lately," Abbey said, returning to the stuffing she was mixing. "You've been working so much this month. I hope you're getting some major overtime for all that. You work all day and then go into the office at night; it's a bit mad. Last night, I heard you come in at three in the morning. They can't expect this to carry on much longer."

Abbey didn't wait for Lucy to respond. Setting aside the stuffing, she moved toward the oven. "I hope you know you aren't fooling me at all." She opened the oven door and checked the thermometer on the turkey cooking inside. "I know exactly what you're doing."

Lucy froze. "You do?"

"This is about—." She looked around the kitchen, making sure they were alone before continuing in a whisper. "Aidan."

Lucy's face felt hot; luckily, her back was to Abbey, making it easy to hide the red burning her cheeks. With trembling hands, Lucy scooped butter into her mashed potatoes.

"What?" Her voice sounded squeaky.

Abbey shut the oven, wiping her hands on the towel tucked into her apron. "You're practically killing yourself with work in order to keep your mind off him. You think if you work until you drop with exhaustion, your thoughts won't revolve around him."

Lucy closed her eyes in relief, releasing a small puff of air. Thinking fast, even though her brain felt like mush, she jumped onto Abbey's train of thought.

"So what if I am? It seems to be working. I wasn't even thinking about him until *you* mentioned his name."

"Have mercy!" Abbey lifted her eyes to the ceiling. "Is it really worth all this trouble? Why not just date him already? You sure do a lot of pining for someone who doesn't want a relationship."

Lucy rolled her eyes. "He doesn't want a relationship either. I can't change that." She sighed heavily. "Anyway, I'm nearly done with this project. I should only need to go in for a few more nights. Including tonight."

Abbey whirled around, looking aghast. "But it's Thanksgiving!"

Lucy went back to overmixing her potatoes. "It's not Thanksgiving in Ireland."

Abbey gasped, placing a hand on her chest, feigning insult. "How dare you! It's Thanksgiving in this house. The turkey is just about perfect. We've got stuffing, rolls, gravy, pumpkin pie." She eyed the bowl in front of Lucy. "And extremely mashed potatoes."

"I'm making green bean casserole, too," Lucy said, setting the mashed potatoes aside. "Just like Mom used to make every Thanksgiving. It seemed to be the one thing she loved to cook. Not that it's difficult, but Mom cooking at all was nothing short of a miracle." Lucy placed her palms together in mock prayer, lifting her eyes to the ceiling. "How lucky we were to have a mom for one day."

Abbey pursed her lips together.

"What? Am I wrong?"

Abbey bit her lower lip. "Mom was different after you

left."

Lucy frowned as she dumped a can of green beans into a casserole dish, using a spatula to spread them evenly.

Abbey held a wet washcloth and began wiping the countertop. "It wasn't immediate; things were pretty bleak right after you left," she said quietly. "When Dad died, she changed."

"The spell broke." Lucy shrugged with no emotion in her tone. "She finally came out of her trance; that's great for you, Abbey."

Grabbing a can of creamy chicken soup, Lucy popped the top and poured the clumpy contents over the beans.

"Ewww." Abbey scrunched her nose as she watched the soup ooze across the beans.

"It looks gross but tastes so good." Lucy began shredding the block of cheddar cheese over the dish. "I never should have left."

"You needed to go." Abbey finished wiping the countertop and sat on the bar stool where Lucy usually sat. "You deserved a life of your own. I understand now how much you gave up to make sure we had food. And how hard you tried to shield me from the reality of horrible parents. You raised me, Lucy, not Mom. I honestly wasn't shocked you left; only shocked you left without me."

Lucy concentrated on grating the cheese, feeling her stomach drop. "I didn't want to leave you. Jeremy wouldn't let you come. I had to make a choice. I chose wrong; I never should have left you."

"I was angry for a long time." Abbey picked at a dark stain on the countertop. "But, I was a spoiled brat. It didn't take long to see how damaged and useless Mom was. I mean, for the first time in my life, I was on my own; no one was around to take care of me. I never realized how much you did for me, for us. For those first months after you left, I was constantly late for school, starving, and had no clean clothes. I was so mad that you left me in that situation. But it forced me to grow up, and I understood why you had to go. We were both kids, but only *I* got to experience a childhood."

"We were dealt a horrible deck." Lucy set the cheese grater down and looked across the counter. "I should have taught you more instead of shielding you. I took on everything so you could have the childhood I couldn't. I hated Mom, and I had to get away. My childhood was stolen because she let Dad destroy her over and over. All she had to do was walk away, slam the door in his face, and we would have had a completely different life."

Abbey straightened in her chair. "Is that what you're so afraid of? A man consuming you to the point you abandon everything else?"

Lucy dropped her gaze, staring into the messy, chunky casserole. "I don't want to be like mom—again." Her voice came out in a whisper. "I was her. It took me far too long to realize it. I finally walked away from Jeremy because he was slowly destroying me. I was becoming exactly like Mom and hated myself for it."

Understanding filled Abbey's eyes. "I get it now. Aidan doesn't want a relationship, and you aren't willing to settle for casual sex."

Lucy felt a lump form in her throat.

Abbey pushed off the chair and carried the washcloth

back to the sink. "I'm so glad you figured that out."

A knot tightened in Lucy's stomach. "This has nothing to do with Aidan. I don't want to talk about him right now."

Abbey smiled. "Oh, yes, let's keep strolling down memory lane; it's such a happy place."

Lucy laughed and slid the casserole into the oven under the browning turkey. "Look, whatever bad choices I made in life, they led me here. Those choices gave me Kaylee and brought you and me together. I'm happy to be in this moment with you."

Abbey's eyes glistened. "And that's Thanksgiving, folks."

They both laughed.

"Thanksgiving was always my favorite holiday as a kid," Lucy said. "Now, Christmas is, but back in the day, I loved Thanksgiving. We got our mom back for the day. Of course, like Cinderella, once the clock struck midnight, she turned back into a drunk pumpkin, and we didn't see her for the rest of the weekend."

Abbey chuckled. "I don't think that's how the fairy tale goes." She clapped her hands together. "Let's make some new traditions. No more talk of our wounded childhood. The Saunders sisters are back together, and it's high time we make everything right."

"Here, here." Lucy grabbed the glass of water next to her.

Abbey held up her glass. "Henceforth, I declare Thanksgiving the day of new beginnings."

"On this day, we won't talk about the past, only the future," Lucy added.

"Sláinte," Abbey stated, pressing her glass forward.

"Sláinte," Lucy repeated.

They clinked glasses and celebrated the small victory.

Abbey's phone buzzed on the counter. A frown crossed her face as she read the text.

"Everything okay?" Lucy asked, watching the smile fade from her sister's face.

"Rob." Abbey lifted the phone, twisting it back and forth. "He has to work late. He says I should start without him."

"Oh, no. He knew you had a whole feast planned, right?"

Abbey waved it off. "He knows, but you know how it is, working late and all that. At least you make time for Kaylee. I wish Rob would hit the office after we're all in bed like you do."

Guilt washed over her. She wasn't leaving the house to work. Lucy gasped, a horrible thought crossing her mind. No! Rob would never do that to Abbey.

Abbey pulled the turkey from the oven and set it on the counter to cool. Lucy took a minute to take her phone and sneak into the living room to text Rob.

Are you sure you can't make it? Abbey really wants you here. We've been cooking all day. It would mean the world to her.

Her phone pinged in response.

Feel awful. Newman project. They want everything done yesterday. Conners is riding my arse hard.

Lucy sighed, both in relief and understanding. The Newman project was extensive and a top priority; every employee knew about it, even if they weren't on the team. It involved a complete office overhaul and needed all hands on deck to ensure the Newman company stayed up and running the entire time. Rob was undoubtedly up to his neck at present. At least, she knew her initial thought was out the window; his excuse was valid.

Sucks. If you can sneak away, even for an hour or two. I'm sure Abbey would thank you.

She added a winking emoji at the end.

I'll do my best.

Lucy knew that was a giant 'no.' Rob would not be joining them tonight. She returned to the kitchen and observed Abbey seamlessly slicing into the turkey.

"You're a real pro at that," she commented.

Kaylee and Lola entered the room.

"It smells good in here," Lola commented.

"Oh wow, this is a proper Thanksgiving feast." Kaylee sounded impressed.

"I try to bring a little bit of America to Ireland," Abbey replied, but the carefree attitude was gone. "Can you girls help with plates, silverware, and cups, please? Oh, and I bought some sparkling grape juice to try. Hopefully, it's close to the stuff you're used to."

"Is Dad coming?" Lola asked, setting a stack of plates next to the food.

Abbey ignored the comment, turning her back to Lola and fiddling with the cork on a wine bottle.

"He's working late, but he said he'll try," Lucy answered for her sister. "Dish up while it's hot; I'm starving."

Abbey sent her sister a thankful glance and poured a generous amount of wine into her glass. The girls filled their plates to overflowing, slowly walking toward the table to avoid spilling. Abbey continued rushing around, pulling glasses from the cupboard, opening the sparkling grape juice, and balancing everything in her hands.

"I've got this," Lucy said, taking the drink and glasses from her sister's hands. "Get some food, and sit down."

Abbey offered a weak smile, and Lucy could tell her sister was trying to cover the fact that Rob's absence hurt her feelings.

Once everyone was seated at the table, Kaylee jumped straight into Christmas. "Can we put up a tree over the weekend?"

Lucy glanced up from her plate. "It's always been our tradition to decorate the day after Thanksgiving. While everyone else is out fighting the Black Friday shopping crowds, we're dancing and decorating to Christmas music."

Abbey stared at her dinner plate, pushing the food around with a fork. "Sure, we have a fake tree and ornaments in the attic. Rob can bring them down—if he ever comes home again."

Lucy caught the last comment, even though Abbey had mumbled it under her breath. Lola and Kaylee were oblivious to the resentful tone in Abbey's voice.

"We still have school tomorrow," Lola pointed out. "I know you have the full weekend off for Thanksgiving in the States, but it isn't a thing here."

"Oh, that's right." Lucy turned her attention to the girls. "It probably isn't utter chaos here either. We should go shopping after school and see what deals we can find."

Kaylee's eyes lit up. "Yes! I bet everything is decorated. I'd love to see the lights and everything Christmasy."

"We have to go to the city center, then," Lola said.

"Oh, I didn't even tell you how amazing the shops are on Grafton Street," Lucy jumped in. "You have to see the Brown and Thomas window; you will love it, Kaylee."

"Sounds great," Abbey mumbled. She continued pushing food around her plate, hardly eating.

No one but Lucy seemed to notice Abbey's silence. Instead, the girls devised a weekend plan, which led to all things Christmas. Lucy and the girls shared their favorite Christmas songs, what movies were on their must-watch list, and wondered if it would snow this year.

Finally, Lucy pushed back from the table, her stomach full. "That was delicious."

"I'm so full." Kaylee rubbed her belly.

"Me too," Lola agreed.

"Take your plates to the sink, please," Lucy said. "Go finish your homework. We'll clean up and meet back here for some pumpkin pie."

"I don't know if I can do homework on a full stomach," Kaylee whined.

Lucy playfully swatted her backside. "I'm sure you'll figure it out. Now, go."

Kaylee squealed as she bounced out of Lucy's reach. Giggling, the girls hurried up the stairs to Lola's room, knowing they had no intention of touching their homework.

A warm smile crossed Lucy's lips as she carried her plate toward the sink. Kaylee was happy here and overjoyed to have Lola back in her life. It was all Lucy had wanted: her daughter to have a real childhood.

She headed back toward the table, noticing Abbey continued to sit, staring at her plate still full of food.

"He really did want to be here," Lucy said softly. "We have a huge, demanding client right now."

"I know," Abbey murmured. "We always do Thanksgiving together; this is the first time he wasn't here. He knows how important this holiday is to me."

Lucy moved toward the counter, pulling plastic containers from the drawers. "He would have been here if there wasn't some sort of emergency."

"I know!" Abbey slammed her fist on the table, her fork bouncing off the plate. "I know all that, Lucy. I know he's working to provide for us. I know he would be here if he could. I know. I know. I know!"

Lucy froze mid-scoop, mashed potatoes plopping off the spoon back into the bowl. She had hit a nerve.

"I'm sorry." Abbey pushed back from the table, taking a deep breath. "I'm irritated. I know Rob works hard. It just feels like he never prioritizes his family; he never puts us first. I'm not asking for all his time, but he knew how important this dinner was to me. I wish he could have taken an hour or two away."

Abbey forcefully shoved her chair in, snatching her plate off the table rough enough to send a bread roll flying across the room. She placed the plate on the counter next to the leftovers.

"I'm angry, and it feels like I'm not allowed to be angry. Then, I feel guilty for having emotions at all. Rob only adds to my guilt; he makes me feel ungrateful." Abbey sighed, running fingers through her hair. "It seems my feelings don't matter. And, I had hoped you, of all people, would at the very least acknowledge and justify my feelings. I need someone to tell me it's okay to be angry, disappointed, and let down. I can feel all those things and still appreciate how hard someone works. "

Lucy moved around the counter, wrapping her arms around her sister. "Oh, Abbey, of course, you're allowed to feel those things. You're right; he should be here. He *should* be making time for you and Lola."

"Thank you," Abbey whispered, moving from the embrace. "Sometimes I feel like you're constantly defending Rob; it's like you aren't on my side."

Lucy nodded. "I'm a peacekeeper by nature. And I understand how busy he is." She smacked her head with her palm. "Look at me; there I go again, making excuses for a grown man. I'm sorry; you are one hundred percent correct. Family should always come first."

Abbey smiled weakly, exhaustion reflected in her eyes. In silence, they packed up the leftovers and cleaned the dishes.

"I need to lie down for a bit," Abbey finally said. "Meet back here in thirty? I'll be ready for pie, wine, and loads of whining."

"Sounds great," Lucy said. "I'm going to call work; tell them I'm taking the night off."

Abbey waved her hand. "You don't have to do that."

"I know, but I want to spend this evening with my family. Plus, you can't be expected to drink that entire bottle of wine alone. Solidarity, sister!"

Abbey let out a genuine laugh. "Thank you."

Lucy waited until Abbey was gone before ascending the stairs to her room on the top floor. Pausing outside Lola's bedroom, she peeked in to see the girls lying on their stomachs, legs kicked up behind them, laughing at something they watched on Lola's tablet. They could easily be mistaken for sisters instead of cousins, their mannerisms nearly identical.

"Pie in thirty."

The pre-teens grunted in acknowledgment without looking up from their video.

Lucy entered her bedroom and looked at the phone in her hand. A wave of guilt washed over her as she pressed in the passcode. By sneaking around with Aidan, she lied to everyone, claiming she had to work late hours. Now, Abbey would feel more guilty believing Lucy was skipping out on work to stay with her. The only thing Lucy was canceling was a booty call with Adian, but she couldn't confess that to Abbey.

Tonight, Abbey needed her, even if she had pretended not to. As children, Thanksgiving was the one holiday they both looked forward to. Their mother was in high spirits all day; she even went shopping for dinner. She wasn't a great cook, making only the green bean casserole; everything else was store-bought and tasted amazing. For that one day, their mother seemed sincerely interested in their lives, asking about school, friends, and after-school activities. After dinner, they watched *Miracle on 34th Street*, the old one with Maureen O'Hara and Natalie Wood, while eating pumpkin pie, loaded with whipped cream, straight out of the pie dish.

After the movie, Mom found a bottle of whiskey and drank until she passed out. Lucy stayed up half the night cleaning the kitchen, washing the dishes, and packing away leftovers she and Abbey would eat for the next few weeks. For Lucy, spending an entire day with a sober mom made the long night worth it.

Lucy understood the significance of this day for Abbey. Rob should have understood, too. It was all Abbey had talked about for several weeks. Rob knew how important this meal was, and he once again chose work over his family.

Even if she pretended otherwise, Abbey needed Lucy here with her tonight. Maybe they could relive their happiest childhood moment, a movie and pumpkin pie. Or they could whine about men while polishing off the wine. Either way, Lucy wanted to spend the evening with her sister.

Staring at the cell phone, she opened Aidan's text threads. For the past month, they had spent at least four nights a week together; it was intense, but it was all they had. She dreaded blowing him off but hoped he would understand.

"Hi, can't get away tonight. My sister needs me."

Ding.

K. Going out with me mates anyway.

Her heart sank. Aidan had already made other plans; she should have been relieved but felt hurt instead. His reply had come quickly; had he been in the process of sending her a text, but she beat him to the punch?

Tears stung at the back of her eyes. Why was his response triggering her this way? She was the one canceling their meet-up. As much as she didn't want to let him down, it would be nice to hear he was at least disappointed. Instead, he had other plans, as if not seeing her was no big deal.

For weeks, Lucy had been lost in work, family, and a secret affair; she seemed to forget Aidan had a life separate from her. He had friends and family, people Lucy didn't know.

A tinge of jealousy overcame her. Who was he going out

with? Males, females, a mixture of both? Their relationship was strictly sexual; they had no rules and no commitment to one another. However, the thought of him with another woman made her stomach churn. She was being ridiculous. The point of their arrangement was to keep emotions out of it, and Lucy seemed to be struggling with that part.

Tossing the phone onto the bed, she flopped down on the edge. A few weeks ago, the idea of a casual relationship seemed thrilling: sneaking around, keeping secrets, and engaging in a world no one knew about. It didn't feel as exciting right now. Instead of butterflies in her stomach, it felt like a giant hole had opened.

It wasn't the first time a fantasy of her creation had let her down. Once, she believed her life with Jeremy would be a big adventure. He lived from moment to moment, taking risks and chances without considering the consequences. In the beginning, they traveled the country in a beat-up car without a care about where they ended up, never knowing where they would sleep that night. Both had little money and would work odd jobs to pay for a few nights in a seedy hotel before moving on to the next town.

Lucy learned very quickly that Jeremy was not the monogamous type. At first, he attempted to hide his infidelity, claiming to have taken a night job, but soon his excuses weakened. He would go to the store for groceries and return three hours later, smelling of perfume. Other times, he went out to the bar, returning home with a wrinkled shirt and traces of lipstick on his neck. And still, she waited and pinned and begged him to stay with her.

Foolishly, she convinced herself she was not like her

mom; her situation was completely different. Jeremy loved her, and no matter how far he strayed, he always came home in the morning. Her father, on the other hand, used her mother for sex and would leave for months on end. Sure, Jeremy was a cheater, but he never abandoned her, at least not at first.

Aidan wasn't like Jeremy. He had been upfront from the start; they were friends with benefits, and that was it. If Aidan saw other women, he was well within his rights to do so. It didn't matter if the thought made her stomach ache. This was the arrangement, and she could walk away at any time.

Maybe Abbey had been right all along. Perhaps Lucy did feel something deeper for Aidan. It didn't matter now; she was in too deep, cared too much, and allowed her fear of what could happen cloud her vision. It would be difficult to walk away at this point, and the truth was, she didn't want to.

Besides, Aidan was the one who suggested they keep things casual. He set up the arrangement, and Lucy unquestioningly agreed to it. They met in *secret* for *sex*. That was a pretty clear sign she was nothing more to him than a late-night booty call. If she tried to change things now, Aidan would be the one walking away.

"Pie!" Kaylee yelled.

Lucy sat up, brushing away the frustrated tears brimming in her eyes.

"I'll be right down!"

In the bathroom, she splashed cold water on her face and looked at the reflection in the mirror. Her eyes were red-rimmed, but she could pass that off as a lack of sleep.

Laughter greeted her as she entered the kitchen, and she couldn't help but smile. This was the reason for uprooting their lives and moving to Ireland: the laughter, joy, and a proper family, a family Lucy had forgotten she had for far too long.

Tonight, she would push Aidan to the back corners of her mind and bask in the laughter and love she needed to heal her for today.

15

Later that night, Lucy tossed and turned, fighting a losing battle against the continuous thoughts racing through her mind. Luckily, Kaylee had fallen asleep in Lola's room, and she didn't have to worry about keeping her daughter awake.

It had been a long time since Lucy had a room all to herself. As a child, she shared a bedroom with Abbey. As a teen, she gave the bedroom to Abbey and slept on the couch in the living room. Then, she lived with Jeremy, and when Kaylee came into the picture, she took turns sleeping with either the baby or Jeremy.

In all of her thirty-three years, Lucy had never had a place all her own. Jeremy had always been in her life at one point or another. Even when they weren't technically together, the lease had always been in both their names.

Jeremy was the last person she wanted to be thinking about right now, but somehow, her thoughts always ended up on him. It was probably because she had spent the last seventeen years of her life trying to get him to settle down.

She was a bit curious if he had noticed they were gone. After a particularly huge argument, she had finally had enough. Without warning or a phone call, she packed up whatever they could carry and left the country.

The fight hadn't been out of the blue; they fought a lot after Kaylee was born. It wasn't so much fighting as it was Lucy pleading and begging Jeremy to stay with them and take an interest in their daughter. But Jeremy made it clear from the moment Lucy announced she was pregnant that he had no desire to be a father. Sadly, she believed he would change once the baby came, and she wasted years lying to herself that he just needed a little more time before realizing he was ready to settle down.

Smiling, she imagined the look on his face when he returned to their apartment and found it empty. They had left all the furniture, but the clothes and belongings were gone, either sold, boxed at her mother's place, or here with them in Ireland. The apartment belonged to Jeremy, and he was welcome to have it.

The pinging from her cell phone shook Lucy from her thoughts.

Stretching out her hand, she felt along the night table until her fingers touched the smooth surface of the cell phone.

The clock flashed 1:04 a.m. as she unlocked the phone and went to her unread messages.

I miss you

The number came up as Unknown Caller. It was probably a misdial. Tossing the phone beside her, she stared at the ceiling.

The phone chimed again.

I want to see you.

Who was this?

Aidan. Her heart skipped a beat. Wait, she saved him as a contact; his name would have come up.

Ding.

Are you there?

Oh no! Jeremy.

He must have finally noticed she was gone and was ready to beg her to come home.

Her mother had betrayed her once again. Jeremy would only have her Irish phone number if her mother had given it to him. It wouldn't surprise Lucy in the least as much as her mother adored Jeremy. Despite how he treated Lucy or Kaylee, she always had some excuse for his bad behavior. And, of course, it was always Lucy's fault he kept leaving; her mother claimed she wasn't trying hard enough to keep him. Yeah, like that worked out so well for her mother.

Lucy looked at the number again; it was local. Jeremy would never fly across an ocean for her, would he? Maybe by her leaving, he realized it was finally time to get his butt into gear. Perhaps he was ready to settle down and even put a ring on her finger.

Dread formed in the pit of her belly. Once upon a time, that had been her dream. But time and distance were funny; they gave her the perspective she needed to get off the train. Only a few months ago, she had wanted to spend the rest of her life with that man; now, the thought made her sick.

Jeremy? Is this you?

Lucy held her breath and waited for a response.

Who's Jeremy? New boyfriend?

Lucy's gut clenched. It wasn't Jeremy.

Relief washed over her, and she felt foolish for ever thinking he would come after her.

The phone vibrated in her hand; the mystery texter was calling her.

Curious, Lucy sat up and pressed the answer button.

"Who is this?" she whispered.

"Lucy?"

"Aidan?" Her heart thundered in her chest. "I didn't recognize the number?"

"It was a mad session" Aidan slurred his words. "Great craic, but I lost me mobile. Luckily, I've 'dis old one."

Lucy's heart fluttered. "You memorized my number?"

Aidan chuckled. "No. I got it from the class lists. Probably breakin' some policy, but sure, what's the harm?"

Tingles raced through her. He was clearly intoxicated but took the time to look up her number.

"I wanted ta hear yar voice," he said softly, like the loud whisper drunk people use when they think they're being quiet.

"Are you drunk calling me?" Lucy chuckled.

"Liquid courage," he admitted.

She melted at the confession, feeling a warm sensation pass over her.

"Drinking on a school night?"

Aidan laughed in response. "I got food from the chipper; it'll soak up the alcohol. I'll be grand by mornin'. That's if I can stop thinkin' 'bout ya. You're keepin' me awake."

A cheesy grin broke across her face, and her pulse raced as her body started to come alive.

"I was lookin' forward to tonight," he continued. "When can I see ya?"

Every nerve in her body reacted to the desperation in his question.

"Lucy?"

Her throat felt dry. "I'm here," she mumbled.

"Oh shite, I shouldn'ta called. You aren't alone, are ya?"

"I'm alone."

"For now. You were waitin' for someone else." His tone changed. "Who's Jeremy?"

Lucy let out a nervous giggle. "Jeremy? He's Kaylee's dad. I thought he was calling for–"

The exact reason you're calling, she finished in her head.

"Sex," Aidan growled.

"No! Well, maybe, but it's not like that; we're not—together. He doesn't even live here. I haven't seen or talked to him in months." Lucy was talking so fast she could hardly keep up with her thoughts.

He was jealous, and that riled her up. His confession and jealousy turned her on in a way she hadn't thought possible. Desire ran through her, pooling in her most intimate parts.

"I gotta go," Lucy said abruptly, ending the call.

Tossing the phone on the bed, she rushed to the bathroom, ignoring all the inner warning bells. This was a bad idea, a terrible idea. But she had an itch only Aidan could scratch.

Lucy exchanged her pajama bottoms for a flowy skirt and, feeling cheeky, slipped off her underwear. Pulling open her closet, she chose a sweater and yanked it over her t-shirt, not bothering to put her bra back on.

Using an app on her phone, she ordered a taxi and quietly tiptoed downstairs. The house was silent. Abbey's bedroom door was closed, but Lola's was wide open. Flashes of light came from inside the room. Lucy sucked in her breath and peeked around the door. The TV was on, but both girls were sound asleep. Ignoring her momentary guilt, she switched off the TV and closed the bedroom door.

Downstairs, all was quiet. Removing the house keys from their hook, she silently made her escape. Swiftly, she walked down the road to where she always met the taxi, never in front of the house where headlights could wake someone. Fifteen minutes later, she stood outside Aidan's apartment building.

Her phone had been pinging nonstop.

Lucy?

Where did you go?

I'm sorry, I shouldn't have called.

You okay?

Did I say something to upset you?

I miss you.

You're driving me crazy.

Sorry, it's the alcohol. Too many shots.

Shivering in the cold, she stared at the keypad that accessed the lobby. This was wild. What was she doing here? He could be passed out by now, and although she knew the code to get into the building, she couldn't get in his apartment unless he opened the door.

Too late to turn back now.

She typed the code into the keypad and entered the building.

A rush of warm air hit her bare legs as the elevator rose closer to his floor.

Her heart hammered in her head, and adrenaline propelled one foot in front of the other. Doubt weaved its way through her mind. They hadn't made a plan; he wasn't expecting her. What if he refused to open the door? It had been over twenty minutes since she had last spoken to him; maybe the alcohol had worn off.

Knocking on the door, she was a bundle of nerves, her stomach in knots.

Aidan pulled open the door. His hair was disheveled, and his eyes were sad. The expression changed from nonchalance to surprise when their eyes met.

"Wh–what're ya doin' here?" he whispered.

The look on his face gave Lucy the confidence she needed.

"Don't talk," she ordered.

Pressing her hands against his chest, she pushed him back into the apartment, kicking the door shut behind them.

"I don't–" Aidan began.

Lucy covered his mouth with her hand. "I said, don't talk."

Aidan's eyes widened in delight as she pushed him further into the room. The back of his legs hit the couch, and he fell to a sitting position. Desire overcame her doubts, and she boldly fluffed up her skirt and straddled his legs. She slid along his thighs until her bare skin rubbed against the bulge of his crotch, sending tingles down to her toes.

Feeling his crotch stiffen, she relaxed, knowing he wanted her, too. Leaning forward, she playfully bit his lip. Fireworks exploded when he kissed her. The heat and desire between them could melt metal.

Aidan's hands were on her thighs, moving along the soft skin to caress her butt. He pulled back from the kiss as he explored the bare skin, giving her a curious look.

"Oops, forgot something," she teased, biting her lip.

Desire burned through his fingertips as he gripped the bare flesh of her buttocks. Their lips met again, this time his tongue exploring her mouth. His hands slipped under her sweater and followed the curve of her spine. His hands were soft and warm.

Lucy broke from the kiss. Gripping the hem of her sweater, she pulled it over her head and tossed it to the floor.

He groaned, taking in the sight of her bare breasts.

"Seems I forgot a few things tonight." She looked at him through her lashes, then added. "I haven't forgotten to take my pill, though."

Seeming to ignore the last comment, he hungrily kissed and suckled each breast. She threw back her head, relishing in each sensation.

Desperately, he flipped her down onto the couch and jumped up. In what seemed like one swift movement, he discarded his clothes and stood naked in front of her. Her eyes wandered down to his enlarged, uncut penis.

A crooked smile hung on his lips as he watched her staring at him. Leaning down, he kissed her gently on the lips, then yanked the skirt down her legs. Once they were both naked, he sat down and pulled her back onto his lap.

"I was really enjoyin' this," he moaned into her hair.

Trailing kisses along her neck, he returned to her breasts, taking his time to give each one undivided attention.

Lucy scooted her hips forward until his tip teased her entrance. As he trailed kisses along the top of her breast, she lightly rubbed along his cock. The tickling sensation drove her wild as her most sensitive part was stimulated.

Aidan took her breast in his mouth and slid inside her. Together, they cried out in pleasure. Desire and need nearly bringing them to the edge. She rocked her hips, taking the lead to move along his length, wanting to feel him deeper inside her.

His lips clamped onto hers, kissing with the desperate need they both felt. Hands tangled in each other's hair until they had to break the kiss and catch their breath. Both were breathing hard, and for a moment, they stopped moving, and their eyes met.

"This is how I wanted me night to end," Aidan breathed. "With you, doing this."

Lucy smiled, leaning back just enough to allow his eyes to wander up and down her body. He made her feel like the most beautiful girl in the world; desire and lust filled his eyes as he drank her in.

"You're gorgeous," he said through gritted teeth.

His lips found hers again, and they kissed, suspended in time for a moment, motionless. Lucy reached behind him and dug her fingers into the couch's back. Her need was too strong, her climax close. It was too intense. She had to break through to the other side.

Moving her hips, she rocked against him, using the couch as leverage to pick up the pace. His eyes rolled to the back of his head, and he leaned against the couch. His fingers gripped her waist, moving her faster against him. Fireworks exploded as pleasure took her over the edge.

Aidan's body tensed; he held her hips still, a groan of pleasure tearing from deep within him as he released himself into her. They panted together for a few moments, neither moving nor breaking their connection.

Finally, Lucy released her grip on the couch, her knuckles white. Sliding off him, she fell against the couch's arm and sighed. Her legs slung lazily over his thighs.

"I love hearin' ya scream me name," he said, grabbing his t-shirt off the floor. "I could listen to that forever."

Lucy felt her face turn red. "I didn't realize I said your name. I'm not usually that vocal, or I didn't think I was."

"I like ya vocal." Aidan glanced at her briefly, using his shirt to clean up. He offered it to her. "Needs ta be washed anyway."

Closing his eyes, he leaned against the couch, giving her a hint of privacy.

"I don't think I've ever done *that* on *this* before." He gave the couch a few pats.

Lucy curled against his side. "I rather enjoyed that."

"Ah, me too."

Lazily, she stroked his chest, running her fingers through the dark hair sprinkled along his pecs.

"I'm sorry I called so late," he said, gently stroking her bare shoulder. "I didn't plan to go to the pub. Me mates invited me. I was about to turn them down, but you canceled on me. I figured I would drink until I stopped thinkin' 'bout ya. Funny thing is, I ended up wasted, and yar still on me mind."

Lucy blushed. "I couldn't sleep anyway."

"I look forward to our nights together," he said, kissing her forehead.

"It's getting more difficult to sneak away," Lucy said honestly.

"I'm sorry all the pressure is on ya," he said. "I enjoy our time, but we can cut back. Maybe we drop down to one night a week?"

Her stomach dropped. Even though fewer nights would make her life a bit easier, she hadn't expected him to suggest cutting back. Was he already growing tired of her?

Pull it together, Lucy chided herself. She would not go down this rabbit hole right now, especially when sitting naked with a good-looking guy. If he wanted to cut back their nights together, she better take full advantage of the current situation.

Turning her attention to Aidan, she glided her hand down his chest and over his stomach. Continuing her journey, her fingers traced the thin trail of hair leading down from his navel.

"I am so fascinated by this foreskin thing," Lucy said.

"Oh really?" Aidan's voice was husky.

Lucy laughed. "Sorry, that probably sounded childish, but I've never actually seen intact foreskin in the flesh before. No pun intended."

He gently stroked her hair. "Please, explore all ya want."

Lucy teased the long, curly hairs surrounding her target.

Aidan tensed. "Oh, you're goin' for it now?"

Lucy slid off the couch and knelt in front of him. "No time like the present. Now, be quiet so I can concentrate."

16

An hour later, Lucy tiptoed into the house, closing the door silently behind her. As tired as she felt, she enjoyed these quiet morning hours before the hustle and bustle of the day began. It was nearly five in the morning; trying to sleep at this point would be useless.

Today would be a 'multiple cups of coffee' kind of day. Flipping on the machine, she refilled the water reserve and snapped it back in place. Opening the small drawer under the machine, she selected a pod and dropped it in place. Choosing a dark blue coffee cup from the drying rack, she placed it under the spout and pressed the start button.

As the coffee machine cranked to life, so did her mind, thoughts bubbling and tumbling over one another. There was no doubt the sex had been fantastic, but the ride home brought every doubt and wishful thought to the surface. Her body was satisfied, but she felt emotionally drained, not the feeling she had hoped for after a few hours with Aidan.

She was her own worst enemy, believing a few nights of

sex would be enough to fulfill her. There was something about Aidan that made her keep coming back for more, and, if she was honest, it was deeper than sex. The more time they spent together, the more difficult being away from him was.

Casual was turning out to be a bad idea; she should have stuck with her original plan and avoided him altogether. Easier said than done. A case in point was how she raced out in the dead of the night, rushing to him simply because he phoned her. He hadn't asked her to come over, but did he know that call would make her drop everything to be with him?

Plain and simple, he booty called her, and it worked. He didn't miss *her*; he missed an easy hook-up. No matter which way she looked at it, the truth was all he had wanted was sex, and he knew just what to say to get it. Damn, this stupid heart and overactive brain. He occupied her thoughts night and day, but was she taking up any real estate in his mind?

After preparing the coffee just as she liked, she crept upstairs, hoping not to wake anyone. Taking a sip of coffee, she opened the door to her room. The bed sheets were tossed back and wrinkled, and an empty wine glass still sat on the nightstand; both reminders of her rush out the door a few hours earlier.

She shimmied the skirt down her thighs, grazing the smooth skin with her thumbs. Memories welled in her mind, the surprised, yet dark, expression on Aidan's face when he realized her butt was bare under the flowing skirt. Desire surged through her as she pulled the sweater over her head, replaying the scene of Aidan groping and kissing her exposed breasts. These thoughts were not going to help get her through the day.

The lukewarm shower did nothing to cool the heatwave burning through her veins. Running soap over her body further fueled an out-of-control fire, reminding her of hands gliding over her skin. He knew every curve of her body and each sensitive spot that sent her over the edge. A new wave of desire washed over her, and she swallowed hard as the bar of soap rubbed lightly against her nipples.

Oh no. This line of thinking needed to stop. She was not going to pleasure herself in the shower, at least not today. Replacing the soap in its holder, she turned the tap until ice-cold water poured onto her head. Holding back a yelp, she stood under the freezing stream until her mind forgot Aidan, and the pulsing between her legs stopped. When, at last, her only thoughts were getting dry, dressed, and warm, she turned off the water and stepped out of the shower.

Wrapping the towel around her, she focused on work and her to-do list. By the time she dressed in fresh panties and jeans, she had a complete list of tasks ready to tackle. She slipped last night's sweater over her head, enjoying its warmth and the cozy feeling it always gave her, fighting to ignore the faint scent of Aidan's place lingering in the wool.

Polishing off the last drops of coffee, she felt ready to take on the day. She gathered her dirty laundry, preparing to make the day full and productive, and returned to the kitchen.

As she waited for her second cup of coffee to brew, she took her laundry into the small utility closet off the kitchen. Abbey told her their laundry room was small by American standards but quite large by Irish ones. They also had the luxury of owning a clothes dryer, which was surprisingly not the norm in this country. Lucy couldn't imagine hanging wet clothes outside on the line; it seemed archaic and outdated, like something her grandmother used to do. Even more odd, some families strung their clothes across the radiators around the house. Lucy could imagine the number of socks she would lose behind the radiator or forgetting about a shirt she hung on a rarely used radiator somewhere in the depths of the house.

Back in the kitchen, Lucy set her laptop on the island countertop and waited for it to power on. With her coffee in hand, she fired up the computer and began working through her emails. Nothing required immediate attention, so she filled a glass with water and moved her workstation to the kitchen table, settling in for the morning.

"Working already?" Abbey asked mid-yawn as she padded into the kitchen. "You and Rob just can't get enough of your jobs."

Lucy did not miss the tinge of resentment oozing in Abbey's statement.

"Need a top-up?" Abbey asked, rummaging through the drying rack for a cup.

Lucy lifted her mug toward her sister. "This one is still full."

"How long have you been up?"

"Not long enough for my hair to dry," Lucy said, sipping her coffee. "I've had some problems sleeping."

Abbey placed her mug under the spout and fired up the coffee machine. "You're working too hard." As the coffee brewed, she tackled the drying rack, stacking the plates and putting them back on the shelf. "It's got to be nearly impossible to shut your mind off. You're either in work mode or mom mode. At some point, you need a break, a chance to zone out."

"That's mom life for you." Lucy deleted all her spam emails. She didn't need Viagra or ads for Walmart; there wasn't a Walmart in Ireland anyway. "You do it too, and you're a super mom, way better than anything I do. Plus, you're starting a business, I don't know where you find time to lounge around."

Abbey gave her a hurt look. "It's not as if I'm laying around all day."

"I didn't say that you are," Lucy said quickly. "It's impressive you're able to shut it off at night and take time for yourself. I need to take lessons from you."

Abbey placed the clean cups back in the cupboard. "What can I say? I love my reality TV and sleep. I need at least an hour to settle down, calm the mind, and then I sleep like a baby."

Lucy pushed back from the table. "I should help you. I'm at a good pausing point."

Abbey shook her head. "It's fine. You're working, and I have a system."

Lucy ignored her comment. "You're working too. Let me at least help pack my child's lunch."

"If you insist. I toss in random food and hope they eat at least two or three things."

Lucy laughed, pulling the lunchboxes from their place on the shelf. "Sounds good to me."

"I do a fruit, a vegetable, a sandwich, and one or two extra things," Abbey explained, pointing toward a shelf. "Everything there is lunch stuff. No crisps, sweets, or fizzy drinks are allowed in lunches."

"Well, that would be my entire lunch out the window," Lucy said. "I used to pack a bag of chips, a candy bar, and a sandwich I never ate. Maybe an apple when we were lucky enough to have fruit in the house."

"You packed the same for me," Abbey said. "Oh, that reminds me, no nuts."

"No PB and J? How will they survive?"

Abbey opened the cutlery drawer and continued emptying the drying rack. "Meat or jam sandwiches?"

"That sounds too healthy," Lucy teased.

Opening the fridge, she pulled out sliced ham and cheese from the drawer and set those on the counter. After retrieving the mayo and mustard, she began constructing the sandwiches.

"I don't know if I ever said thank you," Lucy said, slathering a layer of mayo on the slices of bread.

Abbey finished putting the dishes away and turned to her coffee. "For what?"

"Everything. Does Lola like mustard?"

Abbey swallowed her coffee. "Yes, mustard, ham, cheese, mayo. She'll eat all of it."

Lucy shook the mustard bottle and squirted a healthy amount on each sandwich. "Kaylee loves mustard, too. Anyway, back to thanking you. You were an enormous help, not only in getting us here but also in helping to make the transition smooth. I would never have gotten through all that paperwork without you. Plus, you gave us a place to stay, helped sort out school for Kaylee, and you take care of her as if she were your own daughter. We wouldn't be doing half as well if not for you."

Abbey shrugged. "It's the least I can do. You sacrificed your childhood to raise me."

It was Lucy's turn to shrug. "It was worth it. By the way, how is the new business going? I know you're still in the early stages, but I feel selfish not asking about it sooner."

Lucy felt guilty and too consumed by Aidan to ask how her sister's venture into the business world was going. To be fair, Abbey never brought up the business, seeming to be just as invested in Lucy's love life as she was and pushing for every detail regarding Aidan. But Lucy knew how it felt to be in the caregiver role, always ensuring everyone else was okay and never being asked about her personal life. These were always one-sided relationships, with one person always giving and the other always taking. Lucy wanted to do better for Abbey. Her sister needed someone to share her successes with, especially since she and Rob appeared to be struggling.

Abbey moved to the counter, placing sliced carrots into plastic containers. "It's a huge amount of work, but I know it will be worth it in the end. Maeve is the one with the vision and the drive. I'm just assisting and hoping she chose the right person to help her build this company."

"And it's a travel agency?" Lucy cringed inwardly, embarrassed not to have taken the time to understand the business plan.

"Sort of. It's more about travel experiences," Abbey explained, zipping up Lola's lunch bag. "The vision is to create individualized packages full of experiences and adventures for each client. Depending on their needs, some packages will be more touristy, and others will be off-the-beaten-path adventures. We'll also help with airfare and hotels along the way. I'll focus on Ireland, and Maeve will use her connections with Spain and Italy. As we grow, we hope to branch out to Europe and eventually the U.S."

"That sounds fun," Lucy said, leaning against the counter. "I'm sorry I've been a little selfish lately. I've been wrapped up in my own crap, and I haven't asked about you at all."

"You're asking now." Abbey gave a small smile. "There isn't much to share; it's still early days and very research-heavy. I'm slowly compiling interesting places to visit and building a database. Once the weather clears up, I hope to get out in the field more to test some places for myself."

Lucy rubbed her palms together. "Oh, I would love to trail along. So far, all I've seen of Ireland is Dublin, and there is an entire country for me to discover."

Abbey placed the lunchboxes on the end of the counter as Lucy put items back into the fridge.

"It's a massive transition to move to a new country. On top of that, you started a new job, earned a big promotion, worried about your daughter, dealt with heartbreak, and somehow you still have time for late-night booty calls."

Lucy's head snapped up. "What?"

Abbey tilted her head and gave her sister a sideways glance. "Come on. You're sneaky, but not that sneaky. Have you looked in a mirror today or any day after claiming to work late? I know you love your job, but no one comes home from work with a silly, sex grin. And you, my dear sister, have that look on your face right now. You didn't get up early this morning; you never went to sleep. And even though you claimed to cancel work last night, you still managed to sneak out for a hookup."

Lucy dropped her head like a child caught with her hand in the cookie jar. "How long have you known?"

"A few weeks," Abbey said, pausing to sip her coffee. "My suspicion began when you stopped talking about Aidan. This was shortly after the 'keep it casual' conversation. At first, I thought maybe you took my advice and chose to move on. I figured throwing yourself into work was your way of dealing with things.

"Then, you went to the office one night and came home with a surprising glow about you. Each time you went to *the office*, I found you in the kitchen the following day with a hop in your step. You were far too happy and relaxed to be the stressed-out, overworked woman you attempted to portray."

Lucy swallowed hard around the lump in her throat. "Well done, Sherlock. Why haven't you said anything?"

Abbey gave a stern look. "And what do you want me to say, Lucy? You're a grown-ass woman. If you want to slink off into the night for a secret love affair, I won't stop you. I wish you would have told me, but I can guess why you felt the need to hide it."

"It's not serious," Lucy said quickly.

Abbey turned away and moved toward the cupboard. "Okay."

"I didn't tell you because I didn't think you would approve."

Abbey blew out a breath. "Well, you're right about that. I

think it's a horrible idea. But, like I said, you're a grown woman; my opinion is just an opinion."

Abbey pulled two bowls from the cupboard and placed them on the counter. Flipping on the kettle, she opened one of the drawers and retrieved the rolled oats.

Lucy watched as her sister continued to prepare breakfast for their girls. "I'll be careful."

"Do you even know what that means?" Abbey didn't turn around as she poured boiling water into the bowls. "What is there to be careful about if it's just sex?"

Lucy glared into her back, the condescending tone grating on her nerves.

Finally, Abbey turned back toward Lucy. "Listen, it's your life. You can stop sneaking around, and you can stop lying. I can't take any more lies right now. Just be honest with me."

She returned to stirring the oatmeal. The back door slammed, causing Lucy to jump at the sudden noise. Abbey's back stiffened.

"I didn't expect to see either of you up at this hour." Rob walked into the room, tossing his jacket over the back of a chair. The laptop bag gripped tightly in his hand.

"It's seven," Abbey said in a clipped tone. "Everyone is awake at this hour."

Rob exhaled roughly. "Seven? Oh, I thought it was earlier. This project is going to kill me."

Abbey kept her back to both Rob and Lucy.

Rob glanced toward Lucy. "It's the Newman project; I'm up to my ears. We had a call last night with Charles Newman himself. He's in Sydney this week and doesn't believe in time differences."

"Ugh." Lucy made a face. "I hate when the big bosses involve themselves. They think you'll sprout wings and fly if they ask you to. "

Rob smiled. "We've got another meeting this morning. I hope to catch a few hours of sleep before returning to the office. Tonight, we have dinner with the daughter; she's on the board of directors and is tougher than her old man."

Abbey turned to glare across the kitchen at him. "You're missing dinner again tonight?" Her jaw was clenched. "Can we expect you before dawn?"

Rob sighed. "I'm sorry, Abbs, really I am. I'm sorry I missed last night. If I could have gotten away, I would have, but I have to be there. I'm lead on this project."

"Maybe it would be best to stay in the city then." Anger flashed in Abbey's eyes. "It would save you the drive and the trouble. Wouldn't that make it easier to be at their beck and call?"

Rob put his hands in the air in surrender. "I'm not going to do this right now. I'm exhausted, and I need a shower. I'm here now; that should count for something."

"You're not here." Abbey raised her voice. "You may be standing in this room, but your mind is at work, and your body is half asleep. Are you going to have breakfast with Lola? Walk her to school? Pack her bag? Take five minutes to say hello to her."

"Stop! I'm not doing this," Rob said through gritted teeth. "I'm walking away before I say something I can't take back."

Abbey whirled around, hiding the tears glistening in her eyes as Rob rushed from the room.

"Don't you dare take his side right now!" She leaned over the sink, her arms braced on either side of her.

A wave of guilt washed over Lucy as she bit back the words she was about to say in Rob's defense.

"I won't. I get it; it's not fair. The late nights and the over-commitment to work are hard on you and Lola."

Tears fell from her eyes as Abbey turned, leaning her back against the sink. "Why can't he over-commit to me? Am I a horrible wife?"

"Abbey."

Abbey wiped violently at the tears running down her cheeks. "I am, I know I am. Rob works hard for us. We have a nice life because of him, but all I ever do is yell and get angry. I can't expect him to stop working."

"Yes, you can," Lucy said, stepping around the island. "And maybe you should."

"He loves his job. I can't ask him to quit."

"You're right; Rob is great at his job." Lucy handed Abbey a tissue. "I would even say he is the best in our entire company; that's why he keeps getting promoted. That doesn't mean he can't take a break. You don't have to ask him to quit, but maybe some time off would benefit you both."

Abbey dapped the tissue under her eyes and nose. "I don't think he'll agree with that. He believes the company will fall apart without him."

"Nothing should matter more to him than family. If you want him to prioritize you and Lola, you have to ask. And you shouldn't feel guilty for wanting to spend time with your husband."

"I want him to *want* to spend time with us," Abbey

sighed. "I want him to prioritize us because he wants to, not because I nagged him into it."

"Well, sometimes we need to be reminded," Lucy said, touching Abbey's shoulder. "It's easy to get wrapped up in the day-to-day things and lose sight of what's important. Tell him what you need and what is causing you pain. Maybe he needs to hear how much you miss him to snap you both out of the rut."

"You make it sound easy."

Lucy laughed. "Oh goodness, I know it's not easy. Speaking up is difficult, and pushing through your insecurities is a challenge. I know it's ironic for me to give relationship advice, but what you and Rob have is special. Don't let it fade away because you're afraid of his reaction. Maybe a big blow-up is what he needs to show how much you care."

"I don't even know where to start." Abbey bit her lip and laid her head on Lucy's shoulder. "I feel like we're miles apart."

"He still comes home to you every day," Lucy said. "Even when he works all night, he comes here as soon as the work is done. He could easily stay in the city but chooses to come home to you and Lola. That's something."

"I guess." Abbey shrugged.

Lucy's eyes widened. "Hey, Christmas vacation is coming; why not take a trip?"

"We spend Christmas with his family in Galway." Abbey made a face as if she wasn't looking forward to that particular trip.

"The full two weeks?"

Abbey raised her head and pushed off the sink. "No. We go for Christmas Eve and return a few days later."

"You have plenty of time to go somewhere after," said Lucy, excitement dancing in her eyes.

Abbey reached for her mug, running a fingertip around the rim. "I don't know if he'll be up for it. He'll just make excuses."

Lucy raised one brow. "Like you're doing?"

Abbey's cheeks reddened. "I guess." Suddenly, her eyes brightened as she looked up at Lucy. "Let's all go. You and Kaylee, Me, Rob, and Lola. It can be a group holiday. If you go, and maybe if you ask, he won't say no."

Lucy tapped her fingers on the countertop. "You want me to be a buffer."

"And ask," Abbey muttered.

Lucy sighed. "I'll talk to Kaylee, but *you* have to ask Rob."

Kaylee shuffled into the kitchen. "Talk about what?"

"We're thinking about taking a full family vacation after Christmas," Abbey blurted, a newfound energy surging through her. "We'll go somewhere warm."

"With a beach?" Kaylee's face lit up.

"For sure," Abbey nodded.

"You can talk to Rob while I take the girls to school," Lucy said, smirking at her sister.

Abbey frowned, but Lucy knew her sister would need to convince Rob if they wanted the chance to save their marriage.

Thirty minutes later, Lucy walked toward the school with Kaylee and Lola in tow. The wind bit at her cheeks, and she pulled the scarf tighter around her neck, grateful Kaylee forced her into wearing gloves and a hat.

"This is why we need to go somewhere warm," Kaylee said. "These mornings are freezing."

"A bunch of my friends are going to Tenerife," Lola said. "They go every winter. It's warm, and they stay in these big resorts with pools and all kinds of activities. Julia is forever carrying on about horseback riding."

"No way!" Kaylee shouted. "I want to do that."

"Sounds pricey," Lucy cut in. "Aunt Abbey and I will look into it. She has some connections, and I'm sure she'll find a good deal."

Lucy's heartbeat quickened as the school came into view. Aidan.

Thoughts of their recent lovemaking filled her mind. Even though they had been together only a few hours ago, the anticipation of seeing him again made her breathless. She felt like a schoolgirl with a crush.

Inside the thick gloves, her palms were sweating.

"See you after school," Kaylee called out, breaking Lucy from her trance.

"Love you. Have a good day." Lucy hugged her daughter and watched as she ran to her classmates.

Her heart warmed as a group of girls surrounded Kaylee, laughing and chatting. Seeing her daughter's happiness filled her with pride.

Lucy knew she should leave but couldn't pass up the opportunity to catch a glimpse of Aidan. They rarely saw each other outside his apartment and never fully clothed for long. Of course, they started dressed but, without fail, always ended up naked. Would it be strange to see him now, knowing they wouldn't end up in bed in a matter of minutes?

Her legs turned to Jell-o the minute she saw him crossing the courtyard. He was engrossed in conversation with a fellow teacher and looked good, especially for someone who was heavily intoxicated last night. Dressed in casual clothes and looking relaxed, it seemed he hadn't a care in the world.

Meanwhile, Lucy was a mess. Her heart was about to beat out of her chest, her legs threatening to give out, and she was breathing as if finishing a marathon.

He turned, and their eyes locked. He seemed caught off guard, the surprise evident on his face. Quickly regaining composure, his back straightened, and his demeanor became stoic. He offered her a stiff nod before shifting his attention to the students.

Lucy remained frozen. Her stomach dropped. Was he annoyed by her presence? Within a few seconds of greeting his students, he smiled and laughed, a stark contrast to the greeting she had received moments ago. Without a second glance toward her, he was gone.

That was not the greeting she had hoped for. A nod? Not even a smile or a playful wink? He acted like she was a stranger, someone he had met once or twice, instead of the woman he had greedily made love to only a few hours ago.

Pushing back from the fence, she rushed from the schoolyard, desperately fighting back the tears threatening to fall.

17

Lucy stared at the computer screen, unable to focus, the words blurring together. It was an uphill battle to muster up the motivation for work. Her mind insisted on wandering back to Aidan and his cold greeting.

She felt like a fool. From the minute she arrived on school grounds, she had been a mess. She acted like a love-sick puppy, gripping the fence to steady her wobbly legs and keep her from running straight into his arms.

Aidan looked at her and nodded. *He nodded.* His expression had been blank, his posture stiff, making the nod feel like a dismissal or an obligation he reluctantly needed to fulfill.

Sure, they were *only* sleeping together, but did he have to act that casually?

Then again, what had she expected? He was working and surrounded by kids. Did she think he would run over and kiss her? Slam her against the fence and do inappropriate things with her? No, but she had hoped for more than a nod.

An excited look or a cheesy grin, some gesture to let her know he was crazy about her.

Like an idiot, she cried the entire walk home. Feelings of past rejections reared their ugly heads and harassed her memories. What was her problem, and why did she let him affect her this way? Casual relationships weren't supposed to cause this much pain and confusion; they were supposed to be easy.

Her biggest fear had always been ending up like her mother, yet she always found herself on the same path, falling for men who only wanted sex.

Slamming a fist on the table, she rattled the third cup of coffee, spilling its contents over the rim. Of course, Aidan only wanted her for sex; that was the agreement they made. That was the epitome of friends-with-benefits. The truth was, they weren't friends at all. She knew nothing about him besides a few facts shared here and there, but nothing on a deeper friendship level. Their time together was purely sexual, and she rushed out before the intimate small talk began.

Damn, Abbey for being right all along. Her sister knew what Lucy had tried to deny from the start. Now, it was too late; there was no way she was admitting she wanted more. A future with Aidan was doomed the minute she convinced him all she wanted was sex.

The realization made her stomach churn. There was only one explanation for the way he made her feel. The weak in the knees, gut-wrenching ache to be with him could only mean one thing; she was falling head over heels for this man. Meaningless sex was not enough, and most likely, it never had been. She didn't want casual; she wanted Aidan.

Lucy ran her hands over her face and shoved back from the table, grunting.

"Rough day at the office?" Abbey stood in the kitchen, holding a fresh cup of coffee.

Lucy jumped.

"How long have you been standing there," Lucy snapped.

Abbey raised a brow as she calmly drank her coffee. "Long enough to witness you fighting some unseen demon over there."

Lucy sighed. "Myself, I'm the demon I'm fighting. I'm such, as the locals say, a feckin' eejit."

Abbey looked at her smugly. "Oh, I see, this isn't about work. Could it be about Aidan?"

Lucy glared at her sister. "Yeah, yeah. I said I was an idiot, okay? You were right, and I should have listened."

Abbey lifted a shoulder and continued casually sipping her coffee.

"I like him. I really like him." Lucy ran her fingers through her hair. "Ahh, I sound like a hormonal teenager."

"Adults have hormones, too," Abbey commented, trying to act indifferent while Lucy vented and worked through her emotions.

"I just couldn't stay away." Lucy yanked her mug off the table, spilling more coffee from the nearly full cup.

"Careful there, don't take it out on the poor coffee."

Lucy set the mug down and paced in front of the table. "You told me casual was a horrible idea. You warned me to stay away from Aidan."

"Wait a minute." Abbey held up one finger. "I never said

that."

"Yes, you did." Lucy stopped pacing. "I told you he wanted to be friends with benefits, and you said that was a bad idea."

Abbey nodded. "Ok, I did say that. But I never told you to stay away from Aidan. Is that why you snuck around? Because you thought I disapproved of *him*?"

Lucy bit her lip. "Maybe. I knew you would lecture me about our arrangement, and I thought you didn't like Aidan on some level."

"I like Aidan," Abbey said. "I really like him for you. I told you to fish or cut bait, but that had nothing to do with Aidan and everything to do with you. You have had feelings for him from the moment you two met, but continue insisting it's only ever been about sex."

Lucy sighed. "Good sex."

"It's deeper than that, and you know it." Abbey's tone was gentle. "It takes a lot for sex to be that good every time; normally, it's a clear sign of deeper emotions. And don't give me that crap about Norbert. You were a different person back then, one with severe daddy issues. That sex was good because of the emotional connection you craved at the time."

Lucy looked down, darting her eyes from side to side as she processed those words. "I never thought of it that way."

Abbey bowed. "You're welcome. This therapy session is free of charge."

Lucy gave a half-smile and slowly lowered into the chair. "All that stuff about Aidan doesn't matter, you know. Even if I admit I'm smitten, and yes, maybe I want more than a few hours of sex, it doesn't matter because he doesn't want the same thing."

"Are you sure?"

"He was the one who brought it up. He seemed relieved to hear I didn't want a relationship and was quick to offer causal sex whenever I wanted." She slumped down in the chair. "He hardly even acknowledged me this morning."

"This morning? When you dropped the girls off?" Abbey narrowed her eyes. "What happened?"

Lucy huffed out a breath. "Nothing. I saw him, and when he looked at me, he turned serious and nodded. It was such a stiff nod like I was the annoying sister of your best friend. You know the nod I'm talking about; it's an acknowledgment, so you don't come off rude, but it doesn't invite further communication. It's the brush-off nod."

Abbey stifled a laugh. "Wow, Lucy, you analyzed the crap out of that nod. And this is the real reason for your frustration," Abbey said, pushing her hip off the counter. "But, you only have yourself to blame. You're mad at Aidan for giving you exactly what you requested." She picked up a towel and wiped crumbs into a pile. "*You* didn't want a relationship. He agreed to your terms, and now you're annoyed."

"Honestly, I don't know what I want, and *that* annoys me."

Abbey narrowed her eyes and studied her sister. "I think you're hiding behind that excuse. You use it a lot to justify your frustration. I think you know what you want; you're just afraid of what that means."

Lucy shook her head. "I'm not ready for a relationship."

"Timing doesn't always work in our favor." Abbey

brushed the crumbs into her palm. "Maybe you do want a relationship but are afraid to ask for it. Perhaps you hope Aidan will be the one to ask you and to fight for something more serious. After all you've been through with Jeremy, you deserve a man who will fight for your honor."

Lucy shook her head. "You're such a helpless romantic."

"Everyone needs a little romance."

"I didn't move here for romance." Lucy sat forward, pulling her coffee toward her. "I came here to start over, to heal emotionally, and remove toxic people from my life."

Abbey emptied her palm into the garbage bin. "And starting over doesn't include finding love?"

"How can I fall in love when my heart is still broken?" Lucy toyed with her mug. "I didn't expect Aidan. After that first night, I thought I would never see him again. Never in my wildest dreams did I think he would turn out to be my daughter's teacher; that threw me for a loop."

Abbey carried a wet towel to the table and wiped the spilled coffee.

"I don't know what to do. I never meant to fall for him, but I have." Lucy looked up at Abbey. "There I said it, you're right, I'm mad about him."

Abbey smiled triumphantly. "The first step is admitting you have a problem."

"Haha." Lucy rolled her eyes. "Fine, I have a problem, a huge problem. I can't think straight. He consumes my thoughts day and night. I feel giddy every time he looks at me. I turn to jelly in his presence. I mean, look at me; I'm an emotional wreck just thinking about him. I don't know what to do."

"Tell him," Abbey said. "Tell him exactly what you just told me."

Lucy's eyes widened, and she shook her head vehemently. "I can't do that. Have you been listening? He doesn't want anything serious, and today's little nod makes that pretty clear."

Abbey straightened, the smile fading from her lips. "Listen, you have the same two choices I mentioned before. You either need to tell him how you feel and damn the consequences, or walk away and forget about him. You can't continue like this; you'll drive yourself insane."

"I tried to walk away," Lucy mumbled. "I tried to ignore him. But every time he calls, I go running."

"You do sound like an addict," Abbey said. "Are you hooked on Aidan or the feelings he gives you?"

"Is there a difference?" Lucy asked.

Abbey sighed. "Of course, there is. Addicts live for the high; normally, they need help for their problems because that type of addiction only harms the user. Real personal feelings and connections lead to something deeper, like a relationship, which can heal you."

"A relationship can hurt you too," Lucy mumbled. "Look at Mom, she loved Dad, and all he did was hurt her. Same with Jeremy, we had a real relationship."

"Mom is an addict. She was addicted to alcohol and Dad." Abbey stared down at the counter. "I think you were an addict too. Jeremy made you feel something that wasn't real, and you became addicted to the hope that he was better than Dad. Maybe the addiction was proving you were better than Mom. We both wanted to be better than Mom."

Lucy opened her mouth to protest, but no words came. Abbey made a valid point. What she felt for Jeremy had been real at first, but somewhere along the way, she fell out of love with the person and in love with the idea of what could be.

"You're scared of becoming like Mom, aren't you?" Abbey's voice was soft, gentle. "To be stuck in a relationship you think is real, unable to admit when it's over."

"I was Mom." Lucy felt tears welling in her eyes. "I was just like Mom for so long, and, you're right, Jeremy was my drug. I wanted him to be my knight in shining armor, but he turned out to be the dragon who locked me in the tower.

"I gave him my world, but it was never enough. I lost myself in him, and I'm scared to death I'm doing it again. I've been a fool, sacrificing my wants and needs to keep Aidan in my life. Even knowing all he wants from me is sex."

"Aidan isn't like Jeremy," Abbey said. "I think you put up walls with him, forced his hand, and he said what you wanted to hear."

"You think he wants more?" Lucy asked.

Abbey shrugged. "I think it's possible, but you won't know for sure unless you ask."

Lucy allowed herself to hope for a brief moment.

Then, she thought back to this morning and the indifferent nod. There had been no emotion when he looked at her; his face hadn't lit up, and he gave off an annoyed vibe. His entire demeanor matched their relationship, something causal that meant nothing outside the bedroom.

Lucy felt her lip quiver. "I'm pretty certain he only wants sex."

Abbey's cell phone vibrated along the counter. Picking it

up, she glanced at the caller ID. "Crap, it's Maeve. I have to take this. Don't give up before talking to him; all hope is not lost unless Aidan says it is."

Abbey cheerfully answered the phone and returned to her makeshift office in the living room. Lucy was grateful for the interruption; she was on the verge of tears talking about Aidan. The weeks of sneaking around and throwing herself into work were taking a toll on her.

It was clear Lucy was at a crossroads. She could continue down this path of casual sex, knowing it wouldn't lead anywhere, and end up hurt. Or, she could rip the band-aid off and walk away. It would still hurt if things ended now, but the longer she waited, the more complicated things would become.

Of course, there was Abbey's option; she could confess her newfound feelings. That was a scary thought; once the words were out, she could never take them back. And, if Aidan doubled down on his 'not a relationship type of guy' stance, they would be done. Once two people openly admit they want different things, the dynamics change and the relationship can't survive.

So, once again, Lucy had two options. Keep going as if nothing had changed, or walk away. Pushing her laptop to the side, she placed her head on the table and closed her eyes.

Everything always circled back to Jeremy, and in a way, he destroyed her. In the beginning, their relationship had been thrilling. Like a scene from a movie, he swooped in and whisked her off on a fantasy adventure. Lucy had been seventeen when she walked away from her life. She was a good student and mere months away from graduating, but she dropped out to run off with a man she hardly knew.

Everything seemed perfect for the first two years, but maintaining the nomadic lifestyle was difficult. Over time, they needed to settle in areas for extended periods to work and earn money. But Jeremy was restless; he hated staying in one place for too long. He struggled to find and keep a job, and Lucy was no longer enough for him. Lucy was crushed when Jeremy openly admitted the truth.

"Ah, come on, Luce, I'm a man. I have needs. It means nothing; you're the one I come home to. I love you."

The first cracks began forming in her heart. She was miles from home with nowhere to go. Jeremy had saved her, only to make her feel like a prisoner.

Convinced they loved each other, she allowed it to be enough that he came back to her every night, knowing it was meaningless sex with strangers. After a year, the hours away from her turned into full nights and several days. Each time he came home, she half listened to his flimsy excuses and cried in the shower while he slept. But still, she stayed.

Every time they moved to a new place, she silently prayed things would be different. She let herself believe that if she allowed him freedom, eventually, he would get it out of his system and finally settle down with her. All the while, she refused to believe she was anything like her mother. Even on the nights she passed out drunk, crying for Jeremy, she still told herself she was better than her mother and refused to believe Jeremy was anything like her father.

Shortly after her twenty-first birthday, Lucy discovered she was pregnant. Excitement overwhelmed her as she stared at the double lines on the pregnancy test. Things would be different now. A baby would change everything. Jeremy would be forced to commit to her, and they could finally settle into one place.

Jeremy was less than thrilled.

"A baby?" He yelled. "What are we going to do with a baby? It's hard enough to feed you. Not to mention, I'm putting up with all your whining. Now I have to listen to a crying baby?"

That night, Jeremy stayed away for three weeks. In hopes of making him jealous, she sought out her first one-night stand. But you can't make someone jealous if they aren't around.

She liked to think that if it hadn't been for the pregnancy, she would never have taken him back, but that wasn't true. Jeremy was a master manipulator; in the end, he always convinced her they belonged together.

When Lucy was eight months pregnant, they returned to Oregon and lived in the tiny back bedroom of a small trailer belonging to a guy Jeremy had recently met. Four days after moving in, Jeremy was gone. Lucy woke up alone in a stranger's home, a scribbled note lying on the pillow.

I can't do this. I'm not ready to be a father.

It was the first time Lucy felt truly alone in a long time. With her tail between her legs, she packed what little she had and went home to her mother. Abbey had recently moved in with her boyfriend, and Lucy refused to impose on their life. Instead, she listened to endless lectures and ridicule from the woman she swore never to speak to again.

If only she had been stronger and made a pact with her unborn child to never allow Jeremy back into their lives. She would have saved them both from years of heartache and feeling like a hamster on a wheel of broken promises. Her mother was of little help, constantly berating her life choices and pounding into her the belief that Jeremy needed to be a part of their life.

On the plane to Ireland, Lucy swore she would never go back there. Never give a man the power to dismiss her so easily, to come and go as he pleased with no regard for how it affected her. Not only did she need to guard her heart, but she had a duty to protect her daughter. Lucy despised her mother, hated her for being absent when she was a child, for trying to force her twisted beliefs onto her and her unborn child, and for allowing men to treat both of them like playthings.

Falling into this friends-with-benefits cycle with Aidan had been too easy, like a bad habit she couldn't break. In one instance, she was right back in the loop of sex with no commitment. She couldn't keep going on like this, not when what she felt for him was so much deeper than casual sex.

She was already in over her head, but that wasn't an excuse to continue on a path of self-destruction. Aidan didn't feel the same, and it was hopeless for her to believe he might come to his senses someday. She wasted seventeen years waiting for Jeremy to choose her; she wouldn't put her heart through that again.

A big decision needed to be made, and she couldn't take it lightly. Thankfully, the winter holidays were just around the corner.

"I have some amazing news!" Abbey burst into the room, forcing Lucy back into the present. "That was Maeve. Her friends have an amazing beach house in Spain. They want this rental to be a featured property of our agency."

"That's great," Lucy agreed.

"I haven't gotten to the best part yet," Abbey said, grabbing Lucy's arms. "She wants me to go and stay there for a week. I have to work a little, but it's Spain!"

Lucy's eyes widened. "That's fantastic."

"I'll have to find local excursions, try all the restaurants, and, of course, spend some time on the beach," Abbey said. "The best part is I can take all of you with me."

This was just the break Lucy needed. If she were in another country, she wouldn't be at Aidan's beck and call. Maybe she could finally gain some perspective and reflect on what she truly wanted with him.

18

Lucy opened the pristine glass doors and stepped onto a balcony overlooking the ocean. The mid-day sun danced across the turquoise water, creating a mesmerizing illusion of glitter sprinkled across the surface.

"This is breathtaking!"

"I told you," Abbey said, leaning on the rail beside her sister.

"It sure beats the dreary Irish winter," Lucy said.

"It's the break we all need. Sun, beach, and no commitments, aside from a few excursions I'll need to explore."

Lucy stared at the ocean, hypnotized by the waves growing and peaking before crashing onto the shore. "I always wanted to visit Spain. I've heard of its beauty, but this is far beyond what I imagined. And this balcony, with this view, I'll be spending every morning out here with my coffee and a good book."

"This whole place is heaven." Abbey headed back into the

house. "It's three bedrooms with a fully equipped kitchen. We'll put the girls together, and you can have your own room for a change."

"That will be nice."

"We better unpack. Lola is dying to swim; I'll bet she's already in her suit."

"Really? Isn't the ocean freezing?" Lucy laughed. "It's warm here, but not *that* warm."

Abbey rolled her eyes. "Kids don't care? Remember how cold the Pacific Ocean is? When we were kids, it didn't matter if it was the dead of winter; if we were at the beach, we were leaving soaked."

"True."

In the living room, Rob lounged on one of the two couches, his feet hanging off one end.

"You look comfortable," Lucy commented. "You coming to the beach with us?"

"I may join in after resting my eyes for a few minutes."

Abbey didn't say a word, hardly acknowledging her husband as she headed toward the primary suite down the hall.

Once Abbey was out of sight, Lucy playfully punched his arm. "You should come with us. It would mean the world to Abbey. You two can spend some quality time together."

"Her words?" Rob asked, opening one eye.

"You've been working a lot lately," Lucy continued, trying to sound indifferent. "We've all noticed your absence. Take a break and hang out with your family."

Rob sighed. "They'll have a much better time with you and Kaylee."

"They'll have a better time with *you*." Lucy raised her brows. "You can nap on the beach. Now get ready."

Rob moaned and groaned as he sat up, giving her a playful smirk.

"Now, that's a good boy," she teased as if talking to a dog.

He tossed a pillow at her as she grabbed her suitcase from where it sat near the front door and hurried out of the line of fire.

She passed Kaylee and Lola's shared room and peeked inside. The girls were setting out and showing off their outfits for the week.

"Beach in ten," Lucy told them.

The next room was all hers. The double bed with its fluffy goose-down comforter invited her to climb in and snuggle up, but if she lay down now, it would be well after dark before she got back up again.

Placing the suitcase on its side, she opened the lid and searched out her beachwear. Although she would not be going in the water, it was time to exchange her jeans and hoodie for a flowing skirt, breezy shirt, and sandals.

As she changed, she thought about Abbey and hoped this holiday would help heal the rift between Rob and her sister. The tension between them could be cut with a butter knife. Abbey and Rob had always been the epitome of the perfect couple. From the moment she met Rob, he had been the perfect gentleman. Lucy had been so jealous back then; no man ever looked at her like Rob looked at Abbey.

Rob and Abbey had been her heroes during the darkest moments of her life. Pregnant, alone, and forced to live with her mother again, Lucy fell into a deep depression. What should have been the happiest time of her life, bringing a child into the world, turned into the opposite.

Lucy's father had died years before finally releasing her mother from his hold on her. Her mother quit drinking but remained a bitter shell of the woman she had once been. All the hurt, anger, and disappointment seemed to be pushed directly onto Lucy. It was not the ideal situation for bringing new life into the world.

After a tense week in her childhood home, the contractions began. Without a word, Lucy packed a bag and checked herself into the hospital. She would rather do it alone than deal with her nagging mom while in labor.

Abbey appeared out of the blue within an hour of Lucy's admission.

"I can't believe you moved back and didn't even call me." Abbey tossed her jacket on a chair and sat on the bed beside Lucy. "And you're pregnant? I'm a little insulted you went to Mom before me."

"I didn't want to be a burden," Lucy said, breathing through a contraction. "You've got your own life now. Thank goodness."

Abbey waved away the comment. "Please, there's plenty of room for you. Where is that asshat, anyway?"

Lucy shrugged. "Gone. Haven't seen or heard from him in weeks."

"Dick."

Lucy grabbed Abbey's hand, squeezing as another contraction ripped through her.

"Ok, I've been watching videos on childbirth," Abbey said, sliding off the bed, still holding Lucy's hand. "I'm not a pro, but I'll be your birthing coach. I'm not leaving your side until this baby is born."

Lucy grimaced. "You don't—."

"Hush." Abbey cut her off. "You're right; I don't have to be here. I want to be here. I'm going to be an aunt!"

"What about Rob? Is he okay with you being here?"

"He's the one who practically shoved me out the door," Abbey gushed. "Mom called. She was worried about you and had the common sense to know when she isn't wanted."

Lucy clenched her jaw through the pain.

"And I've already told her you and the baby are coming home with me." Abbey looked at the small table beside the bed. "Do you need ice chips or something?"

"Drugs," Lucy moaned. "I need drugs."

Ten hours later, Abbey held Kaylee for the first time. Twenty-four hours after that, Lucy and Kaylee went to live with Abbey and Rob.

Rob was over the moon to have a baby in the house. He continually surprised Lucy, always offering to help with Kaylee. He changed diapers, rocked her to sleep, and catered to Lucy hand and foot until she fully recovered.

How had Abbey found this gem of a man? Kaylee was Jeremy's child, yet he was nowhere to be seen. Instead, Rob stepped up and heaped affection on Kaylee.

It was Rob who introduced Lucy to the tech world. He taught her basic skills and helped her enroll in technical college, ensuring she took suitable courses.

Abbey and Rob cared for Kaylee so Lucy could earn a certificate in computer science. Then, Rob helped get her a job at his company. It was the first time in her life Lucy felt she was growing up and working in an actual career.

For four years, Lucy and Kaylee lived with Abbey and Rob; it was the happiest she had been in a long time. Not only could she create a stable life for the first time, but she also mended fences with her mother. Their relationship was far from perfect, but having a grandchild brought out a side of her mother Lucy had never seen before. She was a horrible mother but a fantastic grandmother.

Lucy had been present for Lola's entrance into the world. The bond between Lola and Kaylee had begun when they were infants. Lucy and Abbey grew close again, and Rob was a positive male figure in everyone's lives.

Then Jeremy came back.

For weeks, he begged and pleaded with Lucy to take him back. He made endless promises to change, swearing he had matured and was ready to be a father.

"He hasn't changed," Rob warned her. "He's only after the chase. He wants what he can't have. Look at you. You have succeeded without him and made something of yourself, which drives him mad."

Foolishly, Lucy sided with Jeremy. The endless hope and unattainable dream clawed into the back of her mind.

"I think he does want to change," Lucy said. "I can help him like you helped me. Besides, he's Kaylee's father, and I can't keep him from her."

Rob scoffed, huffing out a breath. "It's all a load of crap, Lucy. You are better than that and better than him. He will never change and never amount to anything. He will use you, hurt you, and then he'll leave you."

The words stung. Kind, funny, compassionate Rob had

driven a stake through her heart. Abbey sided with her husband.

"I hope you find your happy ending," Abbey told her, a tinge of sadness in her eyes. "Please don't be a stranger this time, okay? Lola will miss you guys; I'll miss you."

Lucy should never have left with Jeremy. She should have listened to Rob. It would have saved her from years of continual heartbreak. But Rob had given her hope; he was different from other men, and she foolishly believed Jeremy could be like him.

On the beach, Lucy lay back on a blanket in the sand. The sun warmed her skin. The girls laughed and screamed as they played in the water, Rob chasing them through the waves.

"He is such a good dad," Lucy said.

"Mmm-hmm." Abbey watched the three of them, her chin resting on her knees.

"Are you guys okay?" Lucy looked toward her sister, shielding her eyes with her hand.

Abbey wrapped her arms around her legs, pulling them in tightly. "Just a rough patch. It happens, it sucks, but we'll get through it."

"I'm sorry, I haven't been a better sister," Lucy admitted. "I've been distracted with my own issues and given little attention to anything else. But, Abbey, I need you to know I'm here for you. I hope you know you can talk to me."

Abbey shrugged. "It's nothing. I'm being selfish. He's working hard to give us a great life."

"But you aren't happy." Lucy pushed up on her elbows.

"Abbey, if you aren't happy, how great of a life can it be? Don't sell yourself short. You, of all people, deserve the world."

"Maybe you can remind Rob," Abbey muttered. She released her legs and reached down, grasping handfuls of sand and allowing it to drip through her fingers.

"No! *You* remind him." Lucy said. "Talk to him about how you're feeling."

"He likes you better than me." Abbey continued playing with the sand. "He always has. I've always been jealous of the relationship you two have."

"Jealous? Of what?"

"He talks to you, he jokes with you, and you aren't afraid to tell him when he's being a jerk."

Lucy laughed. "We have a very sibling-esque sort of relationship."

"I know, and that's what I'm jealous of. You two are always laughing and joking around. Whenever Rob and I are in the same room, I feel like I'm walking on eggshells."

"He loves you," Lucy said softly.

"Does he?"

"Of course." Lucy sat up, scooting closer to her sister. "Do you honestly think he doesn't?"

Abbey shrugged as if carrying a hundred pounds on her back; her shoulders hardly moved up before slumping forward again. "I'm not sure anymore. He probably *likes* me, but I don't know if he still *loves* me. It feels like he spends long hours at the office because he can't stand to be home with me."

Lucy looked out across the beach, watching Rob

splashing Lola and Kaylee. His laugh echoed across the sand, the wholehearted laugh Lucy always remembered. The more she thought about it, the more she realized she hadn't heard that laugh since moving here.

Lucy put her hand to her chest. "Is this my fault? I'd feel horrible if he was staying away because we moved in. I know we've overstayed a bit, and I take all your attention, but—."

"No!" Abbey grabbed Lucy's hand. "This all started way before you came. It was part of why I pushed you so hard to move here. I was lonely, and my husband, my best friend, was pulling away from me."

Abbey exhaled deeply, releasing Lucy's hand and staring toward the sea. "I can't put all the blame on Rob though. Our lives have changed over the past few years, and I think it started when I went back to work.

"When I was pregnant with Lola, I only wanted to be a housewife. I loved cooking, cleaning, and being there when Lola and Rob came home. I wanted to be that perfect family you see on TV.

"But, they never show how lonely being a housewife can be. I spent so much time alone once Lola was in school; it felt like no one paid attention to me anymore."

Abbey dropped her head to her knees. "Geesh, I sound pathetic."

Lucy shook her head. "You don't."

Abbey continued. "I needed something just for me, so I started a part-time job. It was perfect; I worked while Lola was in school and could do it from the kitchen. Then, Maeve had this crazy idea to start a new business and wanted me to help her. Now, I dedicate more time to that than to housework. I lose track of time and don't always have dinner sorted by the time Rob comes home, and sometimes the house is a mess."

A scowl creased her lips downward. "I get it; it's all been a huge change. Rob is used to coming home to a clean house and dinner on the table. Lately, he comes home to find me still engrossed in work. There are still dishes from breakfast in the sink, and sometimes, I haven't put all the groceries away. I feel his annoyance, but at the same time, is it wrong to ask for some help? I've been doing everything since we met, but it's become mundane and boring. It would be nice if he washed the dishes occasionally."

Abbey sighed, shaking her head. "I should just quit working; then maybe everything would go back to the way it was."

"No, you are building something for yourself, which makes you happy," Lucy protested. "Not to mention, we wouldn't all be here in Spain without that job. This place is amazing."

Abbey's lips cracked with anticipation. "I'm excited about this job; I love building this business. It won't always be so much work. It will be easy once the databases are set up and some excursions are planned out. I love traveling and want to help people have amazing vacations."

"I had no idea all the things you are juggling." Lucy leaned into her sister. "I haven't noticed a messy house, and you seem to always be in the kitchen, cleaning and cooking. You could have asked me for help; I can help you."

"You're a guest in my house," Abbey sighed, ducking her head. "I've been trying extra hard since you moved in. Trying to portray the perfect housewife with the perfect home and family. But, before you came, I had let everything slide to the back burner."

"Oh, Abbey, you don't have to impress me, and you shouldn't be working twice as hard because Kaylee and I live there. We can help, and I don't mind a mess. It's stressful feeling like I can't leave a mug on the counter for more than five minutes." Lucy gave her a weak smile. "I'm sorry I failed to notice you're burning the candle at both ends. Maybe Rob doesn't realize how hard you are working behind the scenes. Does he know how much this business means to you? Because you shouldn't have to give up on your dreams to make a marriage work."

Abbey leaned back, resting her head on Lucy's shoulder. "You know, for someone who seems conflicted in love, you give pretty good relationship advice."

As if on cue, Lucy's phone vibrated next to her, making a muffled whirring sound against the blanket and sand.

Abbey glanced down and noticed the name flashing across the screen. "Speaking of love–."

Lucy ignored the call, focusing on the girls playing in the water.

"Thank you for listening." Abbey pushed up from the blanket. "I know I need to talk to Rob. He may have no idea how I've been feeling. But you should take your own advice and talk to Aidan. You may be surprised to find you both want the same thing."

Lucy glanced at her watch. "That is just a booty call."

"Doesn't he know you aren't home?"

"I haven't exactly spoken to him for a few weeks," Lucy

said sheepishly. "We want different things."

"I think you're wrong," Abbey said. "And I think you're making a huge mistake. You are head over heels for that man, and I think he feels the same way."

19

Lucy stepped into the steaming tub, eagerly anticipating a long soak. After spending the entire day at the beach, followed by some of the best seafood she had ever tasted, she was ready for some alone time.

As soon as they returned from dinner, the girls rushed to their shared room to watch the latest episode of their favorite show. Lucy took that moment to sneak away, leaving Abbey and Rob alone, secretly hoping they would resolve their issues.

The hot water burned at her skin as she sank through the bubbles. Her eyes closed as she lay back, feeling her tense muscles relax. This was heaven.

Through the wall, giggles erupted. Kaylee and Lola were kindred spirits, two souls destined to find one another. These were the moments Lucy was reassured that moving had been the best decision for both of them. If nothing else, Kaylee deserved to be surrounded by adults who wouldn't fail or disappoint her at every turn.

There was no denying that Jeremy was a lousy dad. He was a master manipulator who never really cared about Kaylee. He knew the only way to guarantee Lucy would sleep with him was by giving all his attention to Kaylee. He played her emotions like a fiddle, and it worked every time. Like a prostitute, Lucy traded sex with Jeremy as payment for spending time with Kaylee.

Thank goodness she finally came to her senses. One day, it came like a slap in the face; no matter how she twisted things, Lucy was exactly like her mother. Fear chilled her to the core as she imagined Kaylee continuing the cycle. Would Kaylee try to escape the life Lucy had provided only to be manipulated by a man just like her father?

No! Lucy had to break this cycle.

"I'm done, Jeremy." Lucy pulled him into the back bedroom, not missing the glare Kaylee shot her while shoving headphones over her ears. "I want us to have a real relationship."

Jeremy smirked. "I'll do whatever you want, baby. Let's get naked and talk about it."

Lucy's back stiffened. "No. I'm serious; things need to change. I can't do this anymore."

"Do what?" Jeremy acted oblivious.

"You show up for every few weeks," Lucy said, exasperated. "Then you disappear, and we don't hear from you. You're out there living a completely separate life from us. Yet, you expect Kaylee and I to sit back and wait for your return."

Jeremy reached out to gently caress her cheek. "I just want *you* to wait for me."

She smacked his hand away. "I'm tired of this—arrangement. I want to settle down, maybe have more kids."

Jeremy laughed. "You can't be serious."

"I am serious." Lucy stood her ground. "I want you to choose. If you want to be a free spirit, fine, I want more, and Kaylee sure as hell deserves more."

Jeremy rolled his eyes. "You want me to give her *more* attention? Is that what this is about? Your dad didn't love *you* enough, and you're going to put the pressure on me? What do you want me to do? Take her to the circus, the amusement part? Name it, and I'll do it."

"I want you to act like a father!" Lucy shouted. "I want the three of us to spend time together. I want to be a family."

Jeremy's face turned hard. "I love you. I've always loved you, Lucy; you know that, right?"

"I want you to love *her*." Lucy nodded toward the living room.

Jeremy looked away. "I only want you."

Lucy could feel her heart breaking. "We're a package deal. You can't love me and not her; she's our daughter."

Anger flashed in his eyes. "I never wanted her," he whispered harshly. "I told you that. I want you, and only you. If I have to take her out occasionally to make you happy, I will. But you knew I didn't want to be a father, and that will never change."

He reached for her arm, but Lucy jerked away.

"Come on, baby, we're so good together." Jeremy softened his tone, grabbing hold of her arm and jerking her into him. "Don't you remember the good times we used to have? Traveling around, never knowing where we would end up, making love under the stars."

"I remember sleeping on cold, hard park benches," Lucy mumbled, pressing her palms against his chest. "You left me all the time, on my own. It wasn't all roses and rainbows for me; sure, you had it easy, but I hated that life. I won't ever go back to it."

Jeremy laughed, turning on his carefree charm and releasing his hold on her. "I'm a guy. We're animals, assholes even. " He put his hands on her shoulders. His breath smelled of cigarettes and beer. Lucy felt her stomach turn. Was this really the man she had pined for all these years?

Gently, he moved a strand of hair behind her ear. "I did train you, after all." He leaned down and whispered close to her ear, "I taught you just how to please me."

Bile rose in her throat, and she felt nauseous.

He turned her toward the bed, pressing her back against his chest. "There, right there, is where we are perfect. Just you and me, no one else." Jeremy kissed her neck. "I only come here for you and for this." He violently grabbed her crotch. "If I can't have this, there is nothing for me here."

Lucy shoved him off of her. "Get out! Get out now!"

"If I leave now, I swear to you, I will never come back." His eyes blazed as he glared down at her.

"Get out!" Lucy screamed, shoving and pushing him toward the bedroom door. "Get out! Get out! Get out!"

Kaylee was by her side, wrapping her arms around her waist. "He's gone, Mom."

Lucy slumped against the door jamb, tears streaming down her face. "I'm so sorry, baby, sorry for everything."

They stood holding each other for a long time.

Two weeks later, Lucy packed their bags for Dublin while explaining to her mother all that had transpired.

"You're being overly dramatic," her mom said. "Give the man what he wants. It's a win-win for everyone. Kaylee has a relationship with her father, and you get laid."

"He doesn't want to be a dad," Lucy protested.

"He'll grow to love her; just give him time."

Lucy rolled her eyes and tossed socks and underwear into the suitcase. "Like how Dad grew to love us?"

"That's different."

Lucy huffed out a breath. "I know what it feels like to see your father and know he despises you. I won't do that to Kaylee,

"We're going to Ireland," Lucy said firmly. "I miss Abbey, and I need to get away from here. I'm done with Jeremy and his games; if you don't want to support that decision, that's on you."

She shoved the memories to the back corners of her mind; this was not relaxing. Jeremy was ancient history, and her mother would never change. But what about her? It seemed she had fallen right back in the cycle with Aidan. Their relationship was purely sexual, and Lucy knew she wanted more than Aidan was willing to give.

As if on cue, her cell phone vibrated on the toilet seat where she had left it. Without looking, she knew it was Aidan.

Blood pulsed through her veins. She hated how her body reacted to him. Her fingers itched to read the text, but she kept them submerged, resisting the urge.

Closing her eyes, she tried to push her thoughts of Aidan

away. Instead, she imagined him in the bath with her. Wet hair hanging loosely across his face, doing little to hide the desire burning from his eyes. With a bar of soap, he gently lathered up her leg, moving higher and higher until his fingers lightly grazed the tender folds between her thighs.

Lucy's eyes popped open, and she sat up. That wasn't helping.

Already regretting it, she toweled off her hands and snatched the phone off the toilet.

Happy Christmas

I hope your holidays have been well

I miss you.

Are you around?

A storm of emotions swirled inside as she read each message. Her body and mind were caught in a battle for control. Butterflies battered the walls of her stomach; arousal tingled through her veins; all the while, her brain was flashing warning lights.

Danger! Danger! Heartache ahead!

Ignoring her rational side, she responded.

In Spain. It's warm.

It was all she could do not to confess how much she missed him. They had two very different meanings of the word *miss*. She missed *him*, the person. He missed the sex.

Sounds grand. It's been manky here. Lashing and cold.

Heading to Cork for New Years, don't know why. My family's half mad.

I would rather be there with you.

Or here with you or anywhere with you.

Her heart skipped a beat. Did he mean that?

Maybe she shouldn't have confessed that.

You're in the bath.

The phone rang in her hand; he wanted to video chat.

Her stomach dropped. They just went from a nice, casual chat to a sexually charged one. Now, he knew she was naked and wanted to see for himself. That about summed up their relationship.

Tears burned at the back of her eyes as she stared at the screen, unable to accept the call. She was way over her head, having fallen too far into a relationship that was supposed to be casual. The rules, unwritten as they may be, had been broken, and how she felt about Aidan was way past casual.

It was time to be honest with herself. What she said in that final fight with Jeremy still stood; she wanted more. She wanted a stable relationship and not just a sexual one.

Lucy sighed and set the ringing phone back on the toilet seat. She had to stop this before it went any further.

In a blinding epiphany, she realized she had no idea what came after the casual part of a relationship or how to navigate her way into something more serious. Although her sister was currently struggling, Lucy remembered Abbey and Rob in their earlier days. They had something she hadn't witnessed before, positive communication. They openly shared their thoughts and feelings and genuinely wanted to make each other happy. No man had ever been concerned about Lucy's feelings or happiness.

Moving to Ireland had been the first step toward changing her life, but nothing was different; she had already fallen back into old habits. Casual flings were an addiction, and she had to quit cold turkey.

Every ounce of her being ached to answer that video call. She wanted to hear Aidan's voice and to see his face, especially if she teased him while naked in the bath. But that would be feeding the addiction. Any recovering addict will admit that no matter how much they love the drug, it will never love them back. The drug only wants to consume its users; it will take what it needs and leave them in a worse condition than they started.

When the ringing finally stopped, Lucy sighed in relief. Before she could fully relax, the phone dinged as several text messages came through.

She had enough.

Drying her hands off again, Lucy grabbed the phone and deleted the message thread without reading a single text. *Cold turkey*, she told herself. With a shaking breath, she opened the contact page and stared at Aidan's number. With one button, she could break the cycle, end the addiction, and start her detox. Inhaling, she held her breath and blocked his number before deleting his contact information from her phone.

***

Two months later, Lucy stood in the living room of her new two-bedroom apartment. For the first time in years, she had something all her own. Not to mention, finding housing had been a great distraction now that she had given up on Aidan.

Apartments were few and far between in Dublin, but Lucy got lucky. One of her work colleagues owned this apartment, and the previous tenants had just given their notice. She was able to skip all the hassle and secure the place. The co-worker was more than happy to rent to a friend rather than strangers.

Another perk was that the place came fully furnished and Lucy's co-workers donated all sorts of home goods to the move. Plates, silverware, candles, towels, mats, and other random trinkets filled the cardboard boxes Lucy and Abbey had hauled over this morning. They planned a big shopping spree for the weekend to spruce the place up. Kaylee and Lucy were both excited at the prospect of designing and creating their own space.

"That's the last of it," Lucy said, adding one final cardboard box to the large pile stacked along the wall.

Abbey's eyes glistened. "You don't have to go."

"Oh, no. It's far too late to turn back now." Lucy indicated the collection of boxes. "I'm not moving all that. Besides, it's way beyond time. Kaylee needs her own room, and we'll never feel completely settled until we have our own space. I need to know I can do this on my own."

Abbey hung her head. "I know. But I'm going to miss you. I've gotten used to having you around."

Lucy laughed, heading toward the sliding door leading onto the balcony. "I'm literally one street away from you." Lucy unlocked the door and pulled Abbey outside. "Look, there's your backyard. I can spy on you anytime, and you can do the same. Besides, I plan to drop in unannounced as often as possible."

"Promise?"

"Yes. And Kaylee will be over all the time."

Abbey sighed. "It won't be the same."

"No, it won't. And listen, I know I have a track record for disappearing, but I'm done with that. I'm ready to set down roots. And now that I have you back in my life, I'm not letting you go."

Abbey looked over the railing toward her house. "Wow, you can see straight into my living room."

"And your bedroom," Lucy teased, bumping her elbow against Abbey's arm. "Better close those drapes before you get freaky."

Abbey dropped her gaze.

"It's going to be okay," Lucy said quickly. "Things will get better. Rob loves you."

Abbey shrugged.

A look of concern crossed Lucy's face. "You do want things better, right?"

"I do," Abbey whispered. "I'm not so sure about Rob, though."

"I guess Spain wasn't the miracle fix we hoped it would be," Lucy said. "Maybe with us gone, you'll be forced to communicate. You both were also so good at that."

Abbey sighed, leaning against the railing. "We were, but now he shuts me down whenever I try to talk to him. He doesn't want to talk because he knows it will end in a fight."

"Maybe that's what you need, a good fight," Lucy said.

"Yeah, but I can't force him to talk to me." Abbey's tone dripped with irritation.

Lucy blew out a breath. "The more you ignore it, the

greater the distance will become."

Abbey raised an eyebrow and looked at her sister. "And do you put into practice this advice you dole out? Have *you* told Aidan how you really feel?"

"Don't change the subject." Lucy walked back inside the house. "There is nothing to talk about with Aidan. It was fun and casual, and now it's over; no harm, no foul, and everyone is happy."

"Oh, yeah, you've been *real* happy." Abbey followed her into the living room. "Moping is more like it."

Lucy glared at her sister. "Ok, I admit it, I got a little more attached than I wanted to. Maybe I was in a funk for a while, but it's fine; I'm over it. I got a new apartment and am ready to move on." Lucy tried to sound as if her heart didn't still ache at the mention of his name.

Abbey picked up her purse and jacket from the couch. "Sounds like we both have communication issues." Abbey waved the conversation away. "Anyway, you'll be over for dinner tomorrow, right? It's takeaway night."

"We would never miss that."

"Perfect." Abbey had her hand on the door handle but turned back to Lucy. "Before I forget, and since you're all good on the teacher situation, I need help setting up for the Saint Patrick's Day breakfast at school next week."

Lucy's eyes grew large. "I don't—"

Abbey put up her hand. "We're decorating the hall in the morning after school starts. He'll be in class; you won't see him."

"It's not that—"

Abbey cut her off. "It is that, so let me stop you there. We don't have enough people signed up; this is a big event, and we really could use your help. You can come, decorate, and leave before any students come to the hall for breakfast. You never have to see him."

Lucy shook her head. "I don't think it's a good—."

Abbey pointed at her. "You said you were fine. You're over it, remember?"

"I ghosted him," Lucy spat out.

"Then, say sorry and move on," Abbey continued. "It was just a casual fling, right? I'm sure Aidan doesn't even care."

Lucy's gut twisted. "Fine, I'll help with the decorating only. I can't take extra time off to do more than that."

"Great." Abbey smiled smugly. "I'll see you tomorrow night."

Lucy leaned against the closed door, rubbing her palms over her face as a wave of sadness washed over her. A big part of her wanted to stay with Abbey and live the life they missed out on in their childhood. Abbey had always been the one person who had never abandoned her, even though Lucy continually left her sister. Even after Abbey made her big move to Ireland, she was still always there for Lucy. Although it was over the phone, email, or text messages, she allowed Lucy the space to vent, whine, and cry, often ending every conversation with the invitation to move to Ireland and escape Jeremy for good. Through it all, they were best friends. Lucy would never have made it this far without Abbey's support; she needed that shoulder to cry and lean on.

In a way, Lucy felt she was abandoning Abbey once again. After all Abbey had done for her, Lucy bailed when it seemed Abbey's relationship was falling apart. Lucy couldn't fix whatever was happening between Abbey and Rob, and it scared her to think no one could.

They had to fix things. To Lucy, they were the epitome of a healthy relationship. If they couldn't make things work, what chance did Lucy have?

A loud knocking pulled Lucy from her thoughts. A smile spread across her face as she pulled open the door to her daughter.

"Welcome home!"

20

"How is the new place?" Jenny approached Lucy in the school hall, carrying a clear plastic tub full of decorations. "Abbey's been talking nonstop about your move. She says it's too quiet at her place without you. It must be nice to have your own place. Are you feeling more settled?"

Lucy kept opening her mouth to reply, but Jenny rushed on, not giving her a sliver of space to respond.

"Ah, moving is such a nightmare. All those boxes, packing and unpacking. I should have brought you some wine; that always helps me." Jenny laughed, then turned abruptly as a large clatter echoed through the empty hall. "Oh geez! Áine is such a muppet these days."

Jenny rushed off, leaving Lucy staring after her in confusion.

"Tell us how you really feel, Jenny," Abbey muttered, sidling up to Lucy.

"A muppet?" Lucy laughed. "As in *The Muppet Show*?"

Abbey shrugged, kneeling to remove the lid off the plastic

container. "Who knows, probably."

Bright green shamrocks and paper rainbows spilled from the overfilled tub. Lucy bent down to help sort through the decorations. Abbey set the items into neat piles: Irish flags, green, white, and orange striped banners, and a few random leprechaun cutouts.

"It sounded like you and Jenny were having a very intense, one-sided conversation."

Lucy looked over at her sister. "She's a spitfire. Twenty questions with no chance to answer."

"Hang those on the far wall!" Jenny's voice boomed across the hall in their direction.

Abbey whipped her head from side to side. "Where is she yelling from? How does she even see us?"

Lucy laughed and raised an eyebrow. "I think she just went into the kitchen."

Abbey grabbed a stack of shamrocks. "Well, you heard her; our fearless leader has spoken. Do we have tape or Blu Tack?"

"Blue tag?"

"Blu Tack," Abbey repeated slowly. "It's sticky tack, and it's blue."

Lucy glared at her sister. "You're in a mood today. What do they call it? Cheeky."

"I've been known to be a bit of a spitfire occasionally, too." Abbey gave a devious grin.

"Pure evil," Lucy teased. "I saw some tape and maybe tack-looking stuff on the table over there."

For the next twenty minutes, Lucy and Abbey hung shamrocks, rainbows, banners, and Irish flags along the walls. Parents arrived to help, each shouting a quick hello before being assigned a task. Tables, covered in cheap green and white disposable tablecloths, were set up in long rows for the classes to sit and eat their breakfast. Stacks of paper plates sat next to serving trays and a line of various toppings. The enticing aroma of pancakes and sausages drifted from the kitchen. Lucy's stomach rumbled.

Abbey mentioned she was the lead on this event, but Jenny was clearly a control freak. She rushed around, shouting orders and muttering under her breath, causing Lucy and Abbey to exchange glances while laughing like children. Soon, the hall looked neat, tidy, and inviting. It would only be a few more minutes before kids would file through the doors, leaving a trail of butter, syrup, and sprinkles in their wake.

Lucy wanted to stay and watch the kids' reactions to the hall. But she wasn't ready to face Aidan. Her stomach flipped at the very thought.

Shoving those feelings away, she taped the final rainbow to the wall, stepping back to admire their decorating skills.

"Cheesy enough?" Abbey stood next to her, head tilted as she assessed the wall. "I think so."

Lucy envied Abbey's carefree attitude; she always appeared calm and laid-back. But, maybe it was all a façade, a front she needed the world to perceive. Lucy knew her sister was in pain, but Abbey had a remarkable ability to hide her genuine emotions behind a smile.

"You sure you don't want to stay? Kaylee would love it."

Lucy shook her head. "Can't. I need to work."

Abbey nodded. "Mm-hm, work."

Lucy glared. "Are you mocking me?"

"Yep." Abbey patted her sister's shoulder. "I should make sure they aren't burning the breakfast in there."

Lucy turned back to the nearly empty decoration bin as Abbey headed in the opposite direction. Placing the lid back on top, she pushed it against the wall just as a sharp cry came from inside the kitchen.

"Oh, Jaysus, Áine!" Jenny shouted, bursting from the kitchen just as Abbey pulled open the door. "Oh, sorry, Abbey."

"Áine, are you okay?" Abbey asked as Áine rushed past her, clutching a damp cloth to her arm.

Jenny let out a sigh, replying before Áine could say a word. "She burned her arm on the grill. I'm sure it looks worse than it is, but she wants to go to A&E."

Lucy gave Abbey a questioning look.

"Accident and Emergency, the ER," Abbey said.

Lucy nodded. "Sounds painful."

"It is," Áine replied sharply, glaring at Jenny.

"Yes, of course." Jenny waved her hand as if scooting Áine out the door. "We're short a parent now; two others have already called out. It will be a struggle to keep up."

"I'm sorry," Áine muttered, directing her apology toward Abbey.

Abbey shook her head sympathetically as if it wasn't as big of a deal as Jenny was making it out to be. Áine gave a small smile and headed out the door. Instantly, Jenny and Abbey turned their gaze to Lucy.

A hard stone crashed into the pit of her stomach.

"Please tell me you can stay," Jenny pleaded. "I know you

volunteered for decorations only, but I need one more cook."

Lucy's eyes lit up. Cook? In the kitchen where no one could see her?

"I can flip pancakes."

Jenny clapped her hands together. "Oh, thanks a mill. You're a star. Get in there, and Siobhán will set you up."

Lucy tilted her head toward Abbey, staring at her with wide eyes. "What did I just agree to?"

"You're as white as a ghost," Abbey commented. "Look, I'll be out here helping the kids. I'll make sure *you know who* doesn't set foot in the kitchen."

Lucy placed her open palms together in a silent prayer. "Thank you."

Abbey looked at her sternly. "You should talk to him."

"I know." Lucy looked down. "Just not today, okay?"

Abbey nodded as Lucy moved past her into the kitchen. Her heart fluttered as memories flooded back, reminding her of the last time she was in this small room. Halloween. The day things almost got out of hand with Aidan. Her thighs tingled, remembering his hands skimming along her delicate skin as they kissed.

"You're taking Áine's place?" one of the ladies interrupted her thoughts.

Lucy hoped her cheeks weren't as bright red as they felt. "Yes."

"Ah, grand, you can take over this grill," she pointed with a spatula. "Sorry, I'm Siobhán, and you're Lucy, right? Abbey's sister."

Lucy nodded as Siobhán introduced her to the other helpers, Ciara, Niamh, and Sinéad, the woman from the hallway at the parent-teacher meeting. She felt her face heating up all over again; the last thing she wanted to think about was that awkward meeting when she first realized Aidan was her one-night stand. Quickly, she turned to the empty grill and busied herself, pouring batter in small circles.

Within minutes, they fell into a steady rhythm. Ciara and Niamh mixed batter while Siobhán and Lucy ran the griddles. Sinéad was in charge of grilling sausages. The conversation flowed easily as they discussed families, careers, and travel plans for the upcoming spring break.

As she flipped the bubbling pancakes over, Lucy realized she had never had a good group of girlfriends. Aside from Sherry and Norbert, Lucy had no friends in high school. The friendship with Norbert died off once they stopped sleeping together. When she met Jeremy, he became her whole world. She quit her job at the gas station and stopped hanging out with Sherry altogether.

From the moment they met, her life revolved around Jeremy. Once Kaylee entered the picture, her priorities changed to make her daughter the center of her world. She never stayed in one place long enough to develop healthy friendships; honestly, she didn't know how.

Talking with these women, she longed for deeper connections. She wanted to do more than live in the community; she wanted to be part of it. Abbey was her best friend, and she loved how their relationship grew stronger each day, but she needed other friends, too. It would be nice to find like-minded women to talk with or even find other single mothers to exchange war stories with.

Abbey was forever talking about the Parents' Association

and how she had bonded with several of the ladies. For Abbey, it was more than just a monthly meeting; these ladies were her friends. They got together for coffee mornings and went out for dinner or drinks. It all sounded so lovely. Maybe she should stop making excuses and join the committee herself.

Prickles dotted her skin as Aidan floated to the forefront of her mind.

No. It wasn't the *thought* of him; it *was* him.

As she flipped another batch of pancakes, his voice echoed through the hall. Funny, she hadn't noticed any other teacher even though children had been filing through the hall all morning. It was as if her body was attuned to him. Every nerve responded to the vibration of his voice. This wasn't quite the expected reaction; she figured he would come and go without her noticing.

"Hiya, Abbey, how are ya?"

Aidan was right outside the kitchen door.

Lucy's heart hammered in her chest, and she tried to control her breathing. She could picture Abbey blocking the door and then steering him away.

She hated how he still had this effect on her. Her heart begged her to stop fighting and give in to her feelings. It was difficult to ignore the fairytale playing through her mind. She imagined a love song playing in the background, probably something by Taylor Swift. Aidan would push open the door, and in a cinematic moment, their eyes would lock. Time would slow down, and in perfect sync, they would embrace each other, lips locking in a passionate kiss. Rain droplets would sprinkle over their faces as the students cheered and clapped loudly from behind them, with a smiling Kaylee leading the applause.

It was far too late for any of that now. There was certainly no room for fairy tales or happy endings to this story. Her hands shook as she flipped a pancake, only to toss it directly onto her foot. Batter oozed over the toe of her shoe.

Sinéad nudged Lucy's shoulder with her own. "Just give that one to the kids."

Lucy's jaw dropped.

Sinéad laughed. "I'm only kidding."

Lucy bent down, scooped up the half-cooked pancake, and dropped it into the rubbish bin. Setting the spatula into the sink, she grabbed a towel and mopped the batter off her foot the best she could.

Sinéad washed the spatula and handed it back to Lucy.

"Thanks," she grumbled. "Maybe I need more coffee?"

"It's hard, isn't it?" Sinéad said sympathetically. "Trying to organize everything for these kids and doing it all on your own? Some days, there isn't enough tea in the world to get me through."

Lucy gave a faint appreciative smile, turning back to her grill. She forced herself to concentrate on each step: pour the batter, laugh at jokes, flip the pancake, and place it on the platter. Repeat.

The door creaked behind them.

Lucy's spine stiffened; she knew Aidan was standing in the doorway. Trying to hide the tremble in her wrist, she stared at the steaming pancakes, praying they wouldn't need to be turned until he left.

"Thanks, Ladies." His voice was warm and gentle. "The

kids loved the pancakes."

"Did you get some?" Ciara asked.

Aidan laughed. "I ate a few."

Lucy's knees threatened to buckle at the sound of his laugh. She missed that laugh. But it was greater than that; she missed his smile, his face, the way he looked at her as if she were the only person on earth. It was becoming more than she could bear, and she silently prayed he would leave. She *needed* him to go before she physically fell apart.

The pancakes smoked on the griddle; if she waited much longer to flip them, they would burn.

Feeling his gaze burning into her back, Lucy focused all her attention on the pancakes. Slowly, she moved the spatula under one bubbling pancake and turned it over.

Success!

She continued going with small, slow movements until all the pancakes were successfully tossed over.

The door closed with an almost silent click, but to Lucy, it might as well have been a gong's echoing chime.

Aidan was gone.

Her shoulders drooped forward as guilt washed over her. It hadn't been fair to ghost him like that. Aidan had done nothing wrong, and he deserved better. Their relationship was not serious, but she should have been an adult and ended things with a conversation. Instead, she buried her head in the sand and pretended their time together meant nothing.

"He's so nice," Sinéad said, pulling Lucy back into the moment. "Cute too. I wonder if he's single?"

"Geez, Sinéad, is the ink even dry on your divorce

papers?" Siobhán took on a matronly condensing tone.

Sinéad shrugged. "Calm down. Is it a crime to look? I'm still a hot-blooded woman."

Sinéad raised her eyebrows at Lucy and nudged her shoulder as if they were partners in crime.

"You can't date a teacher anyway," Siobhán added as if she were the authority on the issue.

Lucy's throat grew dry.

"Who says?" Sinéad placed the last of the sausages onto her grill. "Seriously, are there rules against it?"

Siobhán stopped mixing batter and looked at Sinéad, a frown creasing her forehead. "You can't be serious."

"Ah, com'on, I'm not saying I plan on actively pursuing a teacher," Sinéad said, lifting her eyebrows to the sky. "But, since you seem to be the expert, is it realistically off the table? Or is it simply discouraged?"

A light crimson crept up Lucy's neck. Her ears perked up to hear the answers as she moved pancakes from the grill to the serving plate as if uninterested.

"Surely the dating pool isn't so dried up you can only find someone here." Siobhán scoffed, a hand flying to her chest in shock. "It's a bit—desperate."

"Dating is hard." Ciara jumped in. "I hardly have a night out with my husband. I can't imagine trying to juggle single parenthood and dating."

"And you would want to complicate that by dating a teacher?" Siobhán wasn't giving an inch. "How would that look? How do you think your daughter would feel? Her classmates would no doubt tease her to no end."

Sinéad rolled her eyes. "Wow, tell us how you really feel."

Siobhán lifted her palms in defeat. "I'm just saying it's a horrible idea. We haven't even covered how awkward things would get if the relationship ended badly. It sounds messy to me."

"It was all hypothetical," Sinéad promised her. "Aidan's cute, but I'm sure he has his pick of much younger women with less baggage. But, a girl can have a wild fantasy now and again, can't she?"

Jenny burst through the door carrying a bin of dirty dishes. "The last class just sat down. We can stop cooking and start the cleanup." She took the final platter of steaming pancakes and browned sausages. "Lucy, thanks a mill for stepping in. If you need to go, we can finish up. I know you have work."

Lucy was grateful for the chance to escape; she couldn't take much more of the current conversation.

"I do need to get going," she said, wiping her hands on a towel. "I can help with these dishes first?"

Sinéad waved her off. "We've got it. You get going."

"It was great to meet you all," Lucy said as she gathered her things.

"You too," Ciara replied.

"Thanks for your help," Siobhán said.

"See ya at the next one." Sinéad gave a wink.

Lucy hurried out of the kitchen and searched the room for Abbey. Abbey, who was chatting with a few adults, looked up and gave her the "call me" signal with her finger and thumb.

Lucy nodded and rushed out of the hall, anxious to get out of the school and back into the safety of her new home.

Pausing just outside the door, she set her purse down and shrugged into her jacket. Her nerves were shot, and she couldn't stop shaking. Why had Sinéad started asking all those questions? Was she interested in Aidan? A cold, hard knot of jealousy formed in her stomach.

She couldn't forget the tone in Siobhán's voice as she snapped at Sinéad for even thinking about dating a teacher. Lucy had never considered how a relationship with Aidan might affect the other parents. She had gone round and round, contemplating its various effects on Kaylee, but never thought about other parents judging her. Not that it mattered now; there was no relationship. She had bombed that bridge clear out of the water.

Slinging her purse over her shoulder, she headed toward the double doors leading outside. Her brain immediately kicked into work mode; checking her messages was probably a good idea. She pushed through the door with her shoulder while pulling her phone from the purse. Focusing on the phone, she didn't notice someone entering the building as she exited and crashed directly into them.

"Oh, gosh, I'm so sorry," Lucy mumbled, fumbling with the phone as it jumped from her hands.

Catching the phone mid-air, she glanced up at her victim. Aidan.

Of course, it had to be Aidan.

Her cheeks flushed, and her mouth hung open; words escaped her vocabulary.

"You alright there?" he said stiffly, his expression stoic. There was no usual twinkle in his eyes and no smile creasing his lips.

"Ye-yes," she croaked, automatically clearing her throat.

"How'er ya keeping?" His tone sounded clipped as if he asked out of the politeness that came with Irish culture rather than genuinely wanting to know.

Lucy forced herself to speak the words thundering through her brain. "Fine. You?"

"Not great," he answered flatly. "We should talk." He sighed but rushed on before she could interrupt. "Not here, of course, but soon. I have some things to say to ya, and I'd like to know you've received the message." He took a breath and glanced briefly down at his hands. When he looked back at her, his eyes blazed. "I can text or email if you can't stand my presence, but you'll need ta unblock me first."

Pain tore through her gut as if it had been ripped open. She stared at her feet, unable to look him in the eye. Of course, he would be fully aware she had blocked him and was now avoiding him.

"I won't beg; I'm only askin' for some respect," he said curtly. "How about ya message me when you're ready to act like a grown-up? If ya don't get in touch, that's yar choice. I can keep me final thoughts to meself."

The words sliced like a knife as he moved around her and into the building. Tears burned at the back of her eyes. Maybe he cared more than she had given him credit for. But, it had been childish on her part to cut him out without saying a word.

He couldn't possibly have anything nice to say to her at this point, but she owed him a chance to say his peace before the final goodbye, no matter how much it stung.

With her head down, she rushed out the school gates,

gulping in fresh air as if low on oxygen. Her heart ached more than she wanted to admit to anyone, least of all herself. There had been nothing but pain, sadness, and anger in his eyes.

Confusion muddied her thoughts, but it wasn't surprising; she knew little about genuine relationships. Men had come and gone in her life since she was a child, never once explaining their behavior or caring how she felt. The fling with Aidan wasn't supposed to mean anything. He was the one who didn't want a serious relationship; casual was his idea. Why would he be so hell-bent on gaining closure? She thought she had made things easy by walking away.

Had she read the entire situation wrong? Abbey suggested Aidan wanted more, that he had simply gone the casual route as a way to keep seeing her. Lucy's heart skipped a beat.

Aidan was right in saying Lucy needed to grow up. As much as she told herself Aidan meant nothing to her, the truth was she was head over heels in love with him. Whatever they said at the beginning of this fling no longer mattered; her feelings had evolved. It would be impossible to get over him until she admitted to both of them how she felt.

It was time to lay all the cards on the table; if he rejected her, at least then she could let him go. But, as long as there was a thread of hope for them, she would always wonder.

If Aidan wanted to talk to her, she was ready to listen. No matter the cost. She would risk everything to face him, even if his words broke her heart. It was time to lay her emotions bare, and if that meant crumbling and crying at his feet, it was worth the risk.

Lucy paced the living room feeling like a nervous child on the first day of school. Anxiety mixed with anticipation coursed through her veins, and if she couldn't get things under control, she would wear a hole in the carpet.

It had taken her two days to work up the nerve to unblock his phone number. Then, another two days to send the first message. While she was dying to know what he had to say, she dreaded the harsh words he would rain down on her. She hoped, at the very least, they could move past all the hurt and stay friends. If they ever were friends.

It would have been easy to talk via text messages, but she needed to see him. She wanted him to see the pain in her eyes, the uncertainty creasing her brow, and the desire she could no longer keep at bay.

Clutching her phone, she read back through their conversation from a few days ago.

Lucy: I'm ready.

She sent that first text, unsure where to start.

Aidan: OK

Lucy smiled faintly.

Lucy: Can we meet in person?

Aidan: I'm free on Friday.

Lucy: I moved. I have my own place now. Would you like to come here? I can make dinner.

Lucy remembered biting her lower lip, nervous about the response. She stared at the phone screen. It reminded her of the old saying, "A watched pot never boils." That saying needed an update, "a watched phone never rings."

Aidan: I'll call in on Friday. I won't stay long. Send me the Eir Code.

Her heart still squeezed at the final message. He wanted nothing more than to say his peace and be gone.

Lucy checked her reflection for at least the twentieth time. Dressed in jeans and a plain white t-shirt, she intended to keep the vibe casual. The last thing she wanted was to come across as desperate.

Abbey, well aware of this *meeting*, as Lucy now called it, took Kaylee for the night. There had been plenty of innuendos from Abbey, but Lucy figured she would spend tonight crying into some Ben & Jerry's while watching a cheesy rom-com.

The knock on the door sent a ripple of nervous energy through her veins. Her hands shook as she reached for the handle.

Aidan stood in the hallway, his hair a disheveled mess as if he had run his hands through it the entire journey. He glanced up briefly and gave a tight-lipped nod.

"How're ya?" His eyes dropped down to her feet. She

could tell he was nervous, too.

"Alright," she managed to mumble, swallowing over the lump in her throat. Stepping back, she softly said, "Please come in."

He gave another short nod and stepped into her home. The electricity was back; she could feel the intensity between them, setting every nerve on edge. Her body's reaction was so strong she felt forced to grip the doorknob just to stay grounded.

Lucy swiftly closed the door, took a deep breath, and turned to face Aidan. It was now or never. Aidan seemed preoccupied with assessing the living room. He ran a hand along the back of the couch while taking in the small sitting area and TV arrangement. He continued moving toward the balcony, pulling back the curtain and checking the view.

"Nice place. Lucky to 'ave found somethin' in this area."

His tone was cordial and business-like, as if he was here to make a deal and not discuss the downfall of their relationship.

"My sister lives just across the way." Lucy tried to control the tremor in her voice. "I can see straight into her back garden."

"Ay." He dropped the curtain, keeping his back to her. "What happened?"

The words came out in a whisper.

Lucy lost all train of thought. "What happened with Abbey? Nothing, we just—."

"Not with Abbey," he interrupted, his voice barely audible. "With us."

Lucy's face flushed. Of course, he wouldn't care about her

personal life; that wasn't why he came today.

Her spine stiffened, and she nervously gnawed at her lip. Her mind raced with a thousand excuses and reasons for her behavior. Finally, she settled on the truth.

"I guess I got scared."

Aidan turned slowly, his eyebrows furrowed as he studied her face. Lucy moved toward the back of the couch, dropping her gaze and running her fingers along the soft fabric, unable to make eye contact as she awaited his response.

"That wasn't the answer I was expectin'." His tone softened but still held its edge. "I was expectin' loadsa excuses like work is too busy, moving is hard, or it was fun, but you're borin'."

Lucy couldn't help but crack a small smile. Glancing up through her lashes, she was disappointed to find Aidan's face stoic.

"You're not boring," Lucy sighed. "Look, it's not you, it's me, but for real, not just the cliché. The truth is I'm scared, and I'm a big 'ol chicken. I come with a massive amount of baggage and heartache. I have a long history of bad decisions. And I'm really good at running away. That's sort of how I ended up here, in Ireland."

Aidan rubbed a hand over his chin. "What are you so afraid of, Lucy?"

Lucy shrugged, turning her focus to a small piece of thread hanging from the couch's stitching. How was she supposed to answer that? She closed her eyes, searching for the words to make him understand her feelings.

"I thought ya just wanted fun," Aidan said, stepping

closer to the couch. "Come 'ere, if ya wanted to end things, ya coulda just said so. You didn't have to block me and treat me as if I didn't exist. I thought we were a little closer than that."

Lucy shook her head and let out a small laugh of embarrassment. "I know, it was childish."

"So, why didn't ya just talk to me?" Aidan's expression changed; the serious composure fell away. He looked across at her, eyes pleading for an answer as if he knew she was hiding the truth.

She pursed her lips together and inhaled through her nose. "Because I wanted more!" she exclaimed, dropping her gaze back to the loose thread.

"What?" His face scrunched in confusion.

"You heard me," she mumbled, toying with the thread.

"But, ya wanted casual," his voice grew louder. "That was the first thing ya said to me. You weren't ready for anythin' serious."

"No!" Lucy glared at him, a fire igniting inside her. Her fingers dug into the back of the couch, and she forced her voice to remain steady. "*You* wanted causal. *I* didn't want anything. *I* tried to walk away."

Aidan huffed out a breath, which sounded like a laugh. "I only said that 'cause ya looked scared." He gave her a once over. "Similar to how ya look now."

Lucy rolled her eyes. "I was scared, and I'm still scared."

Aidan ran a hand through his hair, turning from her to walk back toward the window. "Maybe the suggestion was half-mad at the time, but I liked ya and wanted a chance to get to know ya better. Plus, we're pretty good at the bedroom stuff, and I wasn't ready to give that up." He hung his head as if suddenly bashful. "Aside from that, I didn't want to jump straight into a relationship either, but I hoped we could figure that part out together in time. Instead, ya—."

"Panicked?" Lucy finished. "Ran away screaming?"

He turned to face her. "Yeah. So, again, what happened?"

"I don't know," Lucy sputtered. "Everything was great and fun, but then—then—."

"Then what?" His fists clenched tightly against his thighs. "Tell me what I did."

"I started falling in love with you." The words were out before she could stop them. Lucy slapped a hand over her mouth, half praying he hadn't heard.

Aidan's jaw dropped, his gaze locking in stunned disbelief.

Lucy's heart thumped frantically in her chest, the pressure building in her lungs, turning each breath into an agonizing effort. It felt as if she stood on a cliff's ledge, balancing on one leg. Aidan could reach out and save her or run in the opposite direction as she toppled over the edge.

All she wanted to do was take the words back, but she couldn't. This was the most honest she had ever been with anyone. There was no point in holding back; she needed to lay it all out.

"I couldn't get you off my mind," she said, concentrating on the dark shades of material covering the couch. "I thought about you day and night. When I was with you, I didn't want to leave, and when I was away, all I could think about was seeing you again. It was too much, too intense, and I know you didn't feel the same way."

Aidan didn't respond. Lucy slowly glanced up to meet his eyes blazing into her.

"That isn't what you want," she whispered, swallowing hard.

Aidan cocked his head to one side. "You have no idea what I want, Lucy Saunders."

His voice came out in a husky baritone as if holding back the floodgates of emotion raging inside him. Lucy expected him to start yelling at any moment. Tears burned the back of her eyes; the last thing she wanted was to have a complete breakdown in front of him. The only way to keep herself from crying was to continue talking.

She broke eye contact, searching the back of the couch for the rogue string to occupy her hands. "I'm afraid of a broken heart. I'm scared you're only interested in sex, and when you get bored of that, you'll be done with me. I thought I was okay with casual, but I want more than just sex. It's not enough for me, and I don't believe it ever was.

"I hate feeling so strongly about you, yet I mean nothing to you. You hardly speak to me outside the bedroom, as if my presence annoys or embarrasses you. I'm jealous when you flirt with other women in front of me or go out with your friends. I don't even know your friends."

"Hold on!" Aidan interrupted her, stepping closer. "Slow down a minute; I can't keep up. Do you honestly think I don't feel anything for you? And I never *see* you outside the bedroom, so how am I supposed to talk to you? You never come to the school; you're the one constantly avoiding me."

"I came to the school." Lucy snapped her head up in defiance. "The day after Thanksgiving, after you went to the bar with your friends. You remember that night? I came to your place; we had good sex, amazing sex. And the next day, you snubbed me."

"What are you on about?" Aidan looked genuinely confused.

"I dropped off Kaylee; I was giddy with excitement to see you again." Lucy felt anger surge through her. "You hardly acknowledged me. I think you gave me a nod. A nod! To the woman you just had sex with. That seems pretty emotionless to me."

Aidan laughed. "Are you being serious?"

"Very." Lucy stuck out her chin stubbornly.

"Ah, Chicken," Aidan laughed again. "What'd ya have me do? I've been half-mad about ya from the moment I met ya. I never see ya in the daytime. It took me off guard, and I could hardly run across the yard and kiss ya. I was holding back because I had ta."

Lucy felt foolish; that was precisely what Abbey had told her.

"And if you want to meet me, mates, you coulda just asked," he continued. "I didn't think that qualified as casual, though."

"Clearly, I want more than casual," Lucy mumbled. "I want something deeper and more stable."

Lucy felt utterly vulnerable, as if she had sliced open a vein and couldn't control the bleeding. She turned from the couch, pacing the area beside it.

"I've traveled the States, partied way too much, slept with too many people, and had more than my share of hangovers. I'm a hot mess but at a huge turning point in my life. I'm ready to settle down. I want Friday nights on the couch with Kaylee. And I want someone in my life to share all the adventures and laughs with. I don't want to wake up with a head full of regrets and nothing to show for it."

Aidan opened his mouth to speak but closed it when Lucy carried on.

"Speaking of Kaylee, what would she think of us dating? Not that we are, but if we did. I mean, how awkward would that be for her? The teenage years are hard enough without your peers picking on you."

"Yar making my head spin with all these thoughts," Aidan managed to interrupt her rant.

Lucy giggled nervously, shaking her head. "I've been doing a lot of deep thinking lately. I guess I just wanted to share it all with you, you know, in the name of honesty or something."

Aidan leaned a hip against the back of the couch. "Well, don't stop on account of me. This is the deepest conversation we've ever had, and I'm enjoying it."

"It's humbling," Lucy replied, dropping her eyes. "I feel raw and vulnerable."

Aidan gave a half-smile. "I like knowing what you're thinking, even if you're wrong."

Lucy laughed nervously. "I'm wrong?"

Aidan pushed off the couch and stepped toward her. Finally, a smug smile creased his lips. "You're wrong about what *I* want."

She couldn't breathe as he stepped closer, standing directly in front of her. He reached out and lightly grazed her arm. Shivers ran through her body, and goosebumps covered her skin.

His breath tickled her ear as he whispered, "I never wanted to be just casual with ya."

She shifted, turning her face toward him. Their lips grazed briefly, sending every fear and worry out the window. All she wanted, in this moment, was him, and damn the consequences.

Their lips locked in a passionate kiss, the desire and need for one another as strong as a magnetic pull refusing to be severed. Instinctively, her arms wrapped around his neck, and she tucked her body tightly against his. The way they fit together so perfectly felt natural as if they were handmade for one another.

One hand cupped her face, softly caressing her cheek before sliding back to intertwine in her hair. Tingles shot through her body as pent-up emotions sparked to life.

Aidan broke the kiss, cupping her face in his hands. His bright blue eyes searched hers as she panted breathlessly.

"I missed you," he murmured, stroking one cheek with the pad of his thumb. "I wish you had just talked to me."

"I was scared and stupid," she whispered, her voice trembling.

His expression turned serious, and his voice deepened. "I want ya pretty bad right now."

Her eyelids felt heavy with arousal. "Me too."

Instead of kissing her again, he untangled from their embrace and stepped back.

Lucy froze, a hard knot forming in the pit of her stomach.

"As much as I want you, I got a few things to say first." His eyes smoldered. "I git that you've been hurt and you're scared, but so am I. I was caught off guard, too. I didn't think I would ever see after that one night together, but then, there you were, in the meetin' room. A parent to one of my students. I was just as shocked as you were, but I had to finish my *work* day. You got to go home and process all those feelings. I'm sorry if I came across as cold or unfeeling; I promise you, inside a fire was ragin'.

"I thought after our second night together, surely that would git you outta me system. But it didn't. As soon as you started ranting about relationships, I panicked. You're right; casual was my idea, and it was stupid. I never wanted that, and I hoped that after some time, you wouldn't want that either."

It was Aidan's turn to pace.

"I should have—."

"Wait," Aidan stopped her. "I'm not done yet."

Lucy nodded, chewing on her bottom lip to keep from speaking.

"What I didn't expect was how horrible you would treat me."

Lucy's eyes snapped up to meet his, her mouth opening in protest.

Aidan held up a finger to quiet her and continued. "You did, Lucy. Maybe horrible is a poor choice of words, but it's how I felt. You think I only wanted sex, but *you* were the one who ran off as soon as we finished. I never asked you to leave; most of the time, I was beggin' ya to stay, but ya always rushed out and made *me* feel like the one being used for sex."

Lucy suddenly felt weak. She dug her fingers into the back of the couch to steady herself.

"And when I finally got up the nerve to confess how much I missed ya, ya ghosted me. Completely shut me off. Blocked me. You broke me heart, Lucy."

Tears burned at the back of her eyes, and a wave of guilt crashed over her heart. Slowly, she walked around the couch and sat on the edge of the cushion.

"Oh, Aidan," she whispered, her voice shaking.

"I haven't been able to eat or sleep or properly function," Aidan continued, moving around the couch toward her. "I think about you all the time. And you didn't even acknowledge me at the Saint Paddy's breakfast. I know you knew I was standing there, but ya kept cooking pancakes and never turned around."

"I couldn't face you," Lucy said; her voice broke, and a tear slid from one eye.

Aidan sat on the couch next to her, his face crumpled. "If I acted like I didn't care, it was because I was willing to be wit ya no matter the cost. Even when I thought *you* were the one who didn't care."

"I was guarded," Lucy mumbled. "Too guarded. I never wanted to hurt you."

"You did," Aidan said matter-of-factly.

"I'm sorry." Lucy reached across to touch his face lightly. "I should have been honest. I'm so used to being the one who gets hurt; it never crossed my mind that I was hurting you."

"That's why I wanted to tell ya in person," Aidan said, grazing the hand still resting on his cheek. "I was angry and hurt. For a few weeks, I didn't ever want to see ya again. But, I couldn't shake ya from me mind, and that made me more angry. Then I realized you probably had no idea how much ya hurt me, because ya didn't know how I felt about ya."

"I thought you would be relieved," Lucy said, dropping her hand onto his thigh. "I felt too much. I didn't know how to handle it. I have massive baggage I need to deal with."

"Where do we go from here?" Aidan asked, intertwining his fingers with hers. "We both admit to wanting more. Is that still what you want?"

"Very much." Lucy smiled up at him. "I want to be with you."

"Good. I don't want to pick up where we left off." Aidan gave her a serious look. "I can't play this hot and cold game anymore. If we're together, then we're together; no ignoring me calls or blocking me. And no more runnin' out in the middle of the night."

Lucy hung her head sheepishly. "That's fair."

Aidan ran a finger along her jawline. "When I make love to ya, I want to wake up next to ya." A mischievous smile played upon his lips. "I hate cold sheets."

"Make love?" Lucy shivered.

"Yes. We're done with casual sex." Aidan straightened his spine. "I want ya, just ya. Let's take a chance on the real thing."

"I don't know—."

Aidan placed his finger on her lips. "Shh, it's all or nothin'. It's as simple as that."

"I don't know if I'm ready—."

Aidan cut her off. "Ya may never know—."

It was Lucy's turn to put a finger against his lips. "As I was trying to say, I don't know if I'm ready, but I'm willing to try."

Aidan's eyes smoldered as he kissed the finger resting on his lips.

Lucy moved toward him, leaning in and kissing him softly. In one swift movement, he pulled her onto his lap. The warmth of his body radiated against her. For a moment, they sat there, locked in an embrace. His lips gently grazed her forehead as he held her.

"Make love to me," Lucy whispered.

Climbing off his lap, she pulled him to stand beside her. She reached for his hand and interlaced their fingers as she led him back to her bedroom.

Standing at the edge of her bed, Lucy turned to face Aidan. The look in his eyes took her breath away. They held a sea of emotions. Desire, but something else too, affection? Adoration? It was hard to put a finger on all the feelings dancing there, but Lucy liked how it made her feel.

Gently, Aidan cupped her chin, tilting it until their lips grazed against each other. A fire ignited inside her; she felt as if sparks would shoot out her fingertips and toes.

Aidan deepened the kiss, moving his hands back to tangle once again in her hair while gently nibbling her lower lip. Fingers caressed the soft skin of her neck as his tongue slid into her mouth.

They sighed simultaneously, and their lips both curled slightly at the gesture.

Lucy ran her hands under his shirt, over his stomach and chest, craving his skin's warmth. Aidan lifted his arms, signaling Lucy to remove the barrier. Returning the favor, Aidan quickly tossed her shirt to the floor, unhooking her bra with a single flick of his fingers.

"Nice," she breathed, breaking the intensity of the moment.

"I've been practicing," he teased, kissing her temple.

Lucy glared at him. "On who?"

"Just me ole blow-up doll." Aidan teased.

Before she could respond, he bent down, grabbed her behind the knees, and flipped her onto the bed. Their lips met again as he gently pressed his body against hers. Running her hands over the soft skin of his shoulders, she felt the skin pimple at each touch. His muscles tensed and relaxed as he moved above her.

Each movement was slow and steady, not the frantic maneuvers of two people engaging in causal, needy sex. Lucy closed her eyes as his hands expertly roamed over her, touching and caressing her body. Aidan knew exactly how to please her; they were no longer fumbling around in unfamiliar territory. She moaned as his hand cupped her breast gently, his lips kissing down her neck, squirming as he hit each tender spot, sending her blood boiling.

Aidan moved off her just long enough to remove the rest of their clothing. Her jeans and panties hit the floor as he tugged his pants off.

"Beautiful," he breathed, kissing her inner thighs. "I missed you so much."

"Same." Lucy struggled to get the single word out.

Her fingers twisted in hair as he continued kissing up her thighs. Her back arched as his tongue found the creases and folds between her legs. Unable to hold back, small gasps escaped her lips as the first climax ripped through her.

As she struggled to catch her breath, Aidan kissed his way

up her body, lightly tracing his lips along the sensitive skin of her belly, teasing his way around the outline of her breasts. Taking one of her perked nipples in his teeth; he sent her gasping for air all over again.

Lucy raked her fingers along the muscles in his back. She needed to feel him, know this moment was real; she ran her hands over his back, sliding down his spine to cup and squeeze his buttocks.

He groaned into her neck, taking a break from the trail of kisses he planted along her jawline. Finding her lips, he lowered his body between her thighs. The warm, slick skin of his chest grazed against her nipples, sending a thrill down her spine.

Lucy felt like she was floating, and a cheesy grin crossed her face. Never had she wanted a man more than in this moment. Sliding her hand between their thighs, she lightly stroked his shaft, gently wrapping her fingers around his girth to lightly stroke.

"Oh, my days," he groaned, breaking their kiss.

Lucy smiled as she toyed with the soft flesh of this foreskin. "I love when you say that," she whispered.

Aidan looked down at her, his eyes dark and intense with desire. For a minute, they stayed lost in the other's gaze. She silently prayed he would always look at her this way.

With her hand still wrapped around him, she moved his uncut tip to lightly caress her opening. They both sucked in a breath as she released her hold, leaving his tip to tease her lower lips.

"Yar so beautiful." The look in his eyes couldn't deny the truth in his words.

He reached down to grip her wrists and extended both her arms over her head, interlacing their fingers, as he slid inside her. Lucy threw back her head; her eyes closed to concentrate fully as waves of pleasure began to build. Squeezing his hands, she cried out as the waves crashed over and over.

A sheepish grin crossed her face. "Sorry, that was a bit unexpected," she whispered.

Aidan panted. "That was the hottest thing I ever seen."

Taking her mouth with his, he began to move again. Her legs tightened around his waist as they moved in sync. Releasing one hand, she stroked and scratched lightly along his back. A low groan rumbled deep in his chest.

He squeezed the hand he still held. His kisses grew in intensity as their movements quickened. Breathing raggedly, he pulled his mouth from hers and let out a low growl. In a quick maneuver, he rolled them over, flipping her up to straddle him. Wiggling his eyebrows, he scanned her body, hungrily taking in every part of her. Still buried inside her, he gripped her hips, guiding them into steady movements that caused his eyes to roll back.

A passionate fire burned between her thighs. She felt both powerful and vulnerable at the same time. Powerful and sexy enough to drive him wild. Vulnerable because her body was entirely on display. She shouldn't have felt self-conscious; Aidan always looked at her as if she were a supermodel. A wave of raw desire cascaded through her as her body took control.

Aidan released his grip on her hips to explore her body greedily. Ripples of pleasure surged like tiny shocks of electricity with each touch. She sucked in a breath as the pad of his thumb found the swollen nub between her thighs, massaging it gently.

Leaning back, Lucy gripped his thighs, arching her back as her climax claimed every nerve. Fireworks shot behind her eyes, and she yelled out his name.

As the intensity continued, Aidan grabbed her hips again, urging her to keep up the current pace. Sleepily, she looked down at him, thrilled by the pleasure etched across his face. Gathering her strength, she continued moving until the orgasm ripped through him.

He pulled her down to greedily kiss her. Breathlessly, she released him and slid down to curl up next to him. They were both sweaty and completely spent. Lucy never wanted this moment to end.

"I forgot to mention one thing," he said once he finally caught his breath. "I think I'm falling in love with ya, too."

22

The hot water streamed down her body, washing away the remnants of a passionate night. As she rinsed the shampoo from her hair, she found it impossible to wipe the smile from her face. Last night had been the first time she had completely given herself to a man, not just her body but her heart.

She had been so foolish in her attempts to push Aidan away, wasting time they could have been together. While Aidan had understood her initial reluctance, he still had the guts to call her out on her crap. She wrongfully projected her fears and past heartache onto Aidan, and he didn't deserve that.

Between their lovemaking, they talked, sharing stories from their past and connecting on a deeper level. Aidan's childhood was one she had always dreamed of. His parents were still together, and although his siblings had their share of rivalries, the family remained close. Aidan had seemed shocked by tales of her childhood, which were so different from the life he had always believed everyone experienced.

Talking about her family led straight into the tale of Jeremy. Although she hadn't planned on sharing that part of her life this early in their relationship, she wanted him to understand that her heart had been damaged and still needed time to heal.

She stepped from the shower and grabbed a white fluffy towel from its hook. As she wiped the condensation off the mirror, a whiff of bacon teased her nostrils, causing her mouth to water and her stomach to growl.

"A man who cooks," she mumbled, nodding at her reflection in a congratulatory manner.

Back in the adjoining bedroom, she pulled a pair of yoga pants off the back of a chair and rummaged around the drawers for a t-shirt. There was no sense bothering with a bra; if the morning went as planned, it would only be in the way.

Pulling a comb through her hair, she padded barefoot into the kitchen. "What's all this?"

She continued combing her hair as she sat at the center island, watching Aidan.

"Pancakes on the griddle, bacon in the pan, and coffee brewing." Aidan used the spatula to point as he spoke. "I figure we worked up an appetite."

Lucy smiled, dipping her head to hide the scarlet rising from her neck. Butterflies fluttered in her stomach, and she hoped to always feel this way around him.

Aidan pulled a mug from the cupboard and filled it with steaming coffee. He added a teaspoon of sugar and a dash of Oat Milk and offered her the cup.

"You know how I like it?" Lucy gave him a quizzical look and took the mug from his hands.

A twinkle danced in his eyes. "I pay attention."

"I was an idiot," she said quietly, looking down into her coffee. "All this time, I thought it was just about sex for you. You called me out pretty harshly last night."

Adian shrugged. "I was hurt, and you needed to know why."

She glanced up at him shyly. "I know. Thank you. I needed to hear it. Sometimes, the truth is brutal, especially since I had no idea I did anything wrong. I never stopped to consider how you were feeling or how my actions might hurt you."

"Ah, sure, look," Aidan said. "Everyone gets wrapped up in their insecurities. I think we hurt each other the most by trying to protect ourselves. It's like collateral damage; no one intends on hurtin' the other, but it happens."

"I'm sorry," she said, cradling the hot mug. "I toyed with your emotions, even though it was unintentional."

Aidan turned back to his cooking. "It got us here."

Lucy smiled at the statement. It was true; all her stupid mistakes and setbacks had brought them to this moment. It was funny how life worked sometimes.

She watched Aidan move with ease around her kitchen. He was wearing track pants but hadn't bothered with a shirt. He appeared to belong in this kitchen as if he made breakfast here every morning.

Heat consumed her as her eyes grazed over his back and shoulder muscles. They tightened and relaxed as he flipped pancakes and turned the bacon. Subconsciously, she licked her lips as her gaze lowered to the pants hanging loosely around his waist. His butt looked firm and tight, clenching as he moved from side to side.

Have mercy; this man was hot and setting her entire body on fire. She squirmed in her chair, aching to touch him, to trace the outline of his shoulder blades with her fingertips.

All her nerves began firing at once, arousal coursing through her body. She could no longer stand it; she needed to feel the heat of his skin.

Rising from the chair, she rounded the counter. Unaware of her movements behind him, he stacked pancakes on a plate. A visible shiver ran through him at her delicate touch, tracing her fingertips lightly across his skin.

"I was sitting over there watching you," she whispered, feathering light kisses along his shoulder blades. "I was itching to touch you."

He exhaled, muscles tightening as he gripped the spatula in one hand and the counter in the other.

His skin was warm and soft as she slowly glided her hands along his sides, continuing to plant soft kisses across his back. Pressing her body against him, her hands traveled across his stomach, and he sucked in a breath.

"The pancakes are going to burn," he panted.

"I'm already on fire," she purred, gliding along his pecs while resting a cheek against his back.

Aidan turned off the griddle and grill and set the spatula on the counter.

Lucy hadn't finished her exploration yet. She resumed kissing the skin on his shoulder while tiptoeing her fingers down to the waistband of his loose-fitting pants. Aidan sighed as she slipped one hand into his boxers, fingering the hair she found there.

His knuckles turned white as he tightened his hold on the countertop, his breath coming out in small moans. Lucy took his length in her hand, stroking lightly. He groaned in response.

He whipped around and surprised Lucy, knocking her off balance. She released him and stepped back, but he grabbed her around her waist, steadying her. His eyes smoldered as he lifted her to sit on the counter, pushing apart her thighs to stand between them.

"I want you for breakfast," he said huskily.

Lucy panted, unable to catch her breath as desire coursed through her. Aidan took her mouth roughly, kissing her deeply as her legs wrapped around his waist.

The jangle of the door knob made Lucy's spine stiffen. Breaking the kiss, she slammed a hand against Aidan's chest and froze.

Kaylee shoved the door open and concentrated on disengaging the key that seemed stuck in the lock.

"I had the best time," she said, not looking up from the door. Kaylee struggled with the stubborn key as Lucy frantically disengaged herself from Aidan, shoving him back.

"Lola had a Rugby match and—." Kaylee's eyes widened as she processed the scene before her.

Aidan and Lucy stared at Kaylee, speechless. Aidan was shirtless, and his hair was a mess. Lucy still sat on the counter, her lips plump and her hair wet from the shower.

"Aidan?" Kaylee looked puzzled as she glanced from her teacher to her mom.

"He came for breakfast," Lucy said quickly.

Kaylee's face changed from puzzled to shocked as realization kicked in.

"Oh, good Lord!" Kaylee slapped her hand dramatically over her eyes. "Ew, gross! I need to wash my eyes."

Kaylee whipped around and rushed into her bedroom, closing the door firmly behind her.

Lucy's face turned dark crimson. Jumping off the counter, she opened her mouth, but no words came out.

Aidan began to laugh.

"What's so funny?" Lucy asked, looking at him with a horrified expression. "This isn't funny."

"It's a little funny." He pursed his lips, trying in vain to stop the smile from bursting across his face. "Oh, come on? Wash out her eyes? That's funny."

Lucy cracked a smile. "Teenage dramatics. Oh my gosh, this is awkward."

Aidan pointed at his crotch. "No, that is awkward. Thank goodness I was behind the counter."

Lucy burst out laughing, glancing down at the bulge in his pants. "I'm so sorry. Oh, what do they call that? Coitus interruptus?"

Aidan rolled his eyes. "All good things must come to an end. I should probably leg it on outta here."

"But you didn't eat," Lucy protested.

He waved her comment away. "Ya need to talk to yar daughter, and ya can't do it while I'm here. Besides, I don't want Kaylee feeling uncomfortable for another minute." Aidan kissed her forehead. "Call me later, okay? Whatever it takes, I want this to work."

Lucy sighed, glancing toward her daughter's closed door. "Me too, but—."

"I know, ya need to talk with Kaylee first," Aidan finished. "We don't have to sort it right now. We'll take things slow."

Lucy nodded as Aidan disappeared into her bedroom. He returned, fully dressed and carrying his jacket.

"Promise you'll call." It came out more as a command than a question.

"I promise." Lucy made an X across her chest.

With a final kiss, he left. The instant the door closed behind him, silence filled the apartment. Lucy sank into the bar stool and stared into her lukewarm coffee.

She had known a conversation with Kaylee was inevitable but thought she would have more time. Lucy and Aidan had only reconnected; they had so much to figure out between themselves without dragging Kaylee into the mix. Now that the secret was out, there was no going back. Whether she wanted to or not, Kaylee needed to be included in the conversation.

Last night was amazing. One of the best nights of her life thus far. She had opened herself to another person, willing to be vulnerable and bare her soul without knowing the outcome.

At first, Aidan was angry, and rightly so; she had treated him like a disposable plaything, but he wanted to work things out. He hadn't come over to berate, belittle, or insult her; he came to have an adult conversation. His words had been challenging to hear, but the end result was worth the few minutes of discomfort.

It dawned on her that the argument with Aidan was one of the healthiest conversations she had ever had with a potential love interest. They may have raised their voices and been upset, but there was no screaming, no name-calling, and no one storming out in a rage.

Jeremy had always blamed her for everything that went wrong in their on-and-off relationship. Anytime she tried to talk to him about her feelings, he would gaslight her and leave in a tantrum, making her feel guilty and at fault for things out of her control.

Aidan was the polar opposite of Jeremy. Throughout the night, they chatted about everything. He listened to her and asked questions to gain a deeper understanding. Jeremy only cared about himself and only talked if *he* was the subject matter. Jeremy was over, and she would never return to that life again. She was making great strides in building a new life here, and it was clear that life would include Aidan.

There was only one thing left to do. Talk to Kaylee. This scared Lucy more than her confrontation with Aidan; after all, this man was her daughter's teacher. With one word, Kaylee could bring this house of cards tumbling down. If Kaylee weren't okay with the relationship, it would have to be over.

Kaylee's door creaked open. She popped her head out, eyes darting back and forth like a rabbit during hunting season.

"Is he gone?"

Lucy nodded. "Yes."

"Good, I gotta pee." Kaylee sprinted out of her room and down the hall to the bathroom.

Lucy held back a laugh. "You could have used the toilet."

"Awkward!" Kaylee called from behind the closed door.

Lucy wasn't sure if it was a bad sign Kaylee wasn't comfortable enough to come out of her room with Aidan in the house. Her heart sped up as anxiety threatened to overcome her. She feared this conversation would mark the end of what Lucy had hoped would be the beginning of something extraordinary.

Pushing up from the bar, she moved to the opposite side of the island. The abandoned pancakes sat on a plate, growing cold. Bacon lay in its congealing grease, and batter remained in the mixing bowl. They would need to eat in the next five minutes or toss it all in the trash.

"Smells good in here." Kaylee walked into the kitchen, looking around as if unsure Aidan had gone. "Did you cook all this?"

"Aidan cooked," Lucy said cautiously, tiptoeing into the impending conversation.

"He cooks?" Kaylee looked surprised. "Bonus points. Wait, you haven't eaten any of it. Is it gross?"

Lucy raised her eyebrows. "You walked in before I got the chance." She blew out a breath. "Sorry, Sweetie, that had to be awkward."

"Super awkward," Kaylee agreed, pulling the plate of pancakes toward her.

"Bacon?" Lucy picked up her coffee mug from the counter and set it in the microwave.

"Sure." Kaylee took a small bite of pancake. "Yum, this is really good."

Lucy placed two strips of bacon on a plate and handed it

to Kaylee. Turning back to the microwave, she retrieved her coffee and took a careful sip.

"You should try some pancakes." Kaylee pushed the plate toward her mother.

"I guess I can give it a go, as they say here." Lucy took a bite. "Wow, that is good."

Kaylee began cutting another pancake into bite-sized pieces. "So, I see you took my advice."

"What advice?"

Kaylee gave a sly smile. "Remember, after Halloween, I said I should set you up with Aidan? I was only kidding, you know."

Lucy felt her face flush. "Well—."

Kaylee's eyes widened. "You were already sleeping with him when I said that. That's why you acted so strange."

Lucy stopped chewing and swallowed hard.

"Exactly, how long have you been sleeping with my teacher?"

Lucy coughed. "First of all, it's not what it looks like."

"Oh really?" Kaylee wasn't buying it. "He didn't sleep here last night and then make you breakfast this morning?"

Lucy's shoulders dropped. "Okay, it's exactly what it looks like."

"Yep," Kaylee said. "So, how long has this been going on?"

"Well, that's complicated." Lucy contemplated the best way to explain things. While they had an open relationship, there was still a fine line between parent and child. Kaylee may be wise beyond her years, but she was still only twelve. "We've been on and off for a while; the timeline is murky."

Kaylee's face screwed up in disgust. "I thought you were done with that."

A rock thudded in Lucy's stomach. "Done with what? Men? Dating?"

Kaylee rolled her eyes. "Casual sex," she said bluntly. "The last thing you need is another man coming and going from your life as he pleases."

Waves of guilt flooded over her. Kaylee was observant and knew far too much about her mother's sex life. Lucy shouldn't be surprised. At six years old, she had known more about sex than any television show would ever teach her. She heard the sighs and moans carrying through the thin walls. Of course, Kaylee would have experienced the same thing.

"This is nothing like that, I promise." Lucy reached across and clutched her daughter's hand. "Aidan is nothing like your father."

Kaylee dropped her gaze, absently pushing a piece of pancake around the plate with a fork. Lucy's heart broke. She never wanted her child to feel the pain and abandonment Lucy had known her entire childhood. A father who was all but absent; those few moments Jeremy did come around weren't for Kaylee's benefit but more a means to an end. Kaylee had always seen right through the façade Jeremy displayed.

"What have I done to you?" Lucy sighed heavily. "I tried to protect and shield you, but I never did. I'm sorry your dad is such a loser. I should have chosen better."

Kaylee's eyes flew up to meet her mother's. "Don't blame yourself for Dad's behavior. You tried to make things better and fought hard to make us a family. Dad never wanted to change, and *you* finally found the courage to get us out of there."

Lucy's eyes welled with prideful tears.

"Dad was a jerk to you, Mom. You deserve to be happy. As far back as I can remember, he never made you happy. Honestly, we were both happiest when he wasn't around."

"How did you get so mature?" Lucy said, wiping at her eyes. "I forget you aren't a little kid anymore. And far too perceptive for both our goods."

Kaylee rolled her eyes at the compliment. She took a bite of the pancake she had been toying with. "Does Aidan make you happy?"

Lucy blushed. "I think he does," she said quietly. "I think he could."

"He's a fun teacher, and I think he's a nice guy." Kaylee took another bite. "And these pancakes really are good."

"We could use a good cook around here." Lucy stabbed her fork into one of Kaylee's bite-sized pieces.

Kaylee cut up another pancake. "So, how did this all start? You're never at school. I only saw you talking to him at the Halloween dance."

"There have been a few awkward moments at your school." Lucy smiled.

"Oh?"

"Nothing scandalous," Lucy said quickly. "I first met him at a pub before I knew he was your teacher."

Kaylee looked up thoughtfully, searching her memories. Her mouth dropped open.

"He was the one-night stand!"

Lucy's eyes widened. "How do you know that term?

And—."

Kaylee rolled her eyes. "I'm twelve, Mom; I know a lot of things that would probably shock you."

True. Lucy also knew a lot of shocking things at that age.

"First clue? You didn't come home that night," Kaylee continued. "It was like our third night in Dublin, and we shared a room, remember?"

"I thought you were having a sleepover in Lola's room?"

"We did. " Kaylee nodded. "But Aunt Abbey came home without you. I got up around five to pee; you still weren't home."

Holding her hands up in surrender, Lucy said, "In my defense, if I had known he was your teacher, I would have run in the opposite direction. I honestly thought I would never see him again."

Kaylee burst out laughing, covering her mouth to hide the chewed-up food. "How did you find out?"

Lucy ducked her head. "Parent-teacher meeting. I walked through the door and saw him sitting there. I nearly wet myself."

Kaylee doubled over in laughter, clutching the counter to keep from falling off her stool.

"I made such a fool of myself," Lucy said, joining the laughter and acting out her actions from that day. "I was pacing and stuttering and acting like a trapped bird. It was so embarrassing."

"I wish I could have seen it," Kaylee said between gasps of air. "It was probably similar to the reaction I had, walking in this morning and seeing my teacher half-naked, making out with my mom."

Lucy put her head in her hands. "So embarassing."

They were both laughing now, wiping tears from their eyes.

After a few minutes, Lucy regained her composure and turned serious. "Kaylee, I hope you know you are the most important thing in the world to me. I never want to hurt you or put you in an uncomfortable situation. This thing with Aidan, if it's too weird—."

Kaylee cut her off. "You deserve to be happy, Mom. It is weird, but I like Aidan. He's only my teacher for a few more months. As long as we don't have to announce your dating status to the class, and you aren't making out in the yard, it's fine."

Lucy laughed. "I won't make it awkward. Aidan and I are still figuring things out, but we'll do that far away from your school."

"Mom, I don't know if I've said it before, but thanks for bringing us here."

Lucy smiled across at her daughter. "You're happy enough? I feel guilty for taking you away from your friends and grandma."

"I was unsure at first and pretty scared," Kaylee admitted. "But I think it's better for both of us. You needed Aunt Abbey and Uncle Rob; I haven't seen you laugh like you do with them in a long time. And the kids here are all nice and friendly; I've already made new friends. It feels like home, like we've always lived here."

Lucy nodded. "I feel the same."

"I love this apartment, too," Kaylee added. "It's the first time we've had a space all to ourselves. I'm not worried Dad will walk through the door unannounced and ruin everything."

Lucy's stomach rolled; she didn't know Kaylee dreaded Jeremy's presence about as much as he dreaded being a father.

"I feel safe here," Kaylee continued. "I'm not afraid something bad will happen or scared to go to school. And I love that Lola is close by. We can yell off the balcony to each other."

Lucy laughed as she pictured the two girls carrying on a conversation for the whole neighborhood to hear.

Kaylee pushed up from the table and carried her plate toward the sink. "You should figure things out with Aidan. He's a great catch. He can cook, he's funny, not bad on the eyes, and he'd be a great stepdad."

Lucy's jaw dropped. "Let's not rush things."

Kaylee gave her mom a side hug. "It'll be weird seeing him hanging out here and having his stuff around, but I'll get used to it."

"That means a lot to me," Lucy said. "You're old enough to understand how the world works, and I want to include you in mine. Remember, your wants and needs will always come first no matter what, so talk to me if things get too complicated."

"Deal." Kaylee headed toward her room. "Just remember the walls are thin, so keep it down in there."

"Kaylee!" Lucy brought a hand to her chest.

Kaylee burst into a fit of giggles and walked into her room.

Lucy turned to the sink and began cleaning up. As much

as she had dreaded that conversation with Kaylee, she was glad to finally share her news. Lucy had always tried to communicate openly with her daughter; it was a bond she never had with her mother.

There were so many things she had yet to teach Kaylee in the hopes of steering her onto a more healthy path. From here on out, she would try harder to protect Kaylee from life's struggles, and, if she were lucky, together, they would break the cycle of self-inflicted pain.

One day, in the not-so-distant future, Lucy would share all the horrid stories from her past with Kaylee. From growing up with absent parents to her relationship with Jeremy, Kaylee should know and learn from these stories.

For now, Lucy was ready to start down a new path. It was time to take a chance on love and plunge into a healthy relationship, one where the man and woman love and trust each other equally. Lucy had never experienced that kind of connection before, and although she had no idea what to expect, she was eager to find out.

23

"Knock, knock!" Lucy let herself into Abbey's house.

After their conversation, Rob called and invited Kaylee to join him and Lola for shopping and a movie in Dundrum. As soon as Kaylee was gone, Lucy rushed to Abbey's, anxious to share everything that transpired with Aidan.

"Lucy?" Abbey called from the living room.

"Yeah, hope it's okay to barge in on you." Lucy dropped her purse on the kitchen counter and shook out of her jacket. "I figured we could have some sister time since Rob and Lola were out of the house. Plus, I presumed you'd call me any minute begging for all the dirty details of my talk with Aidan last night."

Lucy walked into the living room and froze. Abbey sat on the couch, shoulders hunched forward. A small pile of balled-up tissue lay strewn across the coffee table.

Lucy rushed toward the couch. "Abbey? What's wrong?"

Abbey sniffed and looked up at her sister. Her eyes were red-rimmed and watery. "Rob and I talked," she whispered

326

before bursting into tears.

Lucy was dumbfounded. She sat beside Abbey on the couch and waited for her to continue.

Abbey held a scrunched-up tissue and wiped it under her nose.

"Sorry, I'm a mess," Abbey said, sniffing.

Lucy reached over and placed her hand on Abbey's knee. "What happened?"

Abbey shrugged. "He came home last night very excited; he got a new promotion. It's a traveling consultant job. He'll be traveling to all your corporate clients, telling them how to improve their IT. Or something like that; I don't speak computer language."

Lucy nodded. "I know what you're saying."

"Good." Abbey huffed out a laugh. "Anyway, I lost it. I couldn't hold back any longer. I explained how we hardly ever see him now, and if he took that promotion, we would spend weeks apart."

Tears filled Abbey's eyes. "You know what he said?"

Lucy bit her lip and shook her head, not sure she wanted to hear the answer.

"He said he already accepted the promotion." Abbey's lip quivered. "He said it wasn't up for discussion. He starts on Monday, leaving in the afternoon for a week. He didn't even talk to me first; he just took the promotion and planned a trip without consulting me."

Lucy's eyes widened; that was bold, even for Rob.

Tears spilled from her eyes and trailed down her cheeks. "That caused a dam to break, and I snapped. We got in a huge fight. Luckily, the girls weren't here. They were invited for ice cream at Julia's house; I hope that's okay."

Lucy waved it away. "Of course."

Abbey shook her head quickly. "Anyway, we fought. I know it was a long time coming, and I should have forced the conversation before, but I was scared. I was scared it would turn into a major blow-up, and it did. It was."

"Oh, Abbey."

"I told him everything," Abbey continued, sniffing. "I asked him if it was too late to change his mind on the promotion. I told him maybe it would be helpful if he was home more."

Abbey paused, shutting her eyes and releasing a waterfall of tears. "He said he didn't want that." Abbey's voice shook. "He didn't want to be home more."

Lucy blew out a breath, grasping Abbey's knee, urging her to keep talking.

"I told him if he went, things would only get worse between us. He agreed. So, I asked him if he even wanted to fix things, and he shrugged. He didn't even give me a proper answer, just a shrug."

Abbey lost control; her shoulders shook as she cried. "I asked if he even cared about me anymore." She struggled to cry and speak simultaneously. "He didn't know."

Dropping her head into her hands, she cried tiny wails she could no longer hold back.

Lucy felt her insides crumble as tears filled her own eyes. All the pain Abbey had tried to hide was finally at the surface and bubbling over. The truth she longed to hide, mostly from herself, was now out in the open. Lucy felt all the pain and sadness right along with Abbey.

"I'm sorry," Lucy said, the only words she could think of.

After a few long moments, Abbey sniffed. Lucy handed her a fresh tissue from the box in the center of the table.

"Thanks," she said quietly. "He left."

"What?" Lucy asked, shocked. "I just saw him."

"Last night," Abbey told her. "He said he couldn't do this anymore. He admitted things were broken between us but didn't know if they were worth fixing. I guess he needed *more* space from me, so he packed a bag and left. He texted this morning that he wanted to spend the day with Lola."

"He came early to take her to her Rugby match. I'm sorry, Kaylee went home early. I told her she could stay, but she wanted to go. I should have warned you, but I was a mess. I didn't sleep at all last night."

"Why didn't you call me?" Lucy asked. "I would have come for Kaylee and Lola, given you the chance to talk more to Rob."

"He was done talking at that point."

"I could have been here for you," Lucy protested. "You know I would have."

Abbey shook her head. "You had your own issues to work through." Abbey took a fresh tissue and blew her nose. "I need to hear all about that, by the way."

"I've done more than my share of talking," Lucy said.

Abbey pushed up from the couch. "No! It's enough for me right now. I've been crying non-stop all morning, going over and over the argument, wondering if I could have said something different. I need a break from it."

Before Lucy could protest further, Abbey moved into the kitchen.

"I need coffee and a change of subject." Abbey pulled two mugs from the cupboard. "I want to hear about your night with Aidan. I'm assuming from the glow on your face and the way you burst in here this morning, your meeting went all night?"

Lucy blushed. "Yes. But, Abbey, I've been talking non-stop about my complicated love life while ignoring your struggles. We can talk about me and Aidan later."

"No!" Abbey said firmly. "I told you, I don't want to talk about my failing marriage. I don't want to cry anymore. It's too new and raw, and it hurts."

Abbey turned to the coffee machine, absently wiping at her eyes. "Please, Lucy, just for now, can we drop it?"

"Are you sure?" Lucy asked, her eyes full of concern as she looked toward her sister.

"I'm sure," Abbey said softly, popping a pod into the top of the machine. "I don't want to cry. I want to laugh and smile and live vicariously through you. Now, tell me every dirty detail, and don't you dare leave a single thing out."

Over coffee, Lucy recanted her evening with Aidan, from the nervous pacing to the openly honest conversation that transpired.

"Wow, he really called you out," Abbey said, impressed. "It's rare for a man to be that intuned with his emotions, at least in my experience."

Lucy nodded. "I never even thought about how my actions would affect him. I was pretty selfish."

Abbey shrugged. "It comes with experience, I guess. But, didn't I tell you he really liked you all along?"

"I know." Lucy hung her head. "You said it from the start,

and it turned out to be true."

"Where do you go from here?" Abbey turned serious. "I hope you made some smart decisions."

Lucy smiled. "We're going to do this thing the grown-up way. Starting slow."

Abbey let out a loud laugh. "Slow? You two are way past slow. Did you end the night naked?"

Lucy's face flushed. "Okay, maybe not that slow." She sipped her coffee. "I'm no good at relationships. I've been with Jeremy for as long as I can remember. I have so much to learn, and I hope Aidan can be patient."

"He loves you, Lucy." Abbey gave her a knowing look. "He's been all in from the start, I'd say. It may take some work to make the relationship last for the long haul, but I think he'll take the good with the bad as long as he gets to be with you. Just remember to be patient with yourself, give yourself a break if you mess up, and always be willing to apologize for your mistakes."

"You'll be the first person I'll come to for relationship advice, trust me," Lucy promised.

Abbey stared into her coffee. "I'm not sure I'm the best person for that."

"You are, Abbey. Simply because things are difficult right now doesn't mean you failed. You and Rob were together for thirteen years? And who's to say this arrangement isn't just a temporary setback?"

Abbey shook her head. "I can't force him to stay, especially since he doesn't seem to want me anymore."

"Things can change with time," Lucy reminded her. "But that doesn't mean you should give up living in the meantime."

Abbey shrugged again. "One day at a time, I guess."

"Sorry, I know you wanted a good laugh." Lucy changed the subject. "So, let me tell you about the moment Kaylee walked in on us."

Epilogue

Summer

Lucy and Aidan walked hand in hand along the pathway in St. Stephen's Green Park. The day was clear, sunny, and pleasantly warm. Kaylee rushed ahead, pausing at the giant pond to scan the green water.

"I see some," she called out, jumping up and down and pointing toward one end of the pond. "Baby swans. Oh my goodness, they're so cute and fluffy."

Lucy smiled at Aidan. He squeezed her hand before releasing it and joining Kaylee at the pond's edge.

"Well, will ya look at that," he said. "Did ya know baby swans are called cygnets?"

Kaylee tilted her head toward Aidan, looking up at him. "School's out. No more lessons."

Aidan shook his head, laughing. "I'm only making a comment."

"Sure ya are," Kaylee replied, but Lucy caught the sly smile her daughter tried to hide. "First, it's 'guess what baby swans are called,' and the next thing I know, you'll be telling me the genus, species, and migration patterns."

Lucy chuckled. "She's got you all figured out."

Aidan nodded, scratching his head. "Actually, I was 'bout ta mention the *Children of Lir*."

Lucy scrunched her brows. "Who?"

Kaylee rolled her eyes. "I knew you had some lesson up your sleeve." She turned to Lucy. "The *Children of Lir* is a myth about King Lir's children being turned into swans. I'm sure Aidan would love to tell you the story."

Aidan gasped. "You were paying attention."

Kaylee scrunched up her nose and looked back toward the swans. Over her head, Lucy and Aidan exchanged glances, smiling at each other. Witnessing the interactions between her daughter and the man she was falling for warmed Lucy's heart. They loved to tease each other, and Lucy could tell Kaylee was comfortable in Aidan's presence.

For the last three months, Lucy and Aidan took things slow. She wouldn't mess things up this time; she had to break the cycle. No more sex without a deeper connection. She wanted the long talks, the laughter, the sharing of hopes and dreams, the disagreements, and all the ugly that strengthened the bond between two people.

Later that evening, the teasing continued throughout dinner. Lucy shook her head in amusement as she began clearing the table.

"That was amazing," Aidan said, standing up and patting

his stomach.

"I've still got room for popcorn," Kaylee said quickly.

Aidan nodded enthusiastically. "Always room for that."

"I'll tidy up and then get that started." Lucy carried plates toward the sink. "Aidan can get the movie queued up for us."

"After a quick trip to the jacks."

Lucy sighed as she watched him stride down the hallway.

"He should stay the night." Kaylee broke through Lucy's daze.

A patch of red burned up Lucy's neck. "What?"

"Aidan. I'm okay with him staying the night." Kaylee opened the dishwasher and set her plate inside.

Lucy couldn't hide the smile spreading across her face. From the moment Kaylee learned about their relationship, Lucy had never asked Aidan to stay the night. While he came over for dinner and a movie often, he always left before things became uncomfortable. Lucy was thankful Kaylee broached the subject and suggested they all move to the next level.

"Are you sure? We never want you to feel uncomfortable, especially in your own home."

"I'm fine with it," Kaylee said. "It was uncomfortable when he first hung out here. I saw him at school and then here, but we've gotten used to each other."

"You two have a great relationship."

Kaylee looked down at her hands. "I really like him, and I—I never had a—."

"Dad." Lucy finished for her. "I know what you mean, Sweetie. Aidan really likes you, too."

Kaylee smiled but continued studying her hands.

"I like having him in our lives."

"Me too," Kaylee mumbled, dropping her hands as Aidan entered the living room.

"Okay," he said, picking up the tv remote. "We've got action, scary, rom-com, or—ohh, a documentary on trad music."

"Don't you dare!" Kaylee rushed from the small kitchen area toward Aidan.

"Ah, it'll be grand. You'll love it."

Lucy watched as Aidan held the remote just out of Kaylee's reach. Her daughter laughed as she jumped up, trying to grab it from Aidan. Lucy felt as if her heart would burst watching their interaction. Aidan had always been so careful and caring toward Kaylee, ensuring she felt included as they navigated this new journey.

"We are not watching a documentary," Kaylee squealed, pulling on his arm. "Give me that remote."

Smiling, Lucy turned to place the popcorn into the microwave and considered her connection with Aidan. It was beyond anything she had ever felt or imagined. With just a single touch, he sent sparks flying between them. When they were apart, she missed him, counting down the hours until they were together again.

But she still had a lot of work to do within herself. Recently, she began seeing a therapist to help sort through her emotions and past traumas. She knew it would be hard work not to muck up this relationship, but she would give it her best shot. Her past with Jeremy would not tarnish her future with Aidan.

Lucy carried two bowls of popcorn into the living room.

Aidan and Kaylee sat on the couch side-by-side. Kaylee was leaning ever so slightly against Aidan's arm; it was such a small thing to notice, but it meant the world to Lucy. In her mind's eye, pictures played like a movie. She could envision their entire future together. In time, Kaylee would allow Aidan to become the father figure she deserved.

Lucy handed a bowl to Kaylee and plopped down on Aidan's free side, resting her head against his shoulder. This was the new beginning she needed and, unbeknownst to her, the reason she had moved across a continent and an ocean. Her destiny was to find this man who was changing her life in the most remarkable ways. She was still broken, but this path would lead to her healing, and there was no other place she would rather be.

The End

About the Author

Michelle Maree is a hopeless romantic with a slightly over-active imagination. Writing novels has always been her biggest passion. She began her career with a series of children's books, *The Magic Cube* series. Now, she is delving into the world of romance, weaving humor and awkward encounters into each story.

A recent transplant from the United States, Michelle lives with her family in Ireland. She loves exploring new places, going to the beach, curling up with a good book, and watching romantic comedies.

www.catchytitlehere.com

Acknowledgments

First and foremost, thank you to my husband, Kevin. You are my sounding board and the one I always bounce ideas off of, no matter how silly they may sound. Thank you for your patience and for believing in my dreams.

Thank you to Sinéad Kenny, my Irish consultant, for taking the time to ensure Aidan's dialogue was authentic and correcting any inaccuracies in my descriptions of Ireland and the Irish culture. Thank you for your edits and ideas and for believing in this story. And, of course, a huge thank you for the cover design.

Thank you to all my beta-readers for your advice and the sometimes difficult criticism I needed to make this story great.

Thank you to my children for allowing me time to write, edit, and promote this book.

Thank you to my grandmother for instilling in me a love for a good romance novel. I miss you every day.

Thank you to teachers everywhere for all you do and for influencing the lives of children around the world. You all deserve a little love story.

Saving the best for last, thank you to all my readers. I hope this story pulled you into another world and allowed you to escape from everyday life. Thank you for choosing this book and allowing me to share one of my stories with you.

Author's Note

I hope you enjoyed this story as much as I enjoyed writing it.

As an author, reviews are the best way to show others how much you enjoyed and appreciated a book. If you liked this book, it would be fantastic if you would give it a rating on Amazon and/or GoodReads.